OLD PETER'S RUS
&
THE BATTLE OF
AND THE BEASTS

*All the time he was doing this Vanya and Maroosia
were snuggling together close by the stove, thinking
what story they would ask for, and listening to the
crashing of the snow as it fell from the trees outside.
Now that old Peter was at home, the noise made them
feel comfortable and warm. Before, perhaps, it had
made them feel a little frightened.*

In a hut deep in the Russian forests, old Peter's
grandchildren listen as he tells of fire-birds and foxes,
of flying ships and frost, of Sadko and salt, of tzars and
peasants and witches and soldiers, and of the Little
Daughter of the Snow.

First published in 1916, *Old Peter's Russian Tales* is a
wonderful collection of classic Russian folk lore, retold
by a master story-teller. For the first time it is available
in this single volume with Arthur Ransome's second
collection of Russian tales, which were originally
brought together as *The War of the Birds and the
Beasts,* in 1984.

Illustrated by Faith Jaques, and with an introduction
by Hugh Lupton, Arthur Ransome's great-nephew and
himself one of Britain's leading story-tellers, this is a
collection to savour and to share.

Arthur Ransome

OLD PETER'S
RUSSIAN TALES
&
THE BATTLE OF THE BIRDS
AND THE BEASTS

Introduced by Hugh Lupton
Illustrated by Faith Jaques

Arthur Ransome
Trust

ARTHUR RANSOME TRUST
WWW.ARTHUR-RANSOME-TRUST.ORG.UK

Old Peter's Russian Tales
First published by Thomas Nelson 1916
Reissued with illustrations by Faith Jaques 1971
Published by Jonathan Cape Ltd 1984
Published by Jane Nissen Books 2003

The Battle of the Birds and the Beasts
First Published by Jonathan Cape Ltd 1984
as *The War of the Birds and the Beasts*,
edited by Hugh Brogan and illustrated by Faith Jaques
Published by Puffin Books 1986

This combined edition
Published by Arthur Ransome Trust 2016
Text © Arthur Ransome Literary Estate 2016
Introduction © Hugh Lupton 2016
Illustrations © Faith Jaques 2016

Printed by Bell and Bain Ltd, Glasgow

ISBN 978-0-9955681-0-5

Contents

Notes and Acknowledgements   vii

Biographical Notes   ix

Introduction by Hugh Lupton   xi

OLD PETER'S RUSSIAN TALES

The Hut in the Forest   5

The Tale of the Silver Saucer and the
Transparent Apple   10

Sadko   23

Frost   32

The Fool of the World and the Flying Ship   42

Baba Yaga   53

The Cat who became Head-forester   64

Spring in the Forest   73

The Little Daughter of the Snow   75

Prince Ivan, the Witch Baby and
the Little Sister of the Sun   84

The Stolen Turnips, the Magic Tablecloth,
the Sneezing Goat and the Wooden Whistle   97

Little Master Misery   115

A Chapter of Fish   129

The Golden Fish   133

Who Lived in the Skull?   144

CONTENTS

Alenoushka and her Brother   147

The Fire-bird, the Horse of Power and   155
the Princess Vasilissa

The Hunter and his Wife   166

The Three Men of Power – Evening,   172
Midnight and Sunrise

Salt   187

The Christening of the Village   201

THE BATTLE OF THE BIRDS AND THE BEASTS

The Battle of the Birds and the Beasts   215

The Swan Princess   226

Omelya and the Pike   235

The Costly Ring   240

A Chapter of Foxes   249

Concerning the Poor Man Covetous   260

The Little Cattle   265

The Gypsy and Saint George   269

The Blacksmith in Heaven   275

The Soldier and Death   278

The Two Brothers   296

About the Arthur Ransome Trust   303

Notes and Acknowledgements

Our thanks are due to the Arthur Ransome Literary Estate's Senior Executor, Christina Hardyment, for her permission, help and support with this new combined edition of Arthur Ransome's Russian Tales. We are also very grateful to Jane Nissen, who published the previous edition of *Old Peter*, and to Hugh Brogan, who collated and edited the first publication of *The War of the Birds and the Beasts and Other Russian Tales*, in 1984, for their encouragement and advice. Both Jane's edition of *Old Peter*, and previous editions of *The War of the Birds and the Beasts*, benefitted greatly from Faith Jaques's unique illustrations, which do so much to bring Arthur Ransome's tales to life. We are thankful to Faith's Executor, Angela Lett, for her generous permission to maintain the association in this new edition.

Finally, we are very grateful to Hugh Lupton, Arthur Ransome's great-nephew, whose introduction will help both those who are familiar with Ransome's Russian Tales, and those discovering them for the first time, to understand their place in storytelling traditions and their ability to inspire imaginations and enhance lives.

As stated above, Arthur Ransome's second volume of Russian Tales was originally published under the title, *The War of the Birds and the Beasts*. We are re-publishing it under the slightly amended title of *The Battle of the Birds and the Beasts* at Professor Brogan's suggestion, on the grounds that this is a more accurate title for the relevant tale.

Although *The War of the Birds and the Beasts* was first published in 1984, several of the stories therein had been published before. Most notably, *The Soldier and Death*,

NOTES AND ACKNOWLEDGEMENTS

Ransome's "favourite of all Russian Tales" was first published, on its own in book form, by John G Wilson in July, 1920.

The Costly Ring and *Concerning the Poor Man Covetous* were first published in *Country Life*, on 17 January, 1914 and 7 August, 1915 respectively.

The Blacksmith in Heaven was first published in *The Wheatsheaf*, in December, 1919.

GERAINT LEWIS
August, 2016

Biographical Notes

ARTHUR RANSOME

Arthur Ransome was born in Leeds, in 1884, and educated at Rugby School and the Yorkshire College. He abandoned a chemistry degree at the latter in order to pursue his growing passion for writing. Moving to London, he became a publisher's office boy before serving his literary apprenticeship as a ghost-writer, essayist and storyteller in the vibrant, pre-war Bohemian community. In 1913 he travelled to Russia to study folklore and write *Old Peter's Russian Tales*. The First World War turned Ransome into a journalist. He reported on the Eastern Front and the growing political turmoil in Russia for the *Daily News* and *Manchester Guardian*. His political journalism led to his being one of the few Westerners to know the leading Bolsheviks personally and, in consequence to involvement in both diplomatic and intelligence circles. In 1924 he married Trotsky's secretary, Evgenia Shelepina, before returning to Britain, where he continued to work for the *Guardian*. As a political journalist he travelled to Egypt and China; as an essayist he wrote his highly-regarded *Rod and Line* series of fishing essays and numerous other articles. He resigned, in 1929, and between 1930 and 1947 created his famous *Swallows and Amazons* series of children's novels. Ransome received the first Carnegie Medal for Children's Literature, for *Pigeon Post*, in 1937, an honorary MA (Durham) and D. Litt (Leeds) and, in 1953 was made CBE. He died in 1967.

HUGH LUPTON

Hugh Lupton's interest in traditional music, in street theatre, in live poetry, and in myth, resulted in him becoming a professional storyteller in 1981. For twelve years he toured Britain with the "Company of Storytellers". Their work was instrumental in stimulating a nation-wide revival of interest in storytelling. Since the mid-nineties he has worked as a solo performer and collaborator. In 2006 he and Daniel Morden were awarded the Classical Association Prize for "the most significant contribution to the public understanding of the classics". His work with musician Chris Wood has resulted in commissions from Radio 3 and the "Song of the Year" at the BBC folk awards. He tells stories from many cultures, but his particular passion is for the hidden layers of the English landscape and the stories and ballads that give voice to them. His first novel "The Ballad of John Clare'" was published in 2010, he's recently finished a second about the Mabinogion.

FAITH JAQUES

Faith Jaques was a picture book artist and illustrated books by many famous British writers, including Roald Dahl, Alan Ahlberg and Nina Bawden. Her unique style closely resembles classic wood engravings.

Introduction

by Arthur Ransome's great-nephew,
Hugh Lupton

When Arthur Ransome's sister Cecily died, she left her cottage *Greensyke* to my grandmother. It was situated just outside Spark Bridge, about three miles to the south of Coniston Water. For a few years in the late nineteen fifties and early sixties it became a holiday home. My family stayed there every summer.

Maybe I was five or six when we had our first holiday at *Greensyke*. I remember the house clearly. The warm musty smell of the place, more often empty than full, like a fruit that was just beginning to turn. There were always dead butterfies on the window-sill. I remember the tiny kitchen with its traces of leaking gas. I remember the views across the dry stone walled fields. The Old Man of Coniston stood on the horizon. Usually he was wearing his hat of cloud.

And then I remember the bookshelves: All the Beatrix Potters were there, the Babar the Elephant books too. And next to them was a row of dark green volumes (broken by the pink of *Missee Lee*) that we were told had been written by "Great Uncle Arthur" We weren't considered old enough to read them yet (though we pored over the illustrations). At the end of the row, was a quite different book, patterned with red and yellow diagonals. It was pulled out as being "more suitable". With my newly acquired reading skills I could decipher the title: *Old Peter's Russian Tales*.

At bed-times, on one of those early holidays, the book was read aloud to us, one story every evening.

This was my initiation into fairytale. I suppose I must have already known the standard tales – *Cinderella, Jack and the*

Beanstalk, The Three Little Pigs – probably from an anodyne illustrated anthology. They had made no impression. These stories were something else. They were packed with wonders – a talking horse, a flying ship, a house that stood on a chicken's leg, a living child made of snow. They were kind and cruel, happy and sad, they addressed the deep currents and undertows of life that I recognized but could not have named – pity, fear, retribution, trickery, love and death. They were packed with peasant wisdom and they understood suffering. Yes, they were "suitable" for a six year old, but - unlike the *Swallows and Amazons* books that I grew into and grew out of - they have remained "suitable" ever since.

I know now that the Russian fairy tales are the greatest in the world. They have drawn their form from the oral narratives of Europe and the west, an extravagance of invention from the Islamic traditions to the south, a sage and silken exoticism from the eastern border with China, and something strange and archaic from the shamanic traditions of the Siberian north. All have been stirred into the stoic crucible of the Russian folk imagination.

Arthur Ransome first came across the Russian tales in an ethnographic collection in 1912 (probably a translation of Aleksandr Afanasiev's great collection). He immediately recognized the delightful richness of the tradition, but also saw that these dry, distilled texts would never capture the imagination of English readers. He decided to travel to Russia, learn the language and make a collection of his own.

By 1915 he had gathered the stories he wanted to use. Like all good storytellers he describes in his autobiography how he would "read as many variants of a folk-story as I could find, then lay them all aside while writing the story for myself." What he achieves in his retellings is a literary/oral style that honours the pitch and cadence, the repetitions and refrains of a spoken tale. They read aloud brilliantly.

In the summer of 1915, as he was finishing the collection, Ransome fell ill. His friend Harold Williams came to the rescue. He had a Russian wife whose family had an estate at

Vergezha. Ransome finished the book while he was there. He writes about the stay: "At Vergezha all traditional feasts were thoroughly kept up. I came there with Williams at seven in the morning of May 22 to find men bringing in birch-branches to decorate the house for Whitsuntide... At meals we sat at a long table in the dining room. There were benches round the walls and during meals the peasants would drift in and sit there, discussing farm affairs with Arkady Vladimirovich and joining naturally in the general talk." It must have been while he was there, surrounded by the life of an old patriarchal Russia, that the idea of Old Peter and his grandchildren came to him. They enabled Ransome to give a domestic context to the stories without having to resort to "the continual explanation that would have been as destructive of the tales as an endless series of asides."

There is no hint in the book that the old order is about to disintegrate, but hindsight gives the lost world of Old Peter a particular poignancy (played on brilliantly by Marcus Sedgwick in his novel *Blood Red, Snow White*).

The book was published in 1916. It was an instant success. But there remained among Ransome's papers a number of tales that hadn't been included. One or two had appeared in *Country Life*, and one, the splendid *Soldier and Death* had been published as a slender volume in its own right. So in 1984, the centenary of Ransome's birth, his biographer Hugh Brogan trawled Ransome's papers and put together a second collection of Russian Tales – *The War of the Birds and the Beasts*. To my mind, in many ways, it outshines *Old Peter*. It has less of an eye to an audience of children. The tales are a shade darker.

In this new volume the two collections are brought together for the first time.

Arthur Ransome's subsequent career has been well documented: his engagement with the Russian Revolution, his marriage to Evgenia Shelepina (Trotsky's secretary), their return to the Lake District and the long run of children's classics that he wrote during the nineteen-thirties and forties.

INTRODUCTION

By the time I remember him he was an old man and his health was failing. On those holidays in Greensyke we would drive over to Hill Top, near Haverthwaite, for tea. I remember him in a deck chair, or presiding over the tea table, with his shining head and white moustaches. I remember racks of pipes and stacks of fishing rods. I remember jolly "Aunt Genia", with her funny accent, chasing us with a watering can of cold water.

But these scattered memories are over-ridden by my memory of the stories – *Baba Yaga, Prince Ivan and the Witch Baby, Sadko, The Cat who became Head-Forester, The Three Men of Power – Evening, Midnight and Sunrise.* Even the titles evoke an atmosphere that is rich and strange. In his introductory note to *Old Peter's Russian Tales* Arthur Ransome wrote: "No people who really like fairy stories ever grow up altogether. This is a book written far away in Russia, for English children who play in deep lanes with wild roses above them in the high hedges, or by small singing becks that dance down the grey fells at home." I consider myself very lucky to have first heard the stories almost within ear-shot of the singing becks he was remembering.

Access to deep lanes and grey fells is denied to all but a fortunate few of today's children. But the old fairytales, properly told, still speak to them. They have never lost their power. Why? Because they come from somewhere deep in our shared humanity and they do not shy away from what is essentially true. All of us, whether we are six or sixty, recognize that and respond to it – unless (God help us) we have become altogether grown up.

HUGH LUPTON
July 2016

OLD PETER'S
RUSSIAN TALES

Author's Note

The stories in this book are those that Russian peasants tell to their children and each other. In Russia hardly anybody is too old for fairy stories, and I have even heard soldiers on their way to the war talking of very wise and very beautiful princesses as they drank their tea by the side of the road. I think there must be more fairy stories told in Russia than anywhere else in the world. In this book are a few of those I like best. I have taken my own way with them more or less, writing them mostly from memory. They, or versions of them, are to be found in the coloured chap-books, in Afanasiev's great collection, or in solemn, serious volumes of folklorists writing for the learned. My book is not for the learned, or indeed for grown-up people at all. No people who really like fairy stories ever grow up altogether. This is a book written far away in Russia, for English children who play in deep lanes with wild roses above them in the high hedges, or by the small singing becks that dance down the grey fells at home. Russian fairyland is quite different. Under my windows the wavelets of the Volkhov (which has its part in one of the stories) are beating quietly in the dusk. A gold light burns on a timber raft floating down the river. Beyond the river in the blue midsummer twilight are the broad Russian plain and the distant forest. Somewhere in that forest of great trees — a forest so big that the forests of England are little woods beside it — is the hut where old Peter sits at night and tells these stories to his grandchildren.

Vergezha, 1915   A.R.

Author's Note to the 1938 Edition

More than twenty years later, anchored in my boat in an English river, watching the brown sails of the barges towering past the trees, and remembering those summer nights in Russia long ago, I wish a fair wind for the new edition of this book. Fashions change in stories of adventure, but fairy stories (especially those in which there are no fairies or hardly any) live for ever, with a life of their own which depends very little on the mere editors (like me) who pass them on.

Pin Mill on the Orwell, 1938   A.R.

The Hut in the Forest

Outside in the forest there was deep snow. The white snow had crusted the branches of the pine trees, and piled itself up on them till they bent under its weight. Now and then a snow-laden branch would bend too far, and huge lumps of snow fall crashing to the ground under the trees. Then the branch would swing up, and the snow would cover it again with a cold white burden. Sitting in the hut you could hear the crashing again and again out in the forest, as the tired branches flung down their loads of snow. Yes, and now and then there was the howling of wolves far away.

Little Maroosia heard them, and thought of them out there in the dark as they galloped over the snow. She sat closer to Vanya, her brother, and they were both as near as they could get to the door of the stove, where they could see the red fire burning busily, keeping the whole hut warm. The stove filled a quarter of the hut, but that was because it was a bed as well. There were blankets on it, and in those blankets Vanya and Maroosia rolled up and went to sleep at night, as warm as little baking cakes.

The hut was made of pine logs cut from the forest. You could see the marks of the axe. Old Peter was the grandfather of Maroosia and Vanya. He lived alone with them in the hut in the forest, because their father and mother were both dead. Maroosia and Vanya could hardly remember them, and they were very happy with old Peter, who was very kind to them and did all he could to keep them warm and well fed. He let them help him in everything, even in stuffing the windows with moss to keep the cold out when winter began. The moss kept the light out too, but that did not matter. It would be all the jollier in the spring when the sun came pouring in.

Besides old Peter and Maroosia and Vanya there were Vladimir and Bayan. Vladimir was a cat, a big black cat, as stately as an emperor, and just now he was lying in Vanya's arms fast asleep. Bayan was a dog, a tall grey wolf-dog. He could jump over the table with a single bound. When he was in the hut he usually lay underneath the table, because that was the only place where he could lie without being in the way. And, of course, at meal times he was in the way even there. Just now he was out with old Peter.

"I wonder what story it will be tonight?" said Maroosia.

"So do I," said Vanya. "I wish they'd be quick and come back."

Vladimir stirred suddenly in Vanya's lap, and a minute later they heard the scrunch of boots in the snow, and the stamping of old Peter's feet trying to get the snow off his boots. Then the door opened, and Bayan pushed his way in and shook himself, and licked Maroosia and Vanya and startled Vladimir, and lay down under the table and came out again, because he was so pleased to be home. And old Peter came in after him, with his gun on his back and a hare in his hand. He shook himself just like Bayan, and the snow flew off like spray. He hung up his gun, flung the hare into a corner of the hut, and laughed.

"You are snug in here, little pigeons," he said.

Vanya and Maroosia had jumped up to welcome him, and when he opened his big sheepskin coat, they tumbled into it together and clung to his belt. Then he closed the big woolly coat over the top of them and they squealed; and he opened it a little way and looked down at them over his beard, and then closed it again for a moment before letting them out. He did this every night, and Bayan always barked when they were shut up inside.

Then old Peter took his big coat off and lifted down the samovar from the shelf. The samovar is like a big brass tea-urn, with a stout metal tube running through the middle of it in which a fire is lit to make the water boil. When the water boils it is poured through the tap at the bottom onto tea-leaves in the teapot, and the pot is set on the top of the samovar. A little jet of steam rises through a tiny hole in the lid of the samovar, which hums like a bee and makes one feel extra warm and snug when the weather is cold. Old Peter threw in the lighted sticks and charcoal, and made a draught to draw the heat, and then set the samovar on the table with the little fire crackling in its inside. Then he cut some big lumps of black bread. The he took a great saucepan full of soup, that was simmering on the stove, and emptied it into a big wooden bowl. Then he went to the wall where, on three nails, hung three wooden spoons, deep like ladles. There were one big spoon, for old Peter; and two little spoons, one for Vanya and one for Maroosia.

And all the time that old Peter was getting supper ready he was answering questions and making jokes — old ones, of course, that he made every day — about how plump the children were, and how fat was better to eat than butter, and what the Man in the Moon said when he fell out, and what the wolf said who caught his own tail and ate himself up before he found out his mistake.

And Vanya and Maroosia danced about the hut and chuckled.

Then they had supper, all three dipping their wooden spoons in the big bowl together, and eating a tremendous lot of black bread. And, of course, there were scraps for Vladimir and a bone for Bayan.

After that they had tea with sugar but no milk, because they were Russians and liked it that way.

Then came the stories. Old Peter poured another glass of tea for himself, not for the children. His throat was old, he said, and took a lot of keeping wet; and they were young, and would not sleep if they drank tea too near bedtime. Then he threw a log of wood into the stove. Then he lit a short little pipe, full of very strong tobacco, called Mahorka, which has a smell like hot tin. And he puffed, and the smoke got in his eyes, and he wiped them with the back of his big hand.

All the time he was doing this Vanya and Maroosia were snuggling together close by the stove, thinking what story they would ask for, and listening to the crashing of the snow as it fell from the trees outside. Now that old Peter was at home, the noise made them feel comfortable and warm. Before, perhaps it had made them feel a little frightened.

"Well, little pigeons, little hawks, little bear cubs, what is it to be?" said old Peter.

"We don't know," said Maroosia.

"Long hair, short sense, little she-pigeon," said old Peter. "All this time and not thought of a story? Would you like the tale of the little Snow Girl who was not loved so much as a hen?"

"Not tonight, grandfather," said Vanya.

"We'd like that tale when the snow melts," said Maroosia. "Tonight we'd like a story we've never heard before," said Vanya.

"Well, well," said old Peter, combing his great grey beard with his fingers, and looking out at them with twinkling eyes from under his big bushy eyebrows. "Have I ever told you the story of 'The Silver Saucer and the Transparent Apple'?"

"No, no, never," cried Vanya and Maroosia at once.

Old Peter took a last pull at his pipe, and Vanya* and Maroosia wriggled with excitement. Then he drank a sip of tea. Then he began.

* The name Vanya is a form of Ivan often used for a young boy.

The Tale of the Silver Saucer
and the Transparent Apple

There was once an old peasant, and he must have had more brains under his hair than ever I had, for he was a merchant, and used to take things every year to sell at the big fair of Nijni Novgorod. Well, I could never do that. I could never be anything better than an old forester.

"Never mind, grandfather," said Maroosia.

God knows best, and He makes some merchants and some foresters, and some good and some bad, all in His own way. Anyhow this one was a merchant, and he had three daughters. They were none of them so bad to look at, but one of them was as pretty as Maroosia. And she was the best of them too. The others put all the hard work on her, while they did nothing but look at themselves in the looking-glass and complain of what they had to eat. They called the pretty one "Little Stupid", because she was so good and did all their work for them. Oh, they were real bad ones, those two. We wouldn't have them in here for a minute.

Well, the time came round for the merchant to pack up and go to the big fair. He called his daughters, and said, "Little pigeons", just as I say to you. "Little pigeons," says he, "what would you like me to bring you from the fair?"

Says the eldest, "I'd like a necklace, but it must be a rich one."

Says the second, "I want a new dress with gold braid."

But the youngest, the good one, Little Stupid, said nothing at all.

"Now little one," says her father, "what is it you want? I must bring something for you too."

Says the little one, "Could I have a silver saucer and a transparent apple? But never mind if there are none."

The old merchant says, "Long hair, short sense," just as I say to Maroosia; but he promised the little pretty one, who was so good that her sisters called her stupid, that if he could get her a silver saucer and a transparent apple she should have them.

Then they all kissed each other, and he cracked his whip, and off he went, with the little bells jingling on the horses' harness.

The three sisters waited till he came back. The two elder ones looked in the looking-glass, and thought how fine they would look in the new necklace and the new dress; but the little pretty one took care of her old mother, and scrubbed and dusted and swept and cooked, and every day the other two said that the soup was burnt or the bread not properly baked.

Then one day there were a jingling of bells and a clattering of horses' hoofs, and the old merchant came driving back from the fair.

The sisters ran out.

"Where is the necklace?" asked the first.

"You haven't forgotten the dress?" asked the second.

But the little one, Little Stupid, helped her old father off with his coat, and asked him if he was tired.

"Well, little one," says the old merchant, "and don't you want your fairing too? I went from one end of the market to the other before I could get what you wanted. I bought the silver saucer from an old Jew, and the transparent apple from a Finnish hag."

"Oh, thank you, father," says the little one.

"And what will you do with them?" says he.

"I shall spin the apple in the saucer," says the little pretty one, and at that the old merchant burst out laughing.

"They don't call you 'Little Stupid' for nothing," says he.

Well, they all had their fairings, and the two elder sisters, the bad ones, they ran off and put on the new dress and the new necklace, and came out and strutted about, preening themselves like herons, now on one leg and now on the other, to see how they looked. But Little Stupid, she just sat herself down beside the stove, and took the transparent apple and

11

set it in the silver saucer, and she laughed softly to herself. And then she began spinning the apple in the saucer.

Round and round the apple spun in the saucer, faster and faster, till you couldn't see the apple at all, nothing but a mist like a little whirlpool in the silver saucer. And the little good one looked at it, and her eyes shone like yours.

Her sisters laughed at her.

"Spinning an apple in a saucer and staring at it, the little stupid," they said, as they strutted about the room, listening to the rustle of the new dress and fingering the bright round stones of the necklace.

But the little pretty one did not mind them. She sat in the corner watching the spinning apple. And as it spun she talked to it.

"Spin, spin, apple in the silver saucer." This is what she said. "Spin so that I may see the world. Let me have a peep at the little father Tzar on his high throne. Let me see the rivers and the ships and the great towns far away."

And as she looked at the little glass whirlpool in the saucer, there was the Tzar, the little father — God preserve him! — sitting on his high throne. Ships sailed on the seas, their white sails swelling in the wind. There was Moscow with its white stone walls and painted churches. Why, there were the market at Nijni Novgorod, and the Arab merchants with their camels, and the Chinese with their blue trousers and bamboo staves. And then there was the great river Volga, with men on the banks towing ships against the stream. Yes, and she saw a sturgeon asleep in a deep pool.

"Oh! Oh! Oh!" says the little pretty one, as she saw all these things.

And the bad ones, they saw how her eyes shone, and they came and looked over her shoulder, and saw how all the world was there, in the spinning apple and the silver saucer. And the old father came and looked over her shoulder too, and he saw the market at Nijni Novgorod.

"Why, there is the inn where I put up the horses," says he. "You haven't done so badly after all, Little Stupid."

And the little pretty one, Little Stupid, went on staring into the glass whirlpool in the saucer, spinning the apple, and seeing all the world she had never seen before, floating there before her in the saucer, brighter than leaves in sunlight.

The bad ones, the elder sisters, were sick with envy.

"Little Stupid," says the first, "if you will give me your silver saucer and your transparent apple, I will give you my fine new necklace."

"Little Stupid," says the second, "I will give you my new dress with gold braid if you will give me your transparent apple and your silver saucer."

"Oh, I couldn't do that," says the Little Stupid, and she goes on spinning the apple in the saucer and seeing what was happening all over the world.

So the bad ones put their wicked heads together and thought of a plan. And they took their father's axe, and went into the deep forest and hid it under a bush.

The next day they waited till afternoon, when work was done, and the little pretty one was spinning her apple in the saucer. Then they said:

"Come along, Little Stupid; we are all going to gather berries in the forest."

"Do you really want me to come too?" says the little one. She would rather have played with her apple and saucer.

But they said, "Why, of course. You don't think we can carry all the berries ourselves!"

So the little one jumped up, and found the baskets, and went with them to the forest. But before she started she ran to her father, who was counting his money, and was not too pleased to be interrupted, for figures go quickly out of your head when you have a lot of them to remember. She asked him to take care of the silver saucer and the transparent apple for fear she would lose them in the forest.

"Very well, little bird," says the old man, and he put the things in a box with a lock and key to it. He was a merchant, you know, and that sort are always careful about things, and go clattering about with a lot of keys at their belt. I've nothing to lock up, and never had, and perhaps it is just as well, for I could never be bothered with keys.

So the little one picks up all three baskets and runs off after the others, the bad ones, with black hearts under their necklaces and new dresses.

They went deep into the forest, picking berries, and the little one picked so fast that she soon had a basket full. She was picking and picking, and did not see what the bad ones were doing. They were fetching the axe.

The little one stood up to straighten her back, which ached after so much stooping, and she saw her two sisters standing in front of her, looking at her cruelly. Their baskets lay on the ground quite empty. They had not picked a berry. The eldest had the axe in her hand.

The little one was frightened.

"What is it, sisters?" says she; "and why do you look at me with cruel eyes? And what is the axe for? You are not going to cut berries with an axe."

"No, Little Stupid," says the first, "we are not going to cut berries with the axe."

"No, Little Stupid," says the second, "the axe is here for something else."

The little one begged them not to frighten her.

Says the first, "Give me your transparent apple."

Says the second, "Give me your silver saucer."

"If you don't give them up at once, we shall kill you." That is what the bad ones said.

The poor little one begged them. "O darling sisters, do not kill me! I haven't got the saucer or the apple with me at all."

"What a lie!" say the bad ones. "You never would leave it behind."

And one caught her by the hair, and the other swung the axe, and between them they killed the little pretty one, who was called Little Stupid because she was so good.

Then they looked for the saucer and the apple, and could not find them. But it was too late now. So they made a hole in the ground, and buried the little one under a birch tree.

When the sun went down the bad ones came home, and they wailed with false voices, and rubbed their eyes to make the tears come. They made their eyes red and their noses too, and they did not look any prettier for that.

"What is the matter with you, little pigeons?" said the old merchant and his wife. I would not say "little pigeons" to such bad ones. Black-hearted crows is what I would call them.

And they wail and lament aloud:

"We are miserable for ever. Our poor little sister is lost. We looked for her everywhere. We heard the wolves howling. They must have eaten her."

The old mother and father cried like rivers in springtime, because they loved the little pretty one, who was called Little Stupid because she was so good.

But before their tears were dry the bad ones began to ask for the silver saucer and the transparent apple.

"No, no," says the old man; "I shall keep them for ever, in memory of my poor little daughter whom God has taken away."

So the bad ones did not gain by killing their little sister.

"That is one good thing," said Vanya.

"But is that all, grandfather?" said Maroosia.

"Wait a bit, little pigeons. Too much haste set his shoes on fire. You listen, and you will hear what happened," said old Peter. He took a pinch of snuff from a little wooden box, and then he went on with his tale.

Time did not stop with the death of the little girl. Winter came, and the snow with it. Everything was all white, just as it is now. And the wolves came to the doors of the huts, even into the villages, and no one stirred farther than he need. And then the snow melted, and the buds broke on the trees, and the birds began singing, and the sun shone warmer every day. The old people had almost forgotten the little pretty one who lay dead in the forest. The bad ones had not forgotten, because now they had to do the work, and they did not like that at all.

And then one day some lambs strayed away into the forest,

15

and a young shepherd went after them to bring them safely back to their mothers. And as he wandered this way and that through the forest, following their light tracks, he came to a little birch tree, bright with new leaves, waving over a little mound of earth. And there was a reed growing in the mound, and that, you know as well as I, is a strange thing, one reed all by itself under a birch tree in the forest. But it was no stranger than the flowers, for there were flowers round it, some red as the sun at dawn and others blue as the summer sky.

Well, the shepherd looks at the reed, and he looks at those flowers, and he thinks, "I've never seen anything like that before. I'll make a whistle-pipe of that reed, and keep it for a memory till I grow old."

So he did. He cut the reed, and sat himself down on the mound, and carved away at the reed with his knife, and got the pith out of it by pushing a twig through it, and beating it gently till the bark swelled, made holes in it, and there was his whistle-pipe. And then he put it to his lips to see what sort of music he could make on it. But that he never knew, for before his lips touched it the whistle-pipe began playing by itself and reciting in a girl's sweet voice. This is what it sang:

"Play, play, whistle-pipe. Bring happiness to my dear father and to my little mother. I was killed — yes, my life was taken from me in the deep forest for the sake of a silver saucer, for the sake of a transparent apple."

When he heard that the shepherd went back quickly to the village to show it to the people. And all the way the whistle-pipe went on playing and reciting, singing its little song. And every one who heard it said, "What a strange song! But who is it who was killed?"

"I know nothing about it," says the shepherd, and he tells them about the mound and the reed and the flowers, and how he cut the reed and made the whistle-pipe, and how the whistle-pipe does its playing by itself.

And as he was going through the village, with all the people crowding about him, the old merchant, that one who was the father of the two bad ones and of the little pretty one, came along and listened with the rest. And when he heard the words about the silver saucer and the transparent apple, he snatched the whistle-pipe from the shepherd boy. And still it sang:

"Play, play, whistle-pipe! Bring happiness to my dear father and to my little mother. I was killed — yes, my life was taken from me in the deep forest for the sake of a silver saucer, for the sake of a transparent apple."

And the old merchant remembered the little good one, and his tears trickled over his cheeks and down his old beard. Old men love little pigeons, you know. And he said to the shepherd:

"Take me at once to the mound, where you say you cut the reed."

The shepherd led the way, and the old man walked beside him, crying, while the whistle-pipe in his hand went on singing and reciting its little song over and over again.

They came to the mound under the birch tree, and there were the flowers, shining red and blue, and there in the middle of the mound was the stump of the reed which the shepherd had cut.

The whistle-pipe sang on and on.

Well, there and then they dug up the mound, and there was the little girl lying under the dark earth as if she were asleep.

"O God of mine," says the old merchant, "this is my daughter, my little pretty one, whom we called Little Stupid." He began to weep loudly and wring his hands; but the whistle-pipe, playing and reciting, changed its song. This is what it sang:

"My sisters took me into the forest to look for the red berries. In the deep forest they killed poor me for the sake of a silver saucer, for the sake of a transparent apple. Wake me, dear father, from a bitter dream, by fetching water from the well of the Tzar."

How the people scowled at the two sisters! They scowled, they cursed them for the bad ones they were. And the bad ones, the two sisters, wept, and fell on their knees, and confessed everything. They were taken, and their hands were tied, and they were shut up in prison.

"Do not kill them," begged the old merchant, "for then I should have no daughters at all, and when there are no fish in the river we make shift with crays. Besides, let me go to the Tzar and beg water from his well. Perhaps my little daughter will wake up, as the whistle-pipe tells us."

And the whistle-pipe sang again:

"Wake me, wake me, dear father, from a bitter dream, by fetching water from the well of the Tzar. Till then, dear father, a blanket of black earth and the shade of the green birch tree."

So they covered the little girl with her blanket of earth, and the shepherd with his dogs watched the mound night and day. He begged for the whistle-pipe to keep him company, poor lad, and all the days and nights he thought of the sweet face of the little pretty one he had seen there under the birch tree.

The old merchant harnessed his horse, as if he were going to the town; and he drove off through the forest, along the roads, till he came to the palace of the Tzar, the little father of all good Russians. And then he left his horse and cart and waited on the steps of the palace.

The Tzar, the little father, with rings on his fingers and a gold crown on his head, came out on the steps in the morning sunshine; and as for the old merchant, he fell on his knees and kissed the feet of the Tzar, and begged:

"O little father, Tzar, give me leave to take water — just a little drop of water — from your holy well."

"And what will you do with it?" says the Tzar.

"I will wake my daughter from a bitter dream," says the old merchant. "She was murdered by her sisters — killed in the deep forest — for the sake of a silver saucer, for the sake of a transparent apple."

"A silver saucer?" says the Tzar — "a transparent apple? Tell me about that."

And the old merchant told the Tzar everything, just as I have told it to you.

And the Tzar, the little father, he gave the old merchant a glass of water from his holy well. "But," says he, "when your daughterkin wakes, bring her to me, and her sisters with her, and also the silver saucer and the transparent apple."

The old man kissed the ground before the Tzar, and took the glass of water and drove home with it, and I can tell you he was careful not to spill a drop. He carried it all the way in one hand as he drove.

He came to the forest and to the flowering mound under the little birch tree, and there was the shepherd watching with his dogs. The old merchant and the shepherd took away the blanket of black earth. Tenderly, tenderly the shepherd used his fingers, until the little girl, the pretty one, the good one, lay there as sweet as if she were not dead.

Then the merchant scattered the holy water from the glass over the little girl. And his daughterkin blushed as she lay there, and opened her eyes, and passed a hand across them, as if she were waking from a dream. And then she leapt up, crying and laughing, and clung about her old father's neck. And there they stood, the two of them, laughing and crying with joy. And the shepherd could not take his eyes from her, and in his eyes, too, there were tears.

But the old father did not forget what he had promised the Tzar. He set the little pretty one, who had been so good that her wicked sisters had called her Stupid, to sit beside him on the cart. And he brought something from the house in a coffer of wood, and kept it under his coat. And they brought out the two sisters, the bad ones, from their dark prison, and set them in the cart. And the Little Stupid kissed them and cried over them, and wanted to loose their hands, but the old merchant would not let her. And they all drove together till they came to the palace of the Tzar. The shepherd boy could not take his eyes from the little pretty one, and he ran all the way behind the cart.

Well, they came to the palace, and waited on the steps; and the Tzar came out to take the morning air, and he saw the old merchant, and the two sisters with their hands tied, and the little pretty one, as lovely as a spring day. And the Tzar saw her, and could not take his eyes from her. He did not see the shepherd boy, who hid away among the crowd.

Says the great Tzar to his soldiers, pointing to the bad sisters, "These two are to be put to death at sunset. When the sun goes down their heads must come off, for they are not fit to see another day."

Then he turns to the little pretty one, and he says: "Little sweet pigeon, where is your silver saucer, and where is your transparent apple?"

The old merchant took the wooden box from under his coat, and opened it with a key at his belt, and gave it to the little one, and she took out the silver saucer and the transparent apple and gave them to the Tzar.

"O lord Tzar," says she, "O little father, spin the apple in the saucer, and you will see whatever you wish to see — your soldiers, your high hills, your forests, your plains, your rivers, and everything in all Russia."

And the Tzar, the little father, spun the apple in the saucer till it seemed a little whirlpool of white mist, and there he saw glittering towns, and regiments of soldiers marching to war, and ships, and day and night, and the clear stars above the trees. He looked at these things and thought much of them.

Then the little good one threw herself on her knees before him, weeping.

"O little father, Tzar," she says, "take my transparent apple and my silver saucer; only forgive my sisters. Do not kill them because of me. If their heads are cut off when the sun goes down, it would have been better for me to lie under the blanket of black earth in the shade of the birch tree in the forest."

The Tzar was pleased with the kind heart of the little pretty one, and he forgave the bad ones, and their hands were untied, and the little pretty one kissed them, and they kissed her again and said they were sorry.

The old merchant looked up at the sun, and saw how the time was going.

"Well, well," says he, "it's time we were getting ready to go home."

They all fell on their knees before the Tzar and thanked him. But the Tzar could not take his eyes from the little pretty one, and would not let her go.

"Little sweet pigeon," says he, "will you be my Tzaritza, and a kind mother to Holy Russia?"

And the little good one did not know what to say. She blushed and answered, very rightly, "As my father orders, and as my little mother wishes, so shall it be."

The Tzar was pleased with her answer, and he sent a messenger on a galloping horse to ask leave from the little pretty one's old mother. And of course the old mother said that she was more than willing. So that was all right. Then there was a wedding — such a wedding! — and every city in Russia sent a silver plate of bread, and a golden salt-cellar, with their good wishes to the Tzar and Tzaritza.

Only the shepherd boy, when he heard that the little pretty

one was to marry the Tzar, turned sadly away and went off into the forest.

"Are you happy, little sweet pigeon?" says the Tzar.

"Oh yes," says the Little Stupid, who was now Tzaritza and mother of Holy Russia; "but there is one thing that would make me happier."

"And what is that?" says the lord Tzar.

"I cannot bear to lose my old father and my little mother and my dear sisters. Let them be with me here in the palace, as they were in my father's house."

The Tzar laughed at the little pretty one, but he agreed, and the little pretty one ran to tell them the good news. She said to her sisters, "Let all be forgotten, and all be forgiven, and may the evil eye fall on the one who first speaks of what has been!"

For a long time the Tzar lived, and the little pretty one the Tzaritza, and they had many children, and were very happy together. And ever since then the Tzars of Russia have kept the silver saucer and the transparent apple, so that, whenever they wish, they can see everything that is going on all over Russia. Perhaps even now the Tzar, the little father — God preserve him! — is spinning the apple in the saucer, and looking at us, and thinking it is time that two little pigeons were in bed.

*****

"Is that the end?" said Vanya.

"That is the end," said old Peter.

"Poor shepherd boy!" said Maroosia.

"I don't know about that," said old Peter. "You see, if he had married the little pretty one, and had to have all the family to live with him, he would have had them in a hut like ours instead of in a great palace, and so he would never have had room to get away from them. And now, little pigeons, who is going to be first into bed?"

22

Sadko

In Novgorod in the old days there was a young man — just a boy he was — the son of a rich merchant who had lost all his money and died. So Sadko was very poor. He had not a kopeck in the world, except what the people gave him when he played his dulcimer for their dancing. He had blue eyes and curling hair, and he was strong, and would have been merry; but it is dull work playing for other folk to dance, and Sadko dared not dance with any young girl, for he had no money to marry on, and he did not want to be chased away as a beggar. And the young women of Novgorod, they never looked at the handsome Sadko. No; they smiled with their bright eyes at the young men who danced with them, and if they ever spoke to Sadko, it was just to tell him sharply to keep the music going or to play faster.

So Sadko lived alone with his dulcimer, and made do with half a loaf when he could not get a whole, and with crust when he had no crumb. He did not mind so very much what came to him, so long as he could play his dulcimer and walk along the banks of the little* river Volkhov that flows by Novgorod, or on the shores of the lake, making music for himself, and seeing the pale mists rise over the water, and dawn or sunset across the shining river.

"There is no girl in all Novgorod as pretty as my little river," he used to say, and night after night he would sit by the banks of the river or on the shores of the lake, playing the dulcimer and singing to himself.

Sometimes he helped the fishermen on the lake, and they would give him a little fish for his supper in payment for his strong young arms.

And it happened that one evening the fishermen asked him

---

* The Volkhov would be a big river if it were in England, and Sadko and old Peter called it little only because they loved it.

to watch their nets for them on the shore, while they went off to take their fish to sell them in the square at Novgorod.

Sadko sat on the shore, on a rock, and played his dulcimer and sang. Very sweetly he sang of the fair lake and the lovely river — the little river that he thought prettier than all the girls of Novgorod. And while he was singing he saw a whirlpool in the lake, little waves flying from it across the water, and in the middle a hollow down into the water. And in the hollow he saw the head of a great man with blue hair and a gold crown. He knew that the huge man was the Tzar of the Sea. And the man came nearer, walking up out of the depths of the lake — a huge, great man, a very giant, with blue hair falling to his waist over his broad shoulders. The little waves ran from him in all directions as he came striding up out of the water.

Sadko did not know whether to run or stay; but the Tzar of the Sea called out to him in a great voice like wind and water in a storm:

"Sadko of Novgorod, you have played and sung many days by the side of this lake and on the banks of the little river Volkhov. My daughters love your music, and it has pleased me too. Throw out a net into the water, and draw it in, and the waters will pay you for your singing. And if you are satisfied with the payment, you must come and play to us down in the green palace of the sea."

With that the Tzar of the Sea went down again into the waters of the lake. The waves closed over him with a roar, and presently the lake was as smooth and calm as it had ever been.

Sadko thought, and said to himself: "Well, there is no harm done in casting out a net." So he threw a net out into the lake.

He sat down again and played on his dulcimer and sang, and when he had finished his singing the dusk had fallen and the moon shone over the lake. He put down his dulcimer and took hold of the ropes of the net, and began to draw it up out of the silver water. Easily the ropes came, and the net, dripping and glittering in the moonlight.

"I was dreaming," said Sadko; "I was asleep when I saw the Tzar of the Sea, and there is nothing in the net at all."

And then, just as the last of the net was coming ashore, he saw something in it, square and dark. He dragged it out, and found it was a coffer. He opened the coffer, and it was full of precious stones — green, red, gold — gleaming in the light of the moon. Diamonds shone there like little bundles of sharp knives.

"There can be no harm in taking these stones," says Sadko, "whether I dreamed or not."

He took the coffer on his shoulder, and bent under the weight of it, strong though he was. He put it in a safe place. All night he sat and watched by the nets, and played and sang, and planned what he would do.

In the morning the fishermen came, laughing and merry after their night in Novgorod, and they gave him a little fish for watching their nets; and he made a fire on the shore, and cooked it and ate it as he used to do.

"And that is my last meal as a poor man," says Sadko. "Ah me! who knows if I shall be happier?"

Then he set the coffer on his shoulder and tramped away for Novgorod.

"Who is that?" they asked at the gates.

"Only Sadko the dulcimer player," he replied.

"Turned porter?" said they.

"One trade is as good as another," said Sadko, and he walked into the city. He sold a few of the stones, two at a time, and with what he got for them he set up a booth in the market. Small things led to great, and he was soon one of the richest traders in Novgorod.

And now there was not a girl in the town who could look too sweetly at Sadko. "He has golden hair," says one. "Blue eyes like the sea," says another. "He could lift the world on his shoulders," says a third. A little money, you see, opens everybody's eyes.

But Sadko was not changed by his good fortune. Still he walked and played by the little river Volkhov. When work was done and the traders gone, Sadko would take his dulcimer and play and sing on the banks of the river. And still he said, "There is no girl in all Novgorod as pretty as my little river." Every time he came back from his long voyages — for he was trading far and near, like the greatest of merchants — he went at once to the banks of the river to see how his sweetheart fared. And always he brought some little present for her and threw it into the waves.

For twelve years he lived unmarried in Novgorod, and every year made voyages, buying and selling, and always growing richer and richer. Many were the mothers in Novgorod who would have liked to see him married to their daughters. Many were the pillows that were wet with the tears of the young girls, as they thought of the blue eyes of Sadko and his golden hair.

And then, in the twelfth year since he walked into Novgorod with the coffer on his shoulder, he was sailing in a ship on the Caspian Sea, far, far away. For many days the ship sailed on, and Sadko sat on deck and played his dulcimer and sang of

Novgorod and of the little river Volkhov that flows under the walls of the town. Blue was the Caspian Sea, and the waves were like furrows in a field, long lines of white under the steady wind, while the sails swelled and the ship shot over the water.

And suddenly the ship stopped.

In the middle of the sea, far from land, the ship stopped and trembled in the waves, as if she were held by a big hand.

"We are aground!" cry the sailors; and the captain, the great one, tells them to take soundings. Seventy fathoms by the bow it was, and seventy fathoms by the stern.

"We are not aground," says the captain, "unless there is a rock sticking up like a needle in the middle of the Caspian Sea!"

"There is magic in this," say the sailors.

"Hoist more sail," says the captain; and up go the white sails, swelling out in the wind, while the masts bend and creak. But still the ship lay shivering and did not move, out there in the middle of the sea.

"Hoist more sail yet," says the captain; and up go the white sails, swelling and tugging, while the masts creak and groan. But still the ship lay there shivering and did not move.

"There is an unlucky one aboard," says an old sailor. "We must draw lots and find him, and throw him overboard into the sea."

The other sailors agreed to this. And still Sadko sat, and played his dulcimer and sang.

The sailors cut pieces of string, all of a length, as many as there were souls in the ship, and one of those strings they cut in half. Then they made them into a bundle, and each man plucked one string. And Sadko stopped his playing for a moment to pluck a string, and his was the string that had been cut in half.

"Magician, sorcerer, unclean one!" shouted the sailors.

"Not so," said Sadko. "I remember now an old promise I made, and I keep it willingly."

He took his dulcimer in his hand, and leapt from the ship

into the blue Caspian Sea. The waves had scarcely closed over his head before the ship shot forward again, and flew over the waves like a swan's feather, and came in the end safely to her harbour.

"And what happened to Sadko?" asked Maroosia.

"You shall hear, little pigeon," said old Peter, and he took a pinch of snuff. Then he went on.

Sadko dropped into the waves, and the waves closed over him. Down he sank, like a pebble thrown into a pool, down and down. First the water blue, then green, and strange fish with goggle eyes and golden fins swam round him as he sank. He came at last to the bottom of the sea.

And there, on the bottom of the sea, was a palace built of green wood. Yes, all the timbers of all the ships that have been wrecked in all the seas of the world are in that palace, and they are all green, and cunningly fitted together, so that the palace is worth a ten days' journey only to see it. And in front of the palace Sadko saw two big knobbly sturgeons, each a hundred and fifty feet long, lashing their tails and guarding the gates. Now, sturgeons are the oldest of all fish, and these were the oldest of all sturgeons.

Sadko walked between the sturgeons and through the gates of the palace. Inside there was a great hall, and the Tzar of the Sea lay resting in the hall, with his gold crown on his head and his blue hair floating round him in the water, and his great body covered with scales lying along the hall. The Tzar of the Sea filled the hall — and there is room in that hall for a village. And there were fish swimming this way and that in and out of the windows.

"Ah, Sadko," says the Tzar of the Sea, "you took what the sea gave you, but you have been a long time in coming to sing in the palaces of the sea. Twelve years I have lain here waiting for you."

"Great Tzar, forgive," says Sadko.

"Sing now," says the Tzar of the Sea, and his voice was like the beating of waves.

And Sadko played on his dulcimer and sang.

He sang of Novgorod and of the little river Volkhov which he loved. It was in his song that none of the girls of Novgorod were as pretty as the little river. And there was the sound of wind over the lake in his song, the sound of ripples under the prow of a boat, the sound of ripples on the shore, the sound of the river flowing past the tall reeds, the whispering sound of the river at night. And all the time he played cunningly on the dulcimer. The girls of Novgorod had never danced to so sweet a tune when in the old days Sadko played his dulcimer to earn kopecks and crusts of bread.

Never had the Tzar of the Sea heard such music.

"I would dance," said the Tzar of the Sea, and he stood up like a tall tree in the hall.

"Play on," said the Tzar of the Sea, and he strode through the gates. The sturgeons guarding the gates stirred the water with their tails.

And if the Tzar of the Sea was huge in the hall, he was huger still when he stood outside on the bottom of the sea. He grew taller and taller, towering like a mountain. His feet were like small hills. His blue hair hung down to his waist, and he was covered with green scales. And he began to dance on the bottom of the sea.

Great was that dancing. The sea boiled, and ships went down. The waves rolled as big as houses. The sea overflowed its shores, and whole towns were under water as the Tzar danced mightily on the bottom of the sea. Hither and thither rushed the waves, and the very earth shook at the dancing of that tremendous Tzar.

He danced till he was tired, and then he came back to the palace of green wood, and passed the sturgeons, and shrank into himself and came through the gates into the hall, where Sadko still played on his dulcimer and sang.

"You have played well and given me pleasure," says the Tzar of the Sea. "I have thirty daughters, and you shall choose one and marry her, and be a Prince of the Sea."

"Better than all maidens I love my little river," says Sadko; and the Tzar of the Sea laughed and threw his head back, with his blue hair floating all over the hall.

And then there came in the thirty daughters of the Tzar of the Sea. Beautiful they were, lovely, and graceful; but twenty-nine of them passed by, and Sadko fingered his dulcimer and thought of his little river.

There came in the thirtieth, and Sadko cried out aloud. "Here is the only maiden in the world as pretty as my little river!" says he. And she looked at him with eyes that shone like stars reflected in the river. Her hair was dark, like the river at night. She laughed, and her voice was like the flowing of the river.

"And what is the name of your little river?" says the Tzar.

"It is the little river Volkhov that flows by Novgorod," says Sadko; "but your daughter is as fair as the little river, and I would gladly marry her if she will have me."

"It is a strange thing," says the Tzar, "but Volkhov is the name of my youngest daughter."

He put Sadko's hand in the hand of his youngest daughter, and they kissed each other. And as they kissed, Sadko saw a necklace round her neck, and knew it for one he had thrown into the river as a present for his sweetheart.

She smiled, and "Come!" says she, and took him away to a palace of her own, and showed him a coffer; and in that coffer were bracelets and rings and earrings — all the gifts that he had thrown into the river.

And Sadko laughed for joy, and kissed the youngest daughter of the Tzar of the Sea, and she kissed him back.

"O my little river!" says he; "there is no girl in all the world but thou as pretty as my little river."

Well, they were married, and the Tzar of the Sea laughed at the wedding feast till the palace shook and the fish swam off in all directions.

And after the feast Sadko and his bride went off together to her palace. And before they slept she kissed him very tenderly, and she said:

"O Sadko, you will not forget me? You will play to me sometimes, and sing?"

"I shall never lose sight of you, my pretty one," says he, "and as for music, I will sing and play all the day long."

"That's as may be," says she, and they fell asleep.

And in the middle of the night Sadko happened to turn in bed, and he touched the Princess with his left foot, and she was cold, cold, cold as ice in January. And with that touch of cold he woke, and he was lying under the walls of Novgorod, with his dulcimer in his hand, and one of his feet was in the little river Volkhov, and the moon was shining.

"O grandfather! And what happened to him after that?" asked Maroosia.

"There are many tales," said old Peter. "Some say he went into the town, and lived on alone until he died. But I think with those who say that he took his dulcimer and swam out into the middle of the river, and sank under water again, looking for his little Princess. They say he found her, and lives still in the green palaces of the bottom of the sea; and when there is a big storm, you may know that Sadko is playing on his dulcimer and singing, and that the Tzar of the Sea is dancing his tremendous dance down there on the bottom, under the waves."

"Yes, I expect that's what happened," said Vanya. "He'd have found it very dull in Novgorod, even though it is a big town."

Frost

The children, in their little sheepskin coats and high felt boots and fur hats, trudged along the forest path in the snow. Vanya went first, then Maroosia, and then old Peter. The ground was white and the snow was hard and crisp, and all over the forest could be heard the crackling of the frost. And as they walked, old Peter told them the story of the old woman who wanted Frost to marry her daughters.

Once upon a time there were an old man and an old woman. Now the old woman was the old man's second wife. His first wife had died, and had left him with a little daughter: Martha she was called. Then he married again, and God gave him a cross wife, and with her two more daughters, and they were very different from the first.

The old woman loved her own daughters, and gave them red kisel jelly every day, and honey too, as much as they could put into their greedy little mouths. But poor little Martha, the eldest, she got only what the others left. When they were cross they threw away what they left, and then she got nothing at all.

The children grew older, and the stepmother made Martha do all the work of the house. She had to fetch the wood for the stove, and light it and keep it burning. She had to draw the water for her sisters to wash their hands in. She had to make the clothes, and wash them and mend them. She had to cook the dinner, and clean the dishes after the others had done before having a bite for herself.

For all that the stepmother was never satisfied, and was for ever shouting at her: "Look, the kettle is in the wrong place"; "There is dust on the floor"; "There is a spot on the table-cloth" or, "The spoons are not clean, you stupid, ugly, idle hussy." But Martha was not idle. She worked all day long, and got up before the sun, while her sisters never stirred from their beds

32

till it was time for dinner. And she was not stupid. She always had a song on her lips, except when her stepmother had beaten her. And as for being ugly, she was the prettiest little girl in the village.

Her father saw all this, but he could not do anything, for the old woman was mistress at home, and he was terribly afraid of her. And as for the daughters, they saw how their mother treated Martha, and they did the same. They were always complaining and getting her into trouble. It was a pleasure to them to see the tears on her pretty cheeks.

Well, time went on, and the little girl grew up, and the daughters of the stepmother were as ugly as could be. Their eyes were always cross, and their mouths were always complaining. Their mother saw that no one would want to marry either of them while there was Martha about the house, with her bright eyes and her songs and her kindness to everybody.

So she thought of a way to get rid of her stepdaughter, and a cruel way it was.

"See here, old man," says she, "it is high time Martha was married, and I have a bridegroom in mind for her. Tomorrow morning you must harness the old mare to the sledge, and put a bit of food together and be ready to start early, as I'd like to see you back before night."

To Martha she said: "Tomorrow you must pack your things in a box, and put on your best dress to show yourself to your betrothed."

"Who is he?" asked Martha with red cheeks.

"You will know when you see him," said the stepmother.

All that night Martha hardly slept. She could hardly believe that she was really going to escape from the old woman at last, and have a hut of her own, where there would be no one to scold her. She wondered who the young man was. She hoped he was Fedor Ivanovitch, who had such kind eyes, and such nimble fingers on the balalaika, and such a merry way of flinging out his heels when he danced the Russian dance. But although he always smiled at her when they met, she felt she hardly dared to hope that it was he. Early in the morning she got up and said her prayers to God, put the whole hut in order, and packed her things into a little box. That was easy, because she had such few things. It was the other daughters who had new dresses. Any old thing was good enough for Martha. But she put on her best blue dress, and there she was, as pretty a little maid as ever walked under the birch trees in spring.

The old man harnessed the mare to the sledge and brought it to the door. The snow was very deep and frozen hard, and the wind peeled the skin from his ears before he covered them with the flaps of his fur hat.

"Sit down at the table and have a bite before you go," says the old woman.

The old man sat down, and his daughter with him, and drank a glass of tea and ate some black bread. And the old woman put some cabbage soup, left from the day before, in a saucer, and said to Martha, "Eat this, my little pigeon, and get ready for the road." But when she said "my little pigeon", she did not smile with her eyes, but only with her cruel mouth, and Martha was afraid. The old woman whispered to the old man: "I have a word for you, old fellow. You will take Martha to her betrothed, and I'll tell you the way. You go straight along, and then take the road to the right into the forest . . . you know . . . straight to the big fir tree that stands on a hillock, and there you will give Martha to her betrothed and leave her. He will be waiting for her, and his name is Frost."

The old man stared, opened his mouth, and stopped eating. The little maid, who had heard the last words, began to cry.

"Now, what are you whimpering about?" screamed the old woman. "Frost is a rich bridegroom and a handsome one. See how much he owns. All the pines and firs are his, and the birch trees. Anyone would envy his possessions, and he himself is a very bogatir,* a man of strength and power."

The old man trembled, and said nothing in reply. And Martha went on crying quietly, though she tried to stop her

* The bogatirs were strong men, heroes of old Russia.

tears. The old man packed up what was left of the black bread, told Martha to put on her sheepskin coat, set her in the sledge and climbed in, and drove off along the white, frozen road.

The road was long and the country open, and the wind grew colder and colder, while the frozen snow blew up from under the hoofs of the mare and spattered the sledge with white patches. The tale is soon told, but it takes time to happen, and the sledge was white all over long before they turned off into the forest.

They came in the end deep into the forest, and left the road, and over the deep snow through the trees to the great fir. There the old man stopped, told his daughter to get out of the sledge, set her little box under the fir, and said, "Wait here for your bridegroom, and when he comes be sure to receive him with kind words." Then he turned the mare round and drove home, with the tears running from his eyes and freezing on his cheeks before they had had time to reach his beard.

The little maid sat and trembled. Her sheepskin coat was worn through, and in her blue bridal dress she sat, while fits of shivering shook her whole body. She wanted to run away; but she had not strength to move, or even to keep her little white teeth from chattering between her frozen lips.

Suddenly, not far away, she heard Frost crackling among the fir trees, just as he is crackling now. He was leaping from tree to tree, crackling as he came.

He leapt at last into the great fir tree, under which the little maid was sitting. He crackled in the top of the tree, and then called down out of the topmost branches:

"Are you warm, little maid?"

"Warm, warm, little Father Frost."

Frost laughed, and came a little lower in the tree and crackled and crackled louder than before. Then he asked:

"Are you still warm, little maid? Are you warm, little red cheeks?"

The little maid could hardly speak. She was nearly dead, but she answered:

"Warm, dear Frost; warm, little father."

Frost climbed lower in the tree, and crackled louder than ever, and asked:

"Are you still warm, little maid? Are you warm, little red cheeks? Are you warm, little paws?"

The little maid was benumbed all over, but she whispered so that Frost could just hear her:

"Warm, little pigeon, warm, dear Frost."

And Frost was sorry for her, leapt down with a tremendous crackle and a scattering of frozen snow, wrapped the little maid up in rich furs, and covered her with warm blankets.

In the morning the old woman said to her husband, "Drive off now to the forest, and wake the young couple."

The old man wept when he thought of his little daughter, for he was sure that he would find her dead. He harnessed the mare, and drove off through the snow. He came to the tree, and heard his little daughter singing merrily, while Frost crackled and laughed. There she was, alive and warm, with a good fur cloak about her shoulders, a rich veil, costly blankets round her, and a box full of splendid presents.

The old man did not say a word. He was too surprised. He just sat in the sledge staring, while the little maid lifted her box and the box of presents, set them in the sledge, climbed in, and sat down beside him.

They came home, and the little maid, Martha, fell at the feet of her stepmother. The old woman nearly went off her head with rage when she saw her alive, with her fur cloak and rich veil, and the box of splendid presents fit for the daughter of a prince.

"Ah, you slut," she cried, "you won't get round me like that!"

And she would not say another word to the little maid, but went about all day long biting her nails and thinking what to do.

At night she said to the old man:

"You must take my daughters, too, to that bridegroom in the forest. He will give them better gifts than these."

Things take time to happen, but the tale is quickly told. Early next morning the old woman woke her daughters, fed them with good food, dressed them like brides, hustled the old man, made him put clean hay in the sledge and warm blankets, and sent them off to the forest.

The old man did as he was bid — drove to the big fir tree, set the boxes under the tree, lifted out the stepdaughters and set them on the boxes side by side, and drove back home.

They were warmly dressed, these two, and well fed, and at first, as they sat there, they did not think about the cold.

"I can't think what put it into mother's head to marry us both at once," said the first, "and to send us here to be married. As if there were not enough young men in the village. Who can tell what sort of fellows we shall meet here!"

Then they began to quarrel.

"Well," says one of them, "I'm beginning to get the cold shivers. If our fated ones do not come soon, we shall perish of cold."

"It's a flat lie to say that bridegrooms get ready early. It's already dinner-time."

"What if only one comes?"

"You'll have to come another time."

"You think he'll look at you?"

"Well, he won't take you, anyhow."

"Of course he'll take me."

"Take you first! It's enough to make anyone laugh!"

They began to fight and scratch each other, so that their cloaks fell open and the cold entered their bosoms.

Frost, crackling among the trees, laughing to himself, froze the hands of the two quarrelling girls, and they hid their hands in the sleeves of their fur coats and shivered, and went on scolding and jeering at each other.

"Oh, you ugly mug, dirty nose! What sort of a housekeeper will you make?"

"And what about you, boasting one? You know nothing but how to gad about and lick your own face. We'll soon see which of us he'll take."

And the two girls went on wrangling and wrangling till they began to freeze in good earnest.

Suddenly they cried out together:

"Devil take these bridegrooms for being so long in coming! You have turned blue all over."

And together they replied, shivering:

"No bluer than yourself, tooth-chatterer."

And Frost, not so far away, crackled and laughed, and leapt from fir tree to fir tree, crackling as he came.

The girls heard that someone was coming through the forest.

"Listen! there's someone coming. Yes, and with bells on his sledge!"

"Shut up, you slut! I can't hear, and the frost is taking the skin off me."

They began blowing on their fingers.

And Frost came nearer and nearer, crackling, laughing, talking to himself, just as he is doing today. Nearer and nearer he came, leaping from tree-top to tree-top, till at last he leapt into the great fir under which the two girls were sitting and quarrelling.

He leant down, looking through the branches, and asked:

"Are you warm, maidens? Are you warm, little red cheeks? Are you warm, little pigeons?"

"Ugh, Frost, the cold is hurting us. We are frozen. We are waiting for our bridegrooms, but the cursed fellows have not turned up."

Frost came a little lower in the tree, and crackled louder and swifter.

"Are you warm, maidens? Are you warm, my little red cheeks?"

"Go to the devil!" they cried out. "Are you blind? Our hands and feet are frozen!"

Frost came still lower in the branches, and cracked and crackled louder than ever.

"Are you warm, maidens?" he asked.

"Into the pit with you, with all the fiends," the girls screamed at him, "you ugly, wretched fellow! . . ." And as they were cursing at him their bad words died on their lips, for the two girls, the cross children of the cruel stepmother, were frozen stiff where they sat.

Frost hung from the lowest branches of the tree, swaying and crackling while he looked at the anger frozen on their faces. Then he climbed swiftly up again, and crackling and cracking, chuckling to himself, he went off, leaping from fir tree to fir tree, this way and that through the white, frozen forest.

In the morning the old woman says to her husband:

"Now then, old man, harness the mare to the sledge, and put new hay in the sledge to be warm for my little ones, and lay fresh rushes on the hay to be soft for them; and take warm rugs with you, for maybe they will be cold, even in their furs. And look sharp about it, and don't keep them waiting. The frost is hard this morning, and it was harder in the night."

The old man had not time to eat even a mouthful of black bread before she had driven him out into the snow. He put hay and rushes and soft blankets in the sledge, and harnessed the mare, and went off to the forest. He came to the great fir, and found the two girls sitting under it dead, with their anger still to be seen on their frozen, ugly faces.

He picked them up, first one and then the other, and put them in the rushes and the warm hay, covered them with the blankets, and drove home.

The old woman saw him coming, far away, over the shining snow. She ran to meet him, and shouted out:

"Where are the little ones?"

"In the sledge."

She snatched off the blankets and pulled aside the rushes, and found the bodies of her two cross daughters.

Instantly she flew at the old man in a storm of rage. "What have you done to my children, my little red cherries, my little pigeons? I will kill you with the oven fork! I will break your head with the poker!"

The old man listened till she was out of breath and could not say another word. That, my dears, is the only wise thing to do when a woman is in a scolding rage. And as soon as she had no breath left with which to answer him, he said:

"My little daughter got riches for soft words, but yours were always rough of the tongue. And it's not my fault, anyhow, for you yourself sent them into the forest."

Well, at last the old woman got her breath again, and scolded away till she was tired out. But in the end she made her peace with the old man, and they lived together as quietly as could be expected.

As for Martha, Fedor Ivanovitch sought her in marriage, as he had meant to do all along — yes, and married her; and pretty she looked in the furs that Frost had given her. I was at the feast, and drank beer and mead with the rest. And she had the prettiest children that ever were seen — yes, and the best behaved. For if ever they thought of being naughty, the old grandfather told them the story of crackling Frost, and how kind words won kindness, and cross words cold treatment. And now, listen to Frost. Hear how he crackles away! And mind, if ever he asks you if you are warm, be as polite to him as you can. And to do that, the best way is to be good always, like little Martha. Then it comes easy.

*****

The children listened, and laughed quietly, because they knew they were good. Away in the forest they heard Frost, and thought of him crackling and leaping from one tree to another. And just then they came home. It was dusk, for dusk comes early in winter, and a little way through the trees before them they saw the lamp of their hut glittering on the snow. The big dog barked and ran forward, and the children with him. The soup was warm on the stove, and in a few minutes they were sitting at the table, Vanya, Maroosia, and old Peter, blowing at their steaming spoons.

The Fool of the World
and the Flying Ship

There were once upon a time an old peasant and his wife, and they had three sons. Two of them were clever young men who could borrow money without being cheated, but the third was the Fool of the World. He was as simple as a child, simpler than some children, and he never did anyone a harm in his life.

Well, it always happens like that. The father and mother thought a lot of the two smart young men; but the Fool of the World was lucky if he got enough to eat, because they always forgot him unless they happened to be looking at him, and sometimes even then.

But however it was with his father and mother, this is a story that shows that God loves simple folk, and turns things to their advantage in the end.

For it happened that the Tzar of that country sent out

messengers along the highroads and the rivers, even to huts in the forest like ours, to say that he would give his daughter, the Princess, in marriage to anyone who could bring him a flying ship — ay, a ship with wings, that should sail this way and that through the blue sky, like a ship sailing on the sea.

"This is a chance for us," said the two clever brothers; and that same day they set off together, to see if one of them could not build the flying ship and marry the Tzar's daughter, and so be a great man indeed.

And their father blessed them, and gave them finer clothes than ever he wore himself. And their mother made them up hampers of food for the road, soft white rolls, and several kinds of cooked meats, and bottles of vodka. She went with them as far as the highroad, and waved her hand to them till they were out of sight. And so the two clever brothers set merrily off on their adventure, to see what could be done with their cleverness. And what happened to them I do not know, for they were never heard of again.

The Fool of the World saw them set off, with their fine parcels of food, and their fine clothes, and their bottles of vodka.

"I'd like to go too," says he, "and eat good meat, with soft white rolls, and drink vodka, and marry the Tzar's daughter."

"Stupid fellow," says his mother, "what's the good of your going? Why, if you were to stir from the house you would walk into the arms of a bear; and if not that, then the wolves would eat you before you had finished staring at them."

But the Fool of the World would not be held back by words.

"I am going," says he. "I am going. I am going. I am going."

He went on saying this over and over again, till the old woman his mother saw there was nothing to be done, and was glad to get him out of the house so as to be quit of the sound of his voice. So she put some food in a bag for him to eat by the way. She put in the bag some crusts of dry black bread and a flask of water. She did not even bother to go as far as the footpath to see him on his way. She saw the last of him at the door of the hut, and he had not taken two steps before she had gone back into the hut to see to more important business.

No matter. The Fool of the World set off with his bag over his shoulder, singing as he went, for he was off to seek his fortune and marry the Tzar's daughter. He was sorry his mother had not given him any vodka; but he sang merrily for all that. He would have liked white rolls instead of the dry black crusts; but, after all, the main thing on a journey is to have something to eat. So he trudged merrily along the road, and sang because the trees were green and there was a blue sky overhead.

He had not gone very far when he met an ancient old man with a bent back, and a long beard, and eyes hidden under his bushy eyebrows.

"Good day, young fellow," says the ancient old man.

"Good day, grandfather," says the Fool of the World.

"And where are you off to?" says the ancient old man.

"What!" says the Fool; "haven't you heard? The Tzar is going to give his daughter to anyone who can bring him a flying ship."

"And you can really make a flying ship?" says the ancient old man.

"No, I do not know how."

"Then what are you going to do?"

"God knows," says the Fool of the World.

"Well," says the ancient, "if things are like that, sit you down here. We will rest together and have a bite of food. Bring out what you have in your bag."

"I am ashamed to offer you what I have here. It is good enough for me, but it is not the sort of meal to which one can ask guests."

"Never mind that. Out with it. Let us eat what God has given."

The Fool of the World opened his bag, and could hardly believe his eyes. Instead of black crusts he saw fresh white rolls and cooked meats. He handed them out to the ancient, who said, "You see how God loves simple folk. Although your own mother does not love you, you have not been done out of your share of the good things. Let's have a sip at the vodka. . ."

The Fool of the World opened his flask, and instead of water there came out vodka, and that of the best. So the Fool and the ancient made merry, eating and drinking; and when they had done, and sung a song or two together, the ancient says to the Fool:

"Listen to me. Off with you into the forest. Go up to the first big tree you see. Make the sacred sign of the cross three times before it. Strike it a blow with your little hatchet. Fall backwards on the ground, and lie there, full length on your back, until somebody wakes you up. Then you will find the ship made, all ready to fly. Sit you down in it, and fly off whither you want to go. But be sure on the way to give a lift to everyone you meet."

The Fool of the World thanked the ancient old man, said good-bye to him, and went off to the forest. He walked up to a tree, the first big tree he saw, made the sign of the cross three times before it, swung his hatchet round his head, struck a mighty blow on the trunk of the tree, instantly fell backwards flat on the ground, closed his eyes, and went to sleep.

A little time went by, and it seemed to the Fool as he slept that somebody was jogging his elbow. He woke up and opened his eyes. His hatchet, worn out, lay beside him. The big tree was gone, and in its place there stood a little ship, ready and finished. The Fool did not stop to think. He jumped into the ship, seized the tiller, and sat down. Instantly the ship leapt up into the air, and sailed away over the tops of the trees.

The little ship answered the tiller as readily as if she were sailing in water, and the Fool steered for the highroad, and sailed along above it, for he was afraid of losing his way if he tried to steer a course across the open country.

He flew on and on, and looked down, and saw a man lying in the road below him with his ear on the damp ground.

"Good day to you, uncle," cried the Fool.

"Good day to you, Sky-fellow," cried the man.

"What are you doing down there?" says the Fool.

"I am listening to all that is being done in the world."

"Take your place in the ship with me."

The man was willing enough, and sat down in the ship with the Fool, and they flew on together singing songs.

They flew on and on, and looked down, and there was a man on one leg, with the other tied up to his head.

"Good day, uncle," says the Fool, bringing the ship to the ground. "Why are you hopping along on one foot?"

"If I were to untie the other I should move too fast. I should be stepping across the world in a single stride."

"Sit down with us," says the Fool.

The man sat down with them in the ship, and they flew on together singing songs.

They flew on and on, and looked down, and there was a man with a gun, and he was taking aim, but what he was aiming at they could not see.

"Good health to you, uncle," says the Fool. "But what are you shooting at? There isn't a bird to be seen."

"What!" says the man. "If there were a bird that you could see, I should not shoot at it. A bird or a beast a thousand versts away, that's the sort of mark for me."

"Take your seat with us," says the Fool.

The man sat down with them in the ship, and they flew on together. Louder and louder rose their songs.

They flew on and on, and looked down, and there was a man carrying a sack full of bread on his back.

"Good health to you, uncle," says the Fool, sailing down. "And where are you off to?"

"I am going to get bread for my dinner."

"But you've got a full sack on your back."

"That — that little scrap! Why, that's not enough for a single mouthful."

"Take your seat with us," says the Fool.

The Eater sat down with them in the ship, and they flew on together, singing louder than ever.

They flew on and on, and looked down, and there was a man walking round and round a lake.

"Good health to you, uncle," says the Fool. "What are you looking for?"

"I want a drink, and I can't find any water."

"But there's a whole lake in front of your eyes. Why can't you take a drink from that?"

"That little drop!" says the man. "Why, there's not enough water there to wet the back of my throat if I were to drink it at one gulp."

"Take your seat with us," says the Fool.

The Drinker sat down with them, and again they flew on, singing in chorus.

They flew on and on, and looked down, and there was a man walking towards the forest, with a faggot of wood on his shoulders.

"Good day to you, uncle," says the Fool. "Why are you taking wood to the forest?"

"This isn't simple wood," says the man.

"What is it, then?" says the Fool.

"If it is scattered about, a whole army of soldiers leaps up out of the ground."

"There's a place for you with us," says the Fool.

The man sat down with them, and the ship rose up into the air, and flew on, carrying its singing crew.

They flew on and on, and looked down, and there was a man carrying a sack of straw.

"Good health to you, uncle," says the Fool; "and where are you taking your straw?"

"To the village."

"Why, are they short of straw in your village?"

"No; but this is such straw that if you scatter it abroad in the very hottest of the summer, instantly the weather turns cold, and there is snow and frost."

"There's a place here for you too," says the Fool.

"Very kind of you," says the man, and steps in and sits

down, and away they all sail together, singing like to burst their lungs.

They did not meet anyone else, and presently came flying up to the palace of the Tzar. They flew down and cast anchor in the courtyard.

Just then the Tzar was eating his dinner. He heard their loud singing, and looked out of the window and saw the ship come sailing down into his courtyard. He sent his servant out to ask who was the great prince who had brought him the flying ship, and had come sailing down with such a merry noise of singing.

The servant came up to the ship, and saw the Fool of the World and his companions sitting there cracking jokes. He saw they were all moujiks, simple peasants, sitting in the ship; so he did not stop to ask questions, but came back quietly and told the Tzar that there were no gentlemen in the ship at all, but only a lot of dirty peasants.

Now the Tzar was not at all pleased with the idea of giving his only daughter in marriage to a simple peasant, and he began to think how he could get out of his bargain. Thinks he to himself, "I'll set them such tasks that they will not be able to perform, and they'll be glad to get off with their lives, and I shall get the ship for nothing."

So he told his servant to go to the Fool and tell him that before the Tzar had finished his dinner the Fool was to bring him some of the magical water of life.

Now, while the Tzar was giving this order to his servant, the Listener, the first of the Fool's companions, was listening and heard the words of the Tzar and repeated them to the Fool.

"What am I to do now?" says the Fool, stopping short in his jokes. "In a year, in a whole century, I never could find that water. And he wants it before he has finished his dinner."

"Don't you worry about that," says the Swift-goer, "I'll deal with that for you."

The servant came and announced the Tzar's command. "Tell him he shall have it," says the Fool.

His companion, the Swift-goer, untied his foot from beside his head, put it to the ground, wriggled it a little to get the stiffness out of it, ran off, and was out of sight almost before he had stepped from the ship. Quicker than I can tell it you in words he had come to the water of life, and put some of it in a bottle.

"I shall have plenty of time to get back," thinks he, and down he sits under a windmill and goes off to sleep.

The royal dinner was coming to an end, and there wasn't a sign of him. There were no songs and no jokes in the flying ship. Everybody was watching for the Swift-goer, and thinking he would not be in time.

The Listener jumped out and laid his right ear to the damp ground, listened a moment, and said, "What a fellow! He has gone to sleep under the windmill. I can hear him snoring. And there is a fly buzzing with its wings, perched on the windmill close above his head."

"This is my affair," says the Far-shooter, and he picked up his gun from between his knees, aimed at the fly on the windmill, and woke the Swift-goer with the thud of the bullet on the wood of the mill close by his head. The Swift-goer leapt up and ran, and in less than a second had brought the magic water of life and given it to the Fool. The Fool gave it to the servant, who took it to the Tzar. The Tzar had not yet left the table, so that his command had been fulfilled as exactly as ever could be.

"What fellows these peasants are," thought the Tzar. "There is nothing for it but to set them another task." So the Tzar said to his servant, "Go to the captain of the flying ship and give him this message: 'If you are such a cunning fellow, you must have a good appetite. Let you and your companions eat at a single meal twelve oxen roasted whole, and as much bread as can be baked in forty ovens!'

The Listener heard the message, and told the Fool what was coming. The Fool was terrified, and said, "I can't get through even a single loaf at a sitting."

"Don't worry about that," said the Eater. "It won't be more than a mouthful for me, and I shall be glad to have a little snack in place of my dinner."

The servant came, and announced the Tzar's command. "Good," says the Fool. "Send the food along, and we'll know what to do with it."

So they brought twelve oxen roasted whole, and as much bread as could be baked in forty ovens, and the companions had scarcely sat down to the meal before the Eater had finished the lot.

"Why," said the Eater, "what a little! They might have given us a decent meal while they were about it."

The Tzar told his servant to tell the Fool that he and his companions were to drink forty barrels of wine, with forty bucketfuls in every barrel.

The Listener told the Fool what message was coming. "Why," says the Fool, "I never in my life drank more than one bucket at a time."

"Don't worry," says the Drinker. "You forget that I am thirsty. It'll be nothing of a drink for me."

They brought the forty barrels of wine, and tapped them, and the Drinker tossed them down one after another, one gulp for each barrel. "Little enough," says he. "Why, I am thirsty still."

"Very good," says the Tzar to his servant, when he heard that they had eaten all the food and drunk all the wine. "Tell the fellow to get ready for the wedding, and let him go and bathe himself in the bath-house. But let the bath-house be made so hot that the man will stifle and frizzle as soon as he sets foot inside. It is an iron bath-house. Let it be made red hot."

The Listener heard all this and told the Fool, who stopped short with his mouth open in the middle of a joke.

"Don't you worry," says the moujik with the straw.

Well, they made the bath-house red hot, and called the Fool, and the Fool went along to the bath-house to wash himself, and with him went the moujik with the straw.

They shut them both into the bath-house, and thought that that was the end of them. But the moujik scattered his straw before them as they went in, and it became so cold in there that the Fool of the World had scarcely time to wash himself before the water in the cauldrons froze to solid ice. They lay down on the very stove itself, and spent the night there, shivering.

In the morning the servants opened the bath-house, and there were the Fool of the World and the moujik, alive and well, lying on the stove and singing songs.

They told the Tzar, and the Tzar raged with anger. "There is no getting rid of this fellow," says he. "But go and tell him that I send him this message: 'If you are to marry my daughter, you must show that you are able to defend her. Let me see that you have at least a regiment of soldiers.'" Thinks he to himself, "How can a simple peasant raise a troop? He will find it hard enough to raise a single soldier."

The Listener told the Fool of the World, and the Fool began to lament, "This time," says he, "I am done indeed. You, my brothers, have saved me from misfortune more than once, but this time, alas, there is nothing to be done."

"Oh, what a fellow you are!" says the peasant with the faggot of wood. "I suppose you've forgotten about me. Remember that I am the man for this little affair, and don't you worry about it at all."

The Tzar's servant came along and gave his message.

"Very good," says the Fool, "but tell the Tzar that if after this he puts me off again, I'll make war on his country, and take the Princess by force."

And then, as the servant went back with the message, the whole crew on the flying ship set to their singing again, and sang and laughed and made jokes as if they had not a care in the world.

During the night, while the others slept, the peasant with the faggot of wood went hither and thither, scattering his sticks. Instantly where they fell there appeared a gigantic army. Nobody could count the number of soldiers in it — cavalry, foot soldiers, yes, and guns, and all the guns new and bright, and the men in the finest uniforms that ever were seen.

In the morning, as the Tzar woke and looked from the windows of the palace, he found himself surrounded by troops upon troops of soldiers, and generals in cocked hats bowing in the courtyard and taking orders from the Fool of the World, who sat there joking with his companions in the flying ship. Now it was the Tzar's turn to be afraid. As quickly as he could he sent his servants to the Fool with presents of rich jewels and fine clothes, invited him to come to the palace, and begged him to marry the Princess.

The Fool of the World put on the fine clothes, and stood there as handsome a young man as a princess could wish for a husband. He presented himself before the Tzar, fell in love with the Princess and she with him, married her the same day, received with her a rich dowry, and became so clever that all the court repeated everything he said. The Tzar and the Tzaritza liked him very much, and as for the Princess, she loved him to distraction.

Baba Yaga

"Tell us about Baba Yaga," begged Maroosia.

"Yes," said Vanya, "please, grandfather, and about the little hut on hen's legs."

"Baba Yaga is a witch," said old Peter, "a terrible old woman she is, but sometimes kind enough. You know it was she who told Prince Ivan how to win one of the daughters of the Tzar of the Sea, and that was the best daughter of the bunch, Vasilissa the Very Wise. But then Baba Yaga is usually bad, as in the case of Vasilissa the Very Beautiful, who was only saved from her iron teeth by the cleverness of her Magic Doll."

"Tell us the story of the Magic Doll," begged Maroosia.

"I will some day," said old Peter.

"And has Baba Yaga really got iron teeth?" asked Vanya.

"Iron, like the poker and tongs," said old Peter.

"What for?" said Maroosia.

"To eat up little Russian children," said old Peter, "when she can get them. She usually only eats bad ones, because the good ones get away. She is bony all over, and her eyes flash, and she drives about in a mortar, beating it with a pestle, and sweeping up her tracks with a besom, so that you cannot tell which way she has gone."

"And her hut?" said Vanya. He had often heard about it before, but he wanted to hear about it again.

"She lives in a little hut which stands on hen's legs. Sometimes it faces the forest, sometimes it faces the path, and sometimes it walks solemnly about. But in some of the stories she lives in another kind of hut, with a railing of tall sticks, and a skull on each stick. And all night long fire glows in the skulls and fades as the dawn rises."

"Now tell us one of the Baba Yaga stories," said Maroosia.

"Please," said Vanya.

"I will tell you how one little girl got away from her, and

then, if ever she catches you, you will know exactly what to do."

And old Peter put down his pipe and began:

BABA YAGA AND THE LITTLE GIRL WITH THE KIND HEART

Once upon a time there was a widowed old man who lived alone in a hut with his little daughter. Very merry they were together, and they used to smile at each other over a table just piled with bread and jam. Everything went well, until the old man took it into his head to marry again.

Yes, the old man became foolish in the years of his old age, and he took another wife. And so the poor little girl had a stepmother. And after that everything changed. There was no more bread and jam on the table, and no more playing bo-peep, first this side of the samovar and then that, as she sat with her father at tea. It was worse than that, for she never did sit at tea. The stepmother said that everything that went wrong was the little girl's fault. And the old man believed his new wife, and so there were no more kind words for his little daughter. Day after day the stepmother used to say that the little girl was too naughty to sit at table. And then she would throw her a crust and tell her to get out of the hut and go and eat it somewhere else.

And the poor little girl used to go away by herself into the shed in the yard, and wet the dry crust with her tears, and eat it all alone. Ah me! she often wept for the old days, and she often wept at the thought of the days that were to come.

Mostly she wept because she was all alone, until one day she found a little friend in the shed. She was hunched up in a corner of the shed, eating her crust and crying bitterly, when she heard a little noise. It was like this: scratch — scratch. It was just that, a little grey mouse who lived in a hole.

Out he came, his little pointed nose and his long whiskers, his little round ears and his bright eyes. Out came his little humpy body and his long tail. And then he sat up on his hind legs, and curled his tail twice round himself and looked at the little girl.

The little girl, who had a kind heart, forgot all her sorrows, and took a scrap of her crust and threw it to the little mouse. The mouseykin nibbled and nibbled, and there, it was gone, and he was looking for another. She gave him another bit, and presently that was gone, and another and another, until there was no crust left for the little girl. Well, she didn't mind that. You see, she was so happy seeing the little mouse nibbling and nibbling.

When the crust was done the mouseykin looks up at her with his little bright eyes, and "Thank you," he says, in a little squeaky voice. "Thank you," he says "you are a kind little girl, and I am only a mouse, and I've eaten all your crust. But there is one thing I can do for you, and that is to tell you to take care. The old woman in the hut (and that was the cruel stepmother) is own sister to Baba Yaga, the bony-legged, the witch. So if ever she sends you on a message to your aunt, you come and tell me. For Baba Yaga would eat you soon enough with her iron teeth if you did not know what to do."

"Oh, thank you," said the little girl; and just then she heard the stepmother calling to her to come in and clean up the tea things, and tidy the house, and brush out the floor, and clean everybody's boots.

So off she had to go.

When she went in she had a good look at her stepmother, and sure enough she had a long nose, and she was as bony as a fish with all the flesh picked off, and the little girl thought of Baba Yaga and shivered, though she did not feel so bad when she remembered the mouseykin out there in the shed in the yard.

The very next morning it happened. The old man went off to pay a visit to some friends of his in the next village, just as I go off sometimes to see old Fedor, God be with him. And as soon as the old man was out of sight the wicked stepmother called the little girl.

"You are to go today to your dear little aunt in the forest," says she, "and ask her for a needle and thread to mend a shirt."

"But here is a needle and thread," says the little girl.

"Hold your tongue," says the stepmother, and she gnashes her teeth, and they make a noise like clattering tongs. "Hold your tongue," she says. "Didn't I tell you you are to go today to your dear little aunt to ask for a needle and thread to mend a shirt?"

"How shall I find her?" says the little girl, nearly ready to cry, for she knew that her aunt was Baba Yaga, the bony-legged, the witch.

The stepmother took hold of the little girl's nose and pinched it.

"That is your nose," she says. "Can you feel it?"

"Yes," says the poor little girl.

"You must go along the road into the forest till you come to a fallen tree; then you must turn to your left, and then follow your nose and you will find her," says the stepmother. "Now, be off with you, lazy one. Here is some food for you to eat by the way." She gave the little girl a bundle wrapped up in a towel.

The little girl wanted to go into the shed to tell the mouseykin she was going to Baba Yaga, and to ask what she should do. But she looked back, and there was the stepmother at the door watching her. So she had to go straight on.

She walked along the road through the forest till she came to the fallen tree. Then she turned to the left. Her nose was still hurting where the stepmother had pinched it, so she knew she had to go straight ahead. She was just setting out when she heard a little noise under the fallen tree.

"Scratch — scratch."

And out jumped the little mouse, and sat up in the road in front of her.

"O mouseykin, mouseykin," says the little girl, "my stepmother has sent me to her sister. And that is Baba Yaga, the bony-legged, the witch, and I do not know what to do."

"It will not be difficult," says the little mouse, "because of your kind heart. Take all the things you find in the road, and do with them what you like. Then you will escape from Baba Yaga, and everything will be well."

"Are you hungry, mouseykin?" said the little girl.

"I could nibble, I think," says the little mouse.

The little girl unfastened the towel, and there was nothing in it but stones. That was what the stepmother had given the little girl to eat by the way.

"Oh, I'm so sorry," says the little girl. "There's nothing for you to eat."

"Isn't there?" said mouseykin, and as she looked at them the little girl saw the stones turn to bread and jam. The little girl sat down on the fallen tree, and the little mouse sat beside her, and they ate bread and jam until they were not hungry any more.

"Keep the towel," says the little mouse, "I think it will be useful. And remember what I said about the things you find on the way. And now good-bye," says he.

"Good-bye," says the little girl, and runs along.

As she was running along she found a nice new handkerchief lying in the road. She picked it up and took it with her. Then she found a little bottle of oil. She picked it up and took it with her. Then she found some scraps of meat.

"Perhaps I'd better take them too," she said; and she took them.

Then she found a gay blue ribbon, and she took that. Then she found a little loaf of good bread, and she took that too.

"I dare say somebody will like it," she said.

And then she came to the hut of Baba Yaga, the bony-legged, the witch. There was a high fence round it with big gates. When she pushed them open they squeaked miserably, as if it hurt them to move. The little girl was sorry for them.

"How lucky," she says, "that I picked up the bottle of oil!" and she poured the oil into the hinges of the gates.

Inside the railing was Baba Yaga's hut, and it stood on hen's legs and walked about the yard. And in the yard there was standing Baba Yaga's servant, and she was crying bitterly because of the tasks Baba Yaga set her to do. She was crying bitterly and wiping her eyes on her petticoat.

"How lucky," says the little girl, "that I picked up a handkerchief!" And she gave the handkerchief to Baba Yaga's servant, who wiped her eyes on it and smiled through her tears.

Close by the hut was a huge dog, very thin, gnawing a dry crust.

"How lucky," says the little girl, "that I picked up a loaf!" And she gave the loaf to the dog, and he gobbled it up and licked his lips.

The little girl went bravely up to the hut and knocked on the door.

"Come in," says Baba Yaga.

The little girl went in, and there was Baba Yaga, the bony-legged, the witch, sitting weaving at a loom. In a corner of the hut was a thin black cat watching a mouse-hole.

"Good day to you, auntie," says the little girl, trying not to tremble.

"Good day to you, niece," says Baba Yaga.

"My stepmother has sent me to you to ask for a needle and thread to mend a shirt."

"Very well," says Baba Yaga, smiling, and showing her iron teeth. "You sit down here at the loom, and go on with my weaving, while I go and get you the needle and thread."

The little girl sat down at the loom and began to weave.

Baba Yaga went out and called to her servant, "Go, make the bath hot and scrub my niece. Scrub her clean. I'll make a dainty meal of her."

The servant came in for the jug. The little girl begged her, "Be not too quick in making the fire, and carry the water in a sieve." The servant smiled, but said nothing, because she was afraid of Baba Yaga. But she took a very long time about getting the bath ready.

Baba Yaga came to the window and asked:

"Are you weaving, little niece? Are you weaving, my pretty?"

"I am weaving, auntie," says the little girl.

58

When Baba Yaga went away from the window, the little girl spoke to the thin black cat who was watching the mouse-hole.

"What are you doing, thin black cat?"

"Watching for a mouse," says the thin black cat. "I haven't had any dinner for three days."

"How lucky," says the little girl, "that I picked up the scraps of meat!" And she gave them to the thin black cat. The thin black cat gobbled them up, and said to the little girl:

"Little girl, do you want to get out of this?"

"Catkin dear," says the little girl, "I do want to get out of this, for Baba Yaga is going to eat me with her iron teeth."

"Well," says the cat, "I will help you."

Just then Baba Yaga came to the window.

"Are you weaving, little niece?" she asked. "Are you weaving, my pretty?"

"I am weaving, auntie," says the little girl, working away, while the loom went clickety clack, clickety clack.

Baba Yaga went away.

Says the thin black cat to the little girl: "You have a comb in your hair, and you have a towel. Take them and run for it while Baba Yaga is in the bath-house. When Baba Yaga chases after you, you must listen; and when she is close to you, throw away the towel, and it will turn into a big wide river. It will take her a little time to get over that. But when she does, you must listen; and as soon as she is close to you throw away the comb, and it will sprout up into such a forest that she will never get through it at all."

"But she'll hear the loom stop," says the little girl.

"I'll see to that," says the thin black cat.

The cat took the little girl's place at the loom.

Clickety clack, clickety clack; the loom never stopped for a moment.

The girl looked to see that Baba Yaga was in the bath-house, and then she jumped down from the little hut on hen's legs, and ran to the gates as fast as her legs could flicker.

The big dog leapt up to tear her to pieces. Just as he was going to spring on her he saw who she was.

"Why, this is the little girl who gave me the loaf," says he. "A good journey to you, little girl"; and he lay down again with his head between his paws.

When she came to the gates they opened quietly, quietly, without making any noise at all, because of the oil she had poured into their hinges.

Outside the gates there was a little birch tree that beat her in the eyes so that she could not go by.

"How lucky," says the little girl, "that I picked up the ribbon!" And she tied up the birch tree with the pretty blue ribbon. And the birch tree was so pleased with the ribbon that it stood still, admiring itself, and let the little girl go by.

How she did run!

Meanwhile the thin black cat sat at the loom. Clickety clack, clickety clack, sang the loom; but you never saw such a tangle as the tangle made by the thin black cat.

And presently Baba Yaga came to the window.

"Are you weaving, little niece?" she asked. "Are you weaving, my pretty?"

"I am weaving, auntie," says the thin black cat, tangling and tangling, while the loom went clickety clack, clickety clack.

"That's not the voice of my little dinner," says Baba Yaga, and she jumped into the hut, gnashing her iron teeth; and there was no little girl, but only the thin black cat, sitting at the loom, tangling and tangling the threads.

"Grr," says Baba Yaga, and jumps for the cat, and begins banging it about. "Why didn't you tear the little girl's eyes out?"

"In all the years I have served you," says the cat, "you have only given me one little bone; but the kind little girl gave me scraps of meat."

Baba Yaga threw the cat into a corner, and went out into the yard.

"Why didn't you squeak when she opened you?" she asked the gates.

"Why didn't you tear her to pieces?" she asked the dog.

"Why didn't you beat her in the face, and not let her go by?" she asked the birch tree.

"Why were you so long in getting the bath ready? If you had been quicker, she never would have got away," said Baba Yaga to the servant.

And she rushed about the yard, beating them all, and scolding at the top of her voice.

"Ah!" said the gates, "in all the years we have served you, you never even eased us with water; but the kind little girl poured good oil into our hinges."

"Ah!" said the dog, "in all the years I've served you, you never threw me anything but burnt crusts; but the kind little girl gave me a good loaf."

"Ah!" said the little birch tree, "in all the years I've served you, you never tied me up, even with thread; but the kind little girl tied me up with a gay blue ribbon."

"Ah!" said the servant, "in all the years I've served you, you have never given me even a rag; but the kind little girl gave me a pretty handkerchief."

Baba Yaga gnashed at them with her iron teeth. Then she jumped into the mortar and sat down. She drove it along with the pestle, and swept up her tracks with a besom, and flew off in pursuit of the little girl.

The little girl ran and ran. She put her ear to the ground and listened. Bang, bang, bangety bang! she could hear Baba Yaga beating the mortar with the pestle. Baba Yaga was quite close. There she was, beating with the pestle and sweeping with the besom, coming along the road.

As quickly as she could, the little girl took out the towel and threw it on the ground. And the towel grew bigger and bigger, and wetter and wetter, and there was a deep, broad river between Baba Yaga and the little girl.

The little girl turned and ran on. How she ran!

Baba Yaga came flying up in the mortar. But the mortar could not float in the river with Baba Yaga inside. She drove it in, but only got wet for her trouble. Tongs and pokers tumbling down a chimney are nothing to the noise she made as she gnashed her iron teeth. She turned home, and went flying back to the little hut on hen's legs. Then she got together all her cattle and drove them to the river.

"Drink, drink!" she screamed at them; and the cattle drank up all the river to the last drop. And Baba Yaga, sitting in the mortar, drove it with the pestle, and swept up her tracks with the besom, and flew over the dry bed of the river and on in pursuit of the little girl.

The little girl put her ear to the ground and listened. Bang, bang, bangety bang! She could hear Baba Yaga beating the mortar with the pestle. Nearer and nearer came the noise, and there was Baba Yaga, beating with the pestle and sweeping with the besom, coming along the road close behind.

The little girl threw down the comb, and it grew bigger and bigger, and its teeth sprouted up into a thick forest, thicker than this forest where we live — so thick that not even Baba Yaga could force her way through. And Baba Yaga, gnashing her teeth and screaming with rage and disappointment, turned round and drove away home to her little hut on hen's legs.

The little girl ran on home. She was afraid to go in and see her stepmother, so she ran into the shed.

Scratch, scratch! Out came the little mouse.

"So you got away all right, my dear," says the little mouse. "Now run in. Don't be afraid. Your father is back, and you must tell him all about it."

The little girl went into the house.

"Where have you been?" says her father, "and why are you so out of breath?"

The stepmother turned yellow when she saw her, and her eyes glowed, and her teeth ground together until they broke.

But the little girl was not afraid, and she went to her father and climbed on his knee, and told him everything just as it had happened. And when the old man knew that the stepmother had sent his daughter to be eaten by Baba Yaga, he was so angry that he drove her out of the hut, and ever afterwards lived alone with the little girl. Much better it was for both of them.

"And the little mouse?" said Ivan.

"The little mouse," said old Peter, "came and lived in the hut, and every day it used to sit up on the table and eat crumbs, and warm its paws on the little girl's glass of tea."

"Tell us a story about a cat, please, grandfather," said Vanya, who was sitting with Vladimir curled up in his arms.

"The story of a very happy cat," said Maroosia; and then, scratching Bayan's nose, she added, "and afterwards a story about a dog."

"I'll tell you the story of a very unhappy cat who became very happy," said old Peter. "I'll tell you the story of the Cat who became Head-forester."

The Cat who became Head-forester

If you drop Vladimir by mistake, you know he always falls on his feet. And if Vladimir tumbles off the roof of the hut, he always falls on his feet. Cats always fall on their feet, on their four paws, and never hurt themselves. And as in tumbling, so it is in life. No cat is ever unfortunate for very long. The worse things look for a cat, the better they are going to be.

Well, once upon a time, not so very long ago, an old peasant had a cat and did not like him. He was a tom-cat, always fighting; and he had lost one ear, and was not very pretty to look at. The peasant thought he would get rid of his old cat, and buy a new one from a neighbour. He did not care what became of the old tom-cat with one ear, so long as he never saw him again. It was no use thinking of killing him, for it is a life's work to kill a cat, and it's likely enough that the cat would come alive at the end.

So the old peasant he took a sack, and he bundled the tom-cat into the sack, and he sewed up the sack and slung it over his back, and walked off into the forest. Off he went, trudging along in the summer sunshine, deep into the forest. And when he had gone very many versts into the forest, he took the sack with the cat in it and threw it away among the trees.

"You stay there," says he, "and if you do get out in this desolate place, much good may it do you, old quarrelsome bundle of bones and fur!"

And with that he turned round and trudged home again, and bought a nice-looking, quiet cat from a neighbour in exchange for a little tobacco, and settled down comfortably at home with the new cat in front of the stove; and there he may be to this day, so far as I know. My story does not bother with him, but only with the old tom-cat tied up in the sack away there out in the forest.

The bag flew through the air, and plumped down through a bush to the ground. And the old tom-cat landed on his feet inside it, very much frightened but not hurt. Thinks he, this bag, this flight through the air, this bump, means that my life is going to change. Very well; there is nothing like something new now and again.

And presently he began tearing at the bag with his sharp claws. Soon there was a hole he could put a paw through. He went on, tearing and scratching, and there was a hole he could put two paws through. He went on with his work, and soon he could put his head through, all the easier because he had only one ear. A minute or two after that he had wriggled out of the bag, and stood up on his four paws and stretched himself in the forest.

"The world seems to be larger than the village," he said. "I will walk on and see what there is in it."

He washed himself all over, curled his tail proudly up in the air, cocked the only ear he had left, and set off walking under the forest trees.

"I was the head-cat in the village," says he to himself. "If all goes well, I shall be head here too." And he walked along as if he were the Tzar himself.

Well, he walked on and on, and he came to an old hut that had belonged to a forester. There was nobody there, nor had been for many years, and the old tom-cat made himself quite at home. He climbed up into the loft under the roof, and found a little rotten hay.

"A very good bed," says he, and curls up and falls asleep.

When he woke he felt hungry, so he climbed down and went off in the forest to catch little birds and mice. There were plenty of them in the forest, and when he had eaten enough he came back to the hut, climbed into the loft, and spent the night there very comfortably.

You would have thought he would be content. Not he. He was a cat. He said, "This is a good enough lodging. But I have to catch all my own food. In the village they fed me every day, and I only caught mice for fun. I ought to be able to live like that here. A person of my dignity ought not to have to do all the work for himself."

Next day he went walking in the forest. And as he was walking he met a fox, a vixen, a very pretty young thing, gay and giddy like all girls. And the fox saw the cat, and was very much astonished.

"All these years," she said — for though she was young she thought she had lived a long time — "all these years," she said, "I've lived in the forest, but I've never seen a wild beast like that before. What a strange-looking animal! And with only one ear. How handsome!"

And she came up and made her bows to the cat, and said:

"Tell me, great lord, who you are. What fortunate chance has brought you to this forest? And by what name am I to call your Excellency?"

Oh! the fox was very polite. It is not every day that you meet a handsome stranger walking in the forest.

The cat arched his back, and set all his fur on end, and said, very slowly and quietly:

"I have been sent from the far forests of Siberia to be Head-forester over you. And my name is Cat Ivanovitch."

"O Cat Ivanovitch!" says the pretty young fox, and she makes more bows. "I did not know. I beg your Excellency's pardon. Will your Excellency honour my humble house by visiting it as a guest?"

"I will," says the cat. "And what do they call you?"

"My name, your Excellency, is Lisabeta Ivanovna."

"I will come with you, Lisabeta," says the cat.

And they went together to the fox's earth. Very snug, very neat it was inside; and the cat curled himself up in the best place, while Lisabeta Ivanovna, the pretty young fox, made ready a tasty dish of game. And while she was making the meal ready, and dusting the furniture with her tail, she looked at the cat. At last she said, shyly:

"Tell me, Cat Ivanovitch, are you married or single?"

"Single," says the cat.

"And I too am unmarried," says the pretty young fox, and goes busily on with her dusting and cooking.

Presently she looks at the cat again.

"What if we were to marry, Cat Ivanovitch? I would try to be a good wife to you."

"Very well, Lisabeta," says the cat; "I will marry you."

The fox went to her store and took out all the dainties that she had, and made a wedding feast to celebrate her marriage to the great Cat Ivanovitch, who had only one ear, and had come from the far Siberian forests to be Head-forester.

They ate up everything there was in the place.

Next morning the pretty young fox went off busily into the forest to get food for her grand husband. But the old tom-cat stayed at home, and cleaned his whiskers and slept. He was a lazy one, was that cat, and proud.

The fox was running through the forest, looking for game, when she met an old friend, the handsome young wolf, and he began making polite speeches to her.

67

"What had become of you, gossip?" says he. "I've been to all the best earths and not found you at all."

"Let be, fool," says the fox very shortly. "Don't talk to me like that. What are you jesting about? Formerly I was a young, unmarried fox; now I am a wedded wife."

"Whom have you married, Lisabeta Ivanovna?"

"What!" says the fox, "you have not heard that the great Cat Ivanovitch, who has only one ear, has been sent from the far Siberian forests to be Head-forester over all of us? Well, I am now the Head-forester's wife."

"No, I had not heard, Lisabeta Ivanovna. And when can I pay my respects to his Excellency?"

"Not now, not now," says the fox. "Cat Ivanovitch will be raging angry with me if I let anyone come near him. Presently he will be taking his food. Look you. Get a sheep, and make it ready, and bring it as a greeting to him, to show him that he is welcome and that you know how to treat him with respect. Leave the sheep near by, and hide yourself so that he shall not see you; for, if he did, things might be awkward."

"Thank you, thank you, Lisabeta Ivanovna," says the wolf, and off he goes to look for a sheep.

The pretty young fox went idly on, taking the air, for she knew that the wolf would save her the trouble of looking for food.

Presently she met the bear.

"Good day to you, Lisabeta Ivanovna," says the bear; "as pretty as ever, I see you are."

"Bandy-legged one," says the fox; "fool, don't come worrying me. Formerly I was a young, unmarried fox; now I am a wedded wife."

"I beg your pardon," says the bear, "whom have you married, Lisabeta Ivanovna?"

"The great Cat Ivanovitch has been sent from the far Siberian forests to be Head-forester over us all. And Cat Ivanovitch is now my husband," says the fox.

"Is it forbidden to have a look at his Excellency?"

"It is forbidden," says the fox. "Cat Ivanovitch will be raging angry with me if I let anyone come near him. Presently he will be taking his food. Get along with you quickly; make ready an ox, and bring it by way of welcome to him. The wolf is bringing a sheep. And look you. Leave the ox near by, and hide yourself so that the great Cat Ivanovitch shall not see you; or else, brother, things may be awkward."

The bear shambled off as fast as he could go to get an ox.

The pretty young fox, enjoying the fresh air of the forest, went slowly home to her earth, and crept in very quietly, so as not to awake the great Head-forester, Cat Ivanovitch, who had only one ear and was sleeping in the best place.

Presently the wolf came through the forest, dragging a sheep he had killed. He did not dare to go too near the fox's earth, because of Cat Ivanovitch, the new Head-forester. So he stopped, well out of sight, and stripped off the skin of the sheep, and arranged the sheep so as to seem a nice tasty morsel.

Then he stood still, thinking what to do next. He heard a noise, and looked up. There was the bear, struggling along with a dead ox.

"Good day, brother Michael Ivanovitch," says the wolf.

"Good day, brother Levon Ivanovitch," says the bear. "Have you seen the fox, Lisabeta Ivanovna, with her husband, the Head-forester?"

"No, brother," says the wolf. "For a long time I have been waiting to see them."

"Go on and call out to them," says the bear.

"No, Michael Ivanovitch," says the wolf, "I will not go. Do you go; you are bigger and bolder than I."

"No, no, Levon Ivanovitch, I will not go. There is no use in risking one's life without need."

Suddenly, as they were talking, a little hare came running by. The bear saw him first, and roared out:

"Hi, Squinteye! trot along here."

The hare came up, slowly, two steps at a time, trembling with fright.

"Now then, you squinting rascal," says the bear, "do you know where the fox lives, over there?"

"I know, Michael Ivanovitch."

"Get along there quickly, and tell her that Michael Ivanovitch the bear and his brother Levon Ivanovitch the wolf have been ready for a long time, and have brought presents of a sheep and an ox, as greetings to his Excellency . . ."

"His Excellency, mind," says the wolf; "don't forget."

The hare ran off as hard as he could go, glad to have escaped so easily. Meanwhile the wolf and the bear looked about for good places in which to hide.

"It will be best to climb trees," says the bear. "I shall go up to the top of this fir."

"But what am I to do?" says the wolf. "I can't climb a tree for the life of me. Brother Michael, Brother Michael, hide me somewhere or other before you climb up. I beg you, hide me, or I shall certainly be killed."

"Crouch down under these bushes," says the bear, "and I will cover you with the dead leaves."

"May you be rewarded," says the wolf; and he crouched down under the bushes, and the bear covered him up with dead leaves, so that only the tip of his nose could be seen.

Then the bear climbed slowly up into the fir tree, into the very top, and looked out to see if the fox and Cat Ivanovitch were coming.

They were coming; oh yes, they were coming! The hare ran up and knocked on the door, and said to the fox:

"Michael Ivanovitch the bear and his brother Levon Ivanovitch the wolf have been ready for a long time, and have brought presents of a sheep and an ox as greetings to his Excellency."

"Get along, Squinteye," says the fox; "we are just coming."

And so the fox and the cat set out together.

The bear, up in the top of the tree, saw them, and called down to the wolf:

"They are coming, Brother Levon; they are coming, the fox and her husband. But what a little one he is, to be sure!"

"Quiet, quiet," whispers the wolf. "He'll hear you, and then we are done for."

The cat came up, and arched his back and set all his furs on end, and threw himself on the ox, and began tearing the meat with his teeth and claws. And as he tore he purred. And the bear listened, and heard the purring of the cat, and it seemed to him that the cat was angrily muttering, "Small, small, small . . .'

And the bear whispers : "He's no giant, but what a glutton! Why, we couldn't get through a quarter of that, and he finds it not enough. Heaven help us if he comes after us!"

The wolf tried to see, but could not, because his head, all but his nose, was covered with the dry leaves. Little by little he moved his head, so as to clear the leaves away from in front of his eyes. Try as he would to be quiet, the leaves rustled, so little, ever so little, but enough to be heard by the one ear of the cat.

The cat stopped tearing the meat and listened.

"I haven't caught a mouse today," he thought.

Once more the leaves rustled.

The cat leapt through the air and dropped with all four paws, and his claws out, on the nose of the wolf. How the wolf yelped!

The leaves flew like dust, and the wolf leapt up and ran off as fast as his legs could carry him.

Well, the wolf was frightened, I can tell you, but he was not so frightened as the cat.

When the great wolf leapt up out of the leaves, the cat screamed and ran up the nearest tree, and that was the tree where Michael Ivanovitch the bear was hiding in the topmost branches.

"Oh, he has seen me. Cat Ivanovitch has seen me," thought the bear. He had no time to climb down, and the cat was coming up in long leaps.

The bear trusted to Providence, and jumped from the top of the tree. Many were the branches he broke as he fell; many were the bones he broke when he crashed to the ground. He picked himself up and stumbled off, groaning.

The pretty young fox sat still, and cried out, "Run, run,

Brother Levon! . . . Quicker on your pins, Brother Michael! His Excellency is behind you; his Excellency is close behind!"

Ever since then all the wild beasts have been afraid of the cat, and the cat and the fox live merrily together, and eat fresh meat all the year round, which the other animals kill for them and leave a little way off.

And that is what happened to the old tom-cat with one ear, who was sewn up in a bag and thrown away in the forest.

"Just think what would happen to our handsome Vladimir if we were to throw him away!" said Vanya.

Spring in the Forest

Warmer the sun shone, and warmer yet. The pines were green now. All the snow had melted off them, drip, drip, the falling drops of water making tiny wells in the snow under the trees. And the snow under the trees was melting too. Much had gone, and now there were only patches of snow in the forest — like scraps of a big white blanket, shrinking every day.

"Isn't it lucky our blankets don't shrink like that?" said Maroosia.

Old Peter laughed.

"What do you do when the warm weather comes?" he asked. "Do you still wear sheepskin coats? Do you still roll up at night under the rugs?"

"No," said Maroosia; "I throw the rugs off, and put my fluffy coat away till next winter."

"Well," said old Peter, "and God, the Father of us all, He does for the earth just what you do for yourself; but He does it better. For the blankets He gives the earth in winter get smaller and smaller as the warm weather comes, little by little, day by day."

"And then a hard frost comes, grandfather," said Vanya.

"God knows all about that, little one," said old Peter, "and it's for the best. It's good to have a nip or two in the spring, to make you feel alive. Perhaps it's His way of telling the earth to wake up. For the whole earth is only His little one after all."

That night, when it was story-time, Vanya and Maroosia consulted together; and when old Peter asked what the story was to be, they were ready with an answer.

"The snow is all melting away," said Vanya.

"The summer is coming," said Maroosia.

"We'd like the tale of the little snow girl," said Vanya.

" 'The Little Daughter of the Snow,' " said Maroosia.

Old Peter shook out his pipe, and closed his eyes under his bushy eyebrows, thinking for a minute.

Then he began.

The Little Daughter of the Snow

There were once an old man, as old as I am, perhaps, and an old woman, his wife, and they lived together in a hut, in a village on the edge of the forest. There were many people in the village; quite a town it was — eight huts at least, thirty or forty souls, good company to be had for crossing the road. But the old man and the old woman were unhappy, in spite of living like that in the very middle of the world. And why do you think they were unhappy? They were unhappy because they had no little Vanya and no little Maroosia. Think of that. Some would say they were better off without them.

"Would you say that, grandfather?" asked Maroosia.

"You are a stupid little pigeon," said old Peter, and he went on.

Well, these two were very unhappy. All the other huts had babies in them — yes, and little ones playing about in the road outside, and having to be shouted at when anyone came driving by. But there were no babies in their hut, and the old woman never had to go to the door to see where her little one had strayed to, because she had no little one.

And these two, the old man and the old woman, used to stand whole hours, just peeping through their window to watch the children playing outside. They had dogs and a cat, and cocks and hens, but none of these made up for having no children. These two would just stand and watch the children of the other huts. The dogs would bark, but they took no notice; and the cat would curl up against them, but they never felt her; and as for the cocks and hens, well, they were fed, but that was all. The old people did not care for them, and spent all their time in watching the Vanyas and Maroosias who belonged to the other huts.

In the winter the children in their little sheepskin coats . . .

"Like ours?" said Vanya and Maroosia together.

"Like yours," said old Peter.

In their little sheepskin coats, he went on, played in the crisp snow. They pelted each other with snowballs, and shouted and laughed, and then they rolled the snow together and made a snow woman — a regular snow Baba Yaga, a snow witch; such an old fright!

And the old man, watching from the window, saw this, and he says to the old woman:

"Wife, let us go into the yard behind and make a little snow girl; and perhaps she will come alive, and be a little daughter to us."

"Husband," says the old woman, "there's no knowing what may be. Let us go into the yard and make a little snow girl."

So the two old people put on their big coats and their fur hats, and went out into the yard, where nobody could see them.

And they rolled up the snow, and began to make a little snow girl. Very, very tenderly they rolled up the snow to make her little arms and legs. The good God helped the old people, and their little snow girl was more beautiful than ever you could imagine. She was lovelier than a birch tree in spring.

Well, towards evening she was finished — a little girl, all snow, with blind white eyes, and a little mouth, with snow lips tightly closed.

"Oh, speak to us," says the old man.

"Won't you run about like the others, little white pigeon?" says the old woman.

And she did, you know, she really did.

Suddenly, in the twilight, they saw her eyes shining blue like the sky on a clear day. And her lips flushed and opened, and she smiled. And there were her little white teeth. And look, she had black hair, and it stirred in the wind.

She began dancing in the snow, like a little white spirit, tossing her long hair, and laughing softly to herself.

Wildly she danced, like snowflakes whirled in the wind. Her eyes shone, and her hair flew round her, and she sang, while the old people watched and wondered, and thanked God.

This is what she sang:

> "No warm blood in me doth glow,
> Water in my veins doth flow;
> Yet I'll laugh and sing and play
> By frosty night and frosty day -
> Little daughter of the Snow.
>
> "But whenever I do know
> That you love me little, then
> I shall melt away again.
> Back into the sky I'll go -
> Little daughter of the Snow."

"God of mine, isn't she beautiful!" said the old man. "Run, wife, and fetch a blanket to wrap her in while you make clothes for her."

The old woman fetched a blanket, and put it round the shoulders of the little snow girl. And the old man picked her up, and she put her little cold arms round his neck.

"You must not keep me too warm," she said.

Well, they took her into the hut, and she lay on a bench in the corner farthest from the stove, while the old woman made her a little coat.

The old man went out to buy a fur hat and boots from a neighbour for the little girl. The neighbour laughed at the old man; but a rouble is a rouble everywhere, and no one turns it from the door, and so he sold the old man a little fur hat, and a pair of little red boots with fur round the tops.

Then they dressed the little snow girl.

"Too hot, too hot," said the little snow girl. "I must go out into the cool night."

"But you must go to sleep now," said the old woman.

"By frosty night and frosty day," sang the little girl. "No; I will play by myself in the yard all night, and in the morning I'll play in the road with the children."

Nothing the old people said could change her mind.

"I am the little daughter of the Snow," she replied to everything, and she ran out into the yard into the snow.

How she danced and ran about in the moonlight on the white frozen snow!

The old people watched her and watched her. At last they went to bed; but more than once the old man got up in the night to make sure she was still there. And there she was, running about in the yard, chasing her shadow in the moonlight and throwing snowballs at the stars.

In the morning she came in, laughing, to have breakfast with the old people. She showed them how to make porridge for her, and that was very simple. They had only to take a piece of ice and crush it up in a little wooden bowl.

Then after breakfast she ran out in the road, to join the other children. And the old people watched her. Oh, proud they were, I can tell you, to see a little girl of their own out there playing in the road! They fairly longed for a sledge to come driving by, so that they could run out into the road and call to the little snow girl to be careful.

And the little snow girl played in the snow with the other children. How she played! She could run faster than any of them. Her little red boots flashed as she ran about. Not one of the other children was a match for her at snowballing. And when the children began making a snow woman, a Baba Yaga, you would have thought the little daughter of the Snow would have died of laughing. She laughed and laughed, like ringing peals on little glass bells. But she helped in the making of the snow woman, only laughing all the time.

When it was done, all the children threw snowballs at it, till it fell to pieces. And the little snow girl laughed and laughed, and was so quick she threw more snowballs than any of them.

The old man and the old woman watched her, and were very proud.

"She is all our own," said the old woman.

"Our little white pigeon," said the old man.

In the evening she had another bowl of ice-porridge, and then she went off again to play by herself in the yard.

"You'll be tired, my dear," says the old man.

"You'll sleep in the hut tonight, won't you, my love," says the old woman, "after running about all day long?"

But the little daughter of the Snow only laughed. "By frosty night and frosty day," she sang, and ran out of the door, laughing back at them with shining eyes.

And so it went on all through the winter. The little daughter of the Snow was singing and laughing and dancing all the time. She always ran out into the night and played by herself till dawn. Then she'd come in and have her ice-porridge. Then she'd play with the children. Then she'd have ice-porridge again, and off she would go, out into the night.

She was very good. She did everything the old woman told her. Only she would never sleep indoors. All the children of the village loved her. They did not know how they had ever played without her.

It went on so till just about this time of year. Perhaps it was a little earlier. Anyhow the snow was melting, and you could get about the paths. Often the children went together a little way into the forest in the sunny part of the day. The little snow girl went with them. It would have been no fun without her.

And then one day they went too far into the wood, and when they said they were going to turn back, little snow girl tossed her head under her little fur hat, and ran on laughing among the trees. The other children were afraid to follow her. It was getting dark. They waited as long as they dared, and then they ran home, holding each other's hands.

And there was the little daughter of the Snow out in the forest alone.

She looked back for the others, and could not see them. She climbed up into a tree; but the other trees were thick round her, and she could not see farther than when she was on the ground.

She called out from the tree:

"Ai, ai, little friends, have pity on the little snow girl."

An old brown bear heard her, and came shambling up on his heavy paws.

"What are you crying about, little daughter of the Snow?"

"O big bear," says the little snow girl, "how can I help crying? I have lost my way, and dusk is falling, and all my little friends are gone."

"I will take you home," says the old brown bear.

"O big bear," says the little snow girl, "I am afraid of you. I think you would eat me. I would rather go home with someone else."

So the bear shambled away and left her.

An old grey wolf heard her, and came galloping up on his swift feet. He stood under the tree and asked:

"What are you crying about, little daughter of the Snow?"

"O grey wolf," says the little snow girl, "how can I help crying? I have lost my way, and it is getting dark, and all my little friends are gone."

"I will take you home," says the old grey wolf.

"O grey wolf," says the little snow girl, "I am afraid of you. I think you would eat me. I would rather go home with someone else."

So the wolf galloped away and left her.

An old red fox heard her, and came running up to the tree on his little pads. He called out cheerfully:

"What are you crying about, little daughter of the Snow?"

"O red fox," says the little snow girl, "how can I help crying? I have lost my way, and it is quite dark, and all my little friends are gone."

"I will take you home," says the old red fox.

"O red fox," says the little snow girl, "I am not afraid of you. I do not think you will eat me. I will go home with you, if you will take me."

So she scrambled down from the tree, and she held the fox by the hair of his back, and they ran together through the dark forest. Presently they saw the lights in the windows of the huts, and in a few minutes they were at the door of the hut that belonged to the old man and the old woman.

And there were the old man and the old woman crying and lamenting.

"Oh, what has become of our little snow girl?"

"Oh, where is our little white pigeon?"

"Here I am," says the little snow girl. "The kind red fox has brought me home. You must shut up the dogs."

The old man shut up the dogs.

"We are very grateful to you," says he to the fox.

"Are you really?" says the old red fox; "for I am very hungry."

"Here is a nice crust for you," says the old woman.

"Oh," says the fox, "but what I would like would be a nice plump hen. After all, your little snow girl is worth a nice plump hen."

"Very well," says the old woman, but she grumbles to her husband.

"Husband," says she, "we have our little girl again."

"We have," says he; "thanks be for that."

"It seems waste to give away a good plump hen."

"It does," says he.

"Well, I was thinking," says the old woman, and then she tells him what she meant to do. And he went off and got two sacks.

In one sack they put a fine plump hen, and in the other they put the fiercest of the dogs. They took the bags outside and called to the fox. The old red fox came up to them, licking his lips, because he was so hungry.

They opened one sack, and out the hen fluttered. The old red fox was just going to seize her, when they opened the other sack, and out jumped the fierce dog. The poor fox saw his eyes flashing in the dark, and was so frightened that he ran all the way back into the deep forest, and never had the hen at all.

"That was well done," said the old man and the old woman. "We have got our little snow girl, and not had to give away our plump hen."

Then they heard the little snow girl singing in the hut. This is what she sang:

> "Old ones, old ones, now I know
> Less you love me than a hen,
> I shall go away again.
> Good-bye, ancient ones, good-bye,
> Back I go across the sky;

To my motherkin I go -
Little daughter of the Snow."

They ran into the house. There were a little pool of water in front of the stove, and a fur hat, and a little coat, and little red boots were lying in it. And yet it seemed to the old man and the old woman that they saw the little snow girl, with her bright eyes and her long hair, dancing in the room.

"Do not go! do not go!" they begged, and already they could hardly see the little dancing girl.

But they heard her laughing, and they heard her song:

"Old ones, old ones, now I know
Less you love me than a hen,
I shall melt away again.
To my motherkin I go -
Little daughter of the Snow."

And just then the door blew open from the yard, and a cold wind filled the room, and the little daughter of the Snow was gone.

"You always used to say something else, grandfather," said Maroosia.

Old Peter patted her head, and went on.

"I haven't forgotten. The little snow girl leapt into the arms of Frost her father and Snow her mother, and they carried her away over the stars to the far north, and there she plays all through the summer on the frozen seas. In winter she comes back to Russia, and some day, you know, when you are making a snow woman, you may find the little daughter of the Snow standing there instead."

"Wouldn't that be lovely!" said Maroosia.

Vanya thought for a minute, and then he said:

"I'd love her much more than a hen."

Prince Ivan, the Witch Baby and the Little Sister of the Sun

Once upon a time, very long ago, there was a little Prince Ivan who was dumb. Never a word had he spoken from the day that he was born — not so much as a "Yes" or a "No", or a "Please" or a "Thank you". A great sorrow he was to his father because he could not speak. Indeed, neither his father nor his mother could bear the sight of him, for they thought, "A poor sort of Tzar will a dumb boy make!" They even prayed, and said, "If only we could have another child, whatever it is like, it could be no worse than this tongue-tied brat who cannot say a word." And for that wish they were punished, as you shall hear. And they took no sort of care of the little Prince Ivan, and he spent all his time in the stables, listening to the tales of an old groom.

He was a wise man was the old groom, and he knew the past and the future, and what was happening under the earth. Maybe he had learnt his wisdom from the horses. Anyway, he knew more than other folk, and there came a day when he said to Prince Ivan:

"Little Prince," says he, "today you have a sister, and a bad one at that. She has come because of your father's prayers and your mother's wishes. A witch she is, and she will grow like a seed of corn. In six weeks she'll be a grown witch, and with her iron teeth she will eat up your father, and eat up your mother, and eat up you too, if she gets the chance. There's no saving the old people; but if you are quick, and do what I tell you, you may escape, and keep your soul in your body. And I love you, my little dumb Prince, and do not wish to think of your little body between her iron teeth. You must go to your father and ask him for the best horse he has, and then gallop like the wind, and away to the end of the world."

The little Prince ran off and found his father. There was his father, and there was his mother, and a little baby girl was in his mother's arms, screaming like a little fury.

"Well, she's not dumb," said his father, as if he were well pleased.

"Father," says the little Prince, "may I have the fastest horse in the stable?" And those were the first words that ever left his mouth.

"What!" says his father, "have you got a voice at last? Yes, take whatever horse you want. And see, you have a little sister; a fine little girl she is too. She has teeth already. It's a pity they are black, but time will put that right, and it's better to have black teeth than to be born dumb."

Little Prince Ivan shook in his shoes when he heard of the black teeth of his little sister, for he knew that they were iron. He thanked his father and ran off to the stable. The old groom saddled the finest horse there was. Such a horse you never saw. Black it was, and its saddle and bridle were trimmed with shining silver. And little Prince Ivan climbed up and sat on the great black horse, and waved his hand to the old groom, and galloped away, on and on over the wide world.

"It's a big place, this world," thought the little Prince. "I wonder when I shall come to the end of it." You see, he had never been outside the palace grounds. And he had only ridden a little Finnish pony. And now he sat high up, perched on the back of the great black horse, who galloped with hoofs that thundered beneath him, and leapt over rivers and streams and hillocks, and anything else that came in his way.

On and on galloped the little Prince on the great black horse. There were no houses anywhere to be seen. It was a long time since they had passed any people, and little Prince Ivan began to feel very lonely, and to wonder if indeed he had come to the end of the world, and could bring his journey to an end.

Suddenly, on a wide, sandy plain, he saw two old, old women sitting in the road.

They were bent double over their work, sewing and sewing,

and now one and now the other broke a needle, and took a new one out of a box between them, and threaded the needle with thread from another box, and went on sewing and sewing. Their old noses nearly touched their knees as they bent over their work.

Little Prince Ivan pulled up the great black horse in a cloud of dust, and spoke to the old women.

"Grandmothers," said he, "is this the end of the world? Let me stay here and live with you, and be safe from my baby sister, who is a witch and has iron teeth. Please let me stay with you, and I'll be very little trouble, and thread your needles for you when you break them."

"Prince Ivan, my dear," said one of the old women, "this is not the end of the world, and little good would it be to you to stay with us. For as soon as we have broken all our needles and used up all our thread we shall die, and then where would you be? Your sister with the iron teeth would have you in a minute."

The little Prince cried bitterly, for he was very little and all alone. He rode on farther over the wide world, the black horse galloping and galloping, and throwing the dust from his thundering hoofs.

He came into a forest of great oaks, the biggest oak trees in the whole world. And in that forest was a dreadful noise — the crashing of trees falling, the breaking of branches, and the whistling of things hurled through the air. The Prince rode on, and there before him was the huge giant, Tree-rooter, hauling the great oaks out of the ground and flinging them aside like weeds.

"I should be safe with him," thought little Prince Ivan, "and this, surely, must be the end of the world."

He rode close up under the giant, and stopped the black horse, and shouted up into the air.

"Please, great giant," says he, "is this the end of the world? And may I live with you and be safe from my sister, who is a witch, and grows like a seed of corn, and has iron teeth?"

"Prince Ivan, my dear," says Tree-rooter, "this is not the end of the world, and little good would it be to you to stay with me. For as soon as I have rooted up all these trees I shall die, and then where would you be? Your sister would have you in a minute. And already there are not many big trees left."

And the giant set to work again, pulling up the great trees and throwing them aside. The sky was full of flying trees.

Little Prince Ivan cried bitterly, for he was very little and was all alone. He rode on farther over the wide world, the black horse galloping and galloping under the tall trees, and throwing clods of earth from his thundering hoofs.

He came among the mountains. And there was a roaring and a crashing in the mountains as if the earth was falling to pieces. One after another whole mountains were lifted up into the sky and flung down to earth, so that they broke and scattered into dust. And the big black horse galloped through the mountains, and little Prince Ivan sat bravely on his back. And there, close before him, was the huge giant Mountain-tosser, picking up the mountains like pebbles and hurling them to little pieces and dust upon the ground.

"This must be the end of the world," thought the little Prince; "and at any rate I should be safe with him."

"Please, great giant," says he, "is this the end of the world? And may I live with you and be safe from my sister, who is a witch, and has iron teeth, and grows like a seed of corn?"

"Prince Ivan, my dear," says Mountain-tosser, resting for a moment and dusting the rocks off his great hands, "this is not the end of the world, and little good would it be to you to stay with me. For as soon as I have picked up all these mountains and thrown them down again I shall die, and then where would you be? Your sister would have you in a minute. And there are not very many mountains left."

And the giant set to work again, lifting up the great mountains and hurling them away. The sky was full of flying mountains.

Little Prince Ivan wept bitterly, for he was very little and was all alone. He rode on farther over the wide world, the black horse galloping and galloping along the mountain paths, and throwing the stones from his thundering hoofs.

At last he came to the end of the world, and there, hanging in the sky above him, was the castle of the little sister of the Sun. Beautiful it was, made of cloud, and hanging in the sky, as if it were built of red roses.

"I should be safe up there," thought little Prince Ivan, and just then the Sun's little sister opened the window and beckoned to him.

Prince Ivan patted the big black horse and whispered to it, and it leapt up high into the air and through the window, into the very courtyard of the castle.

"Stay here and play with me," said the little sister of the Sun; and Prince Ivan tumbled off the big black horse into her arms, and laughed because he was so happy.

Merry and pretty was the Sun's little sister, and she was very kind to little Prince Ivan. They played games together, and when she was tired she let him do whatever he liked and run about her castle. This way and that he ran about the battlements of rosy cloud, hanging in the sky over the end of the world.

But one day he climbed up and up to the topmost turret of the castle. From there he could see the whole world. And far, far away, beyond the mountains, beyond the forests, beyond the wide plains, he saw his father's palace where he had been born. The roof of the palace was gone, and the walls were broken and crumbling. And little Prince Ivan came slowly down from the turret, and his eyes were red with weeping.

"My dear," says the Sun's little sister, "why are your eyes so red?"

"It is the wind up there," says little Prince Ivan.

And the Sun's little sister put her head out of the window of the castle of cloud and whispered to the winds not to blow so hard.

But next day little Prince Ivan went up again to that topmost turret, and looked far away over the wide world to the ruined palace. "She has eaten them all with her iron teeth," he said to himself. And his eyes were red when he came down.

"My dear," says the Sun's little sister, "your eyes are red again."

"It is the wind," says little Prince Ivan.

And the Sun's little sister put her head out of the window and scolded the wind.

But the third day again little Prince Ivan climbed up the stairs of cloud to that topmost turret, and looked far away to the broken palace where his father and mother had lived. And he came down from the turret with the tears running down his face.

"Why, you are crying, my dear!" says the Sun's little sister. "Tell me what it is all about."

So little Prince Ivan told the little sister of the Sun how his sister was a witch, and how he wept to think of his father and mother, and how he had seen the ruins of his father's palace far away, and how he could not stay with her happily until he knew how it was with his parents.

"Perhaps it is not yet too late to save them from her iron teeth, though the old groom said that she would certainly eat them, and that it was the will of God. But let me ride back on my big black horse."

"Do not leave me, my dear," says the Sun's little sister. "I am lonely here by myself."

"I will ride back on my big black horse, and then I will come to you again."

"What must be, must," says the Sun's little sister; "though she is more likely to eat you than you are to save them. You shall go. But you must take with you a magic comb, a magic brush, and two apples of youth. These apples would make young once more the oldest things on earth."

Then she kissed little Prince Ivan, and he climbed up on his big black horse, and leapt out of the window of the castle down on the end of the world, and galloped off on his way back over the wide world.

He came to Mountain-tosser, the giant. There was only one mountain left, and the giant was just picking it up. Sadly he was picking it up, for he knew that when he had thrown it away his work would be done and he would have to die.

"Well, little Prince Ivan," says Mountain-tosser, "this is the end"; and he heaves up the mountain. But before he could toss it away the little Prince threw his magic brush on the plain, and the brush swelled and burst, and there were range upon range of high mountains, touching the sky itself.

"Why," says Mountain-tosser, "I have enough mountains now to last me for another thousand years. Thank you kindly, little Prince."

And he set to work again, heaving up mountains and tossing them down, while little Prince Ivan galloped on across the wide world.

He came to Tree-rooter, the giant. There were only two of the great oaks left, and the giant had one in each hand.

"Ah me, little Prince Ivan," says Tree-rooter, "my life is come to its end; for I have only to pluck up these two trees and throw them down, and then I shall die."

"Pluck them up," says little Prince Ivan. "Here are plenty more for you." And he threw down his comb. There was a noise of spreading branches, of swishing leaves, of opening buds, all together, and there before them was a forest of great oaks stretching farther than the giant could see, tall though he was.

"Why," says Tree-rooter, "here are enough trees to last me for another thousand years. Thank you kindly, little Prince."

And he set to work again, pulling up the big trees, laughing joyfully and hurling them over his head, while little Prince Ivan galloped on across the wide world.

He came to the two old women. They were crying their eyes out.

"There is only one needle left!" says the first.

"There is only one bit of thread in the box!" sobs the second.

"And then we shall die!" they say both together, mumbling with their old mouths.

"Before you use the needle and thread, just eat these apples," says little Prince Ivan, and he gives them the two apples of youth.

The two old women took the apples in their old shaking fingers and ate them, bent double, mumbling with their old lips. They had hardly finished their last mouthfuls when they sat up straight, smiled with sweet red lips, and looked at the little Prince with shining eyes. They had become young girls again, and their grey hair was black as the raven.

"Thank you kindly, little Prince," say the two young girls. "You must take with you the handkerchief we have been sewing all these years. Throw it to the ground, and it will turn into a lake of water. Perhaps some day it will be useful to you."

"Thank you," says the little Prince, and off he gallops, on and on over the wide world.

He came at last to his father's palace. The roof was gone, and there were holes in the walls. He left his horse at the edge of the garden, and crept up to the ruined palace and peeped through a hole. Inside, in the great hall, was sitting a huge baby girl, filling the whole hall. There was no room for her to move. She had knocked off the roof with a shake of her head. And she sat there in the ruined hall, sucking her thumb.

And while Prince Ivan was watching through the hole he heard her mutter to herself:

> "Eaten the father, eaten the mother,
> And now to eat the little brother."

And she began shrinking, getting smaller and smaller every minute.

Little Prince Ivan had only just time to get away from the hole in the wall when a pretty little baby girl came running out of the ruined palace.

"You must be my little brother Ivan," she called out to him, and came up to him smiling. But as she smiled the little Prince saw that her teeth were black; and as she shut her mouth he heard them clink together like pokers.

"Come in," says she, and she took little Prince Ivan with her to a room in the palace, all broken down and cobwebbed. There was a dulcimer lying in the dust on the floor.

"Well, little brother," says the witch baby, "you play on the dulcimer and amuse yourself while I get supper ready. But don't stop playing, or I shall feel lonely." And she ran off and left him.

Little Prince Ivan sat down and played tunes on the dulcimer — sad enough tunes. You would not play dance music if you thought you were going to be eaten by a witch.

But while he was playing a little grey mouse came out of a crack in the floor. Some people think that this was the wise old groom, who had turned into a little grey mouse to save Ivan from the witch baby.

"Ivan, Ivan," says the little grey mouse, "run while you may. Your father and mother were eaten long ago, and well they deserved it. But be quick, or you will be eaten too. Your pretty little sister is putting an edge on her teeth!"

Little Prince Ivan thanked the mouse, and ran out from the

ruined palace, and climbed up on the back of his big black horse, with its saddle and bridle trimmed with silver. Away he galloped over the wide world. The witch baby stopped her work and listened. She heard the music of the dulcimer, so she made sure he was still there. She went on sharpening her teeth with a file, and growing bigger and bigger every minute. And all the time the music of the dulcimer sounded among the ruins.

As soon as her teeth were quite sharp she rushed off to eat little Prince Ivan. She tore aside the walls of the room. There was nobody there — only a little grey mouse running and jumping this way and that on the strings of the dulcimer.

When it saw the witch baby the little mouse ran across the floor and into the crack and away, so that she never caught it. How the witch baby gnashed her teeth! Poker and tongs, poker and tongs — what a noise they made! She swelled up, bigger and bigger, till she was a baby as high as the palace. And then she jumped up so that the palace fell to pieces about her. Then off she ran after little Prince Ivan.

Little Prince Ivan, on the big black horse, heard a noise behind him. He looked back, and there was the huge witch, towering over the trees. She was dressed like a little baby, and her eyes flashed and her teeth clanged as she shut her mouth. She was running with long strides, faster even than the black horse could gallop — and he was the best horse in all the world.

Little Prince Ivan threw down the handkerchief that had been sewn by the two old women who had eaten the apples of youth. It turned into a deep, broad lake, so that the witch baby had to swim — and swimming is slower than running. It took her a long time to get across, and all that time Prince Ivan was galloping on, never stopping for a moment.

The witch baby crossed the lake and came thundering after him. Close behind she was, and would have caught him; but the giant Tree-rooter saw the little Prince galloping on the big black horse, and the witch baby tearing after him. He pulled up the great oaks in armfuls, and threw them down just in front of the witch baby. He made a huge pile of the big trees, and the witch baby had to stop and gnaw her way through them with her iron teeth.

It took her a long time to gnaw through the trees, and the black horse galloped and galloped ahead. But presently Prince Ivan heard a noise behind him. He looked back, and there was the witch baby, thirty feet high, racing after him, clanging with her teeth. Close behind she was, and the little Prince sat firm on the big black horse, and galloped and galloped. But she would have caught him if the giant Mountain-tosser had not seen the little Prince on the big black horse, and the great witch baby running after him. The giant tore up the biggest mountain in the world and flung it down in front of her, and another on the top of that. She had to bite her way through them, while the little Prince galloped and galloped.

At last little Prince Ivan saw the cloud castle of the little sister of the Sun, hanging over the end of the world and gleaming in the sky as if it were made of roses. He shouted with hope, and the black horse shook his head proudly and galloped on. The witch baby thundered after him. Nearer she came and nearer.

"Ah, little one," screams the witch baby, "you shan't get away this time!"

The Sun's little sister was looking from a window of the castle in the sky, and she saw the witch baby stretching out to grab little Prince Ivan. She flung the window open, and just in time the big black horse leapt up, and through the window and into the courtyard, with little Prince Ivan safe on its back.

How the witch baby gnashed her iron teeth!

"Give him up!" she screams.

"I will not," says the Sun's little sister.

"See you here," says the witch baby, and she makes herself smaller and smaller and smaller, till she was just like a real little girl. "Let us be weighed in the great scales, and if I am heavier than Prince Ivan, I can take him; and if he is heavier than I am, I'll say no more about it."

The Sun's little sister laughed at the witch baby and teased her, and she hung the great scales out of the cloud castle so that they swung above the end of the world.

Little Prince Ivan got into one scale, and down it went.

"Now," says the witch baby, "we shall see."

And she made herself bigger and bigger and bigger, till she was as big as she had been when she sat and sucked her thumb in the hall of the ruined palace. "I am the heavier," she shouted, and gnashed her iron teeth. Then she jumped into the other scale.

She was so heavy that the scale with the little Prince in it shot up into the air. It shot up so fast that little Prince Ivan flew up into the sky, up and up and up, and came down on the topmost turret of the cloud castle of the little sister of the Sun.

The Sun's little sister laughed, and closed the window, and went up to the turret to meet the little Prince. But the witch baby turned back the way she had come, and went off, gnashing her iron teeth until they broke. And ever since then little Prince Ivan and the little sister of the Sun play together in the castle of cloud that hangs over the end of the world. They borrow the stars to play at ball, and put them back at night whenever they remember.

"So when there are no stars?" asked Maroosia.

"It means that Prince Ivan and the Sun's little sister have gone to sleep over their games and forgotten to put their toys away."

The Stolen Turnips,
the Magic Tablecloth, the Sneezing Goat
and the Wooden Whistle

This is the story which old Peter used to tell whenever either Vanya or Maroosia was cross. This did not often happen; but it would be no use to pretend that it never happened at all. Sometimes it was Vanya who scolded Maroosia, and sometimes it was Maroosia who scolded Vanya. Sometimes there were two scoldings going on at once. And old Peter did not like crossness in the hut, whoever did the scolding. He said it spoilt his tobacco and put a sour taste in the tea. And, of course, when the children remembered that they were spoiling their grandfather's tea and tobacco they stopped just as quickly as they could, unless their tongues had run right away with them — which happens sometimes, you know, even to grown-up people. This story used to be told in two ways. It was either the tale of an old man who was bothered by a cross old woman, or the tale of an old woman who was bothered by a cross old man. And the moment old Peter began the story both children would ask at once, "Which is the cross one?" — for then they would know which of them old Peter thought was in the wrong.

"This time it's the old woman," said their grandfather, "but as like as not, it will be the old man next."

And then any quarrelling there was came to an end, and was forgotten before the end of the story. This is the story.

An old man and an old woman lived in a little wooden house. All round the house there was a garden, crammed with flowers, and potatoes, and beetroots, and cabbages. And in one corner of the house there was a narrow wooden stairway which went up and up, twisting and twisting, into a high tower. In the top of the tower was a dovecot, and on the top of the dovecot was a flat roof.

Now, the old woman was never content with the doings of the old man. She scolded all day, and she scolded all night.

97

If there was too much rain, it was the old man's fault; and if there was a drought, and all green things were parched for lack of water, well, the old man was to blame for not altering the weather. And though he was old and tired, it was all the same to her how much work she put on his shoulders. The garden was full. There was no room in it at all, not even for a single pea. And all of a sudden the old woman sets her heart on growing turnips.

"But there is no room in the garden," says the old man.

"Sow them on the top of the dovecot," says the old woman.

"But there is no earth there."

"Carry earth up and put it there," says she.

So the old man laboured up and down with his tired old bones, and covered the top of the dovecot with good black earth. He could only take up a very little at a time, because he was old and weak, and because the stairs were so narrow and dangerous that he had to hold on with both hands and carry the earth in a bag which he held in his teeth. His teeth were strong enough, because he had been biting crusts all his life. The old woman left him nothing else, for she took all the crumb for herself. The old man did his best, and by evening the top of the dovecot was covered with earth, and he had sown it with turnip seed.

Next day, and the day after that and every day, the old woman scolded the old man till he went up to the dovecot to see how those turnip seeds were getting on.

"Are they ready to eat yet?"

"They are not ready to eat."

"Is the green sprouting?"

"The green is sprouting."

And at last there came a day when the old man came down from the dovecot and said: "The turnips are doing finely — quite big they are getting; but all the best ones have been stolen away."

"Stolen away?" cried the old woman, shaking with rage. "And have you lived all these years and not learned how to keep thieves from a turnip-bed, on the top of a dovecot, on the top of a tower, on the top of a house? Out with you, and don't you dare to come back till you have caught the thieves."

The old man did not dare to tell her that the door had been bolted, although he knew it had, because he had bolted it himself. He hurried away out of the house, more because he wanted to get out of earshot of her scolding than because he had any hope of finding the thieves. "They may be birds," thinks he, "or the little brown squirrels. Who else could climb so high without using the stairs? And how is an old man like me to get hold of them, flying through the tops of the high trees and running up and down the branches?"

And so he wandered away without his dinner into the deep forest.

But God is good to old men. Hasn't He given me two little pigeons, who nearly always are as merry as all little pigeons should be? And God led the old man through the forest, though the old man thought he was just wandering on, trying to lose himself and forget the scolding voice of the old woman.

And after he had walked a long way through the dark green forest, he saw a little hut standing under the pine trees. There was no smoke coming from the chimney, but there was such a chattering in the hut you could hear it far away. It was like coming near a rookery at evening, or disturbing a lot of starlings. And as the old man came slowly nearer to the hut, he thought he saw little faces looking at him through the window and peeping through the door. He could not be sure, because they were gone so quickly. And all the time the chattering went on louder and louder, till the old man nearly put his hands to his ears.

And then suddenly the chattering stopped. There was not a sound — no noise at all. The old man stood still. A squirrel dropped a fir cone close by, and the old man was startled by the fall of it, because everything else was so quiet.

"Whatever there is in the hut, it won't be worse than the old woman," says the old man to himself. So he makes the sign of the Holy Cross, and steps up to the little hut and takes a look through the door.

There was no one to be seen. You would have thought the hut was empty.

The old man took a step inside, bending under the little low door. Still he could see nobody, only a great heap of rags and blankets on the sleeping-place on the top of the stove. The hut was as clean as if it had only that minute been swept by Maroosia herself. But in the middle of the floor there was a scrap of green leaf lying, and the old man knew in a moment that it was a scrap of green leaf from the top of a young turnip.

And while the old man looked at it, the heap of blankets and rugs on the stove moved, first in one place and then in another. Then there was a little laugh. Then another. And suddenly there was a great stir in the blankets, and they were all thrown back helter-skelter, and there were dozens and dozens of little queer children, laughing and laughing and laughing, and looking at the old man. And every child had a little turnip, and showed it to the old man and laughed.

Just then the door of the stove flew open, and out tumbled more of the little queer children, dozens and dozens of them. The more they came tumbling out into the hut, the more there seemed to be chattering in the stove and squeezing to get out one over the top of another. The noise of chattering and laughing would have made your head spin. And every one of the children out of the stove had a little turnip like the others, and waved it about and showed it to the old man, and laughed like anything.

"Ho," says the old man, "so you are the thieves who have stolen the turnips from the top of the dovecot?"

"Yes," cried the children, and the chatter rattled as fast as hailstones on the roof. "Yes! yes! yes! *We* stole the turnips."

"How did you get on to the top of the dovecot when the door into the house was bolted and fast?"

At that the children all burst out laughing, and did not answer a word.

"Laugh you may," said the old man, "but it is I who get the scolding when the turnips fly away in the night."

"Never mind! never mind!" cried the children. "We'll pay for the turnips."

"How can you pay for them?" asks the old man. "You have nothing to pay with."

All the children chattered together, and looked at the old man and smiled. Then one of them said to the old man, "Are you hungry, grandfather?"

"Hungry!" says the old man. "Why, yes, of course I am, my dear. I've been looking for you all day, and I had to start without my dinner."

"If you are hungry, open the cupboard behind you."

The old man opened the cupboard.

"Take out the tablecloth."

The old man took out the tablecloth.

"Spread it on the table."

The old man spread the tablecloth on the table.

"Now!" shouted the children, chattering like a thousand nests full of young birds, "we'll all sit down and have dinner."

They pulled out the benches and gave the old man a chair at one end, and all crowded round the table ready to begin.

"But there's no food," said the old man.

How they laughed!

"Grandfather," one of them sings out from the other end of the table, "you just tell the tablecloth to turn inside out."

"How?" says he.

"Tell the tablecloth to turn inside out. That's easy enough."

"There's no harm in doing that," thinks the old man; so he says to the tablecloth as firmly as he could, "Now then you, tablecloth, turn inside out!"

The tablecloth hove itself up into the air, and rolled itself this way and that as if it were in a whirlwind, and then suddenly laid itself flat on the table again. And somehow or other it had covered itself with dishes and plates and wooden spoons with pictures on them, and bowls of soup and mushrooms and kasha, and meat and cakes and fish and ducks, and everything else you could think of, ready for the best dinner in the world.

The chattering and laughing stopped, and the old man and those dozens and dozens of little queer children set to work and ate everything on the table.

"Which of you washes the dishes?" asked the old man, when they had all done.

The children laughed.

"Tell the tablecloth to turn outside in."

"Tablecloth," says the old man, "turn outside in."

Up jumped the tablecloth with all the empty dishes and dirty plates and spoons, whirled itself this way and that in the air, and suddenly spread itself out flat again on the table, as clean and white as when it was taken out of the cupboard. There was not a dish or a bowl, or a spoon or a plate, or a knife to be seen; no, not even a crumb.

"That's a good tablecloth," says the old man.

"See here, grandfather," shouted the children: "you take the tablecloth along with you, and say no more about those turnips."

"Well, I'm content with that," says the old man. And he folded up the tablecloth very carefully and put it away inside his shirt, and said he must be going.

"Good-bye," says he, "and thank you for the dinner and the tablecloth."

"Good-bye," say they, "and thank you for the turnips."

The old man made his way home, singing through the forest in his creaky voice until he came near the wooden house where he lived with the old woman. As soon as he came near there he slipped along like any mouse. And as soon as he put his head inside the door the old woman began:

"Have you found the thieves, you old fool?"

"I found the thieves."

"Who were they?"

"They were a whole crowd of little queer children."

"Have you given them a beating they'll remember?"

"No, I have not."

"What? Bring them to me, and I'll teach them to steal my turnips!"

"I haven't got them."

"What have you done with them?"

"I had dinner with them."

Well, at that the old woman flew into such a rage she could hardly speak. But speak she did — yes, and shout too and scream — and it was all the old man could do not to run away out of the cottage. But he stood still and listened, and thought of something else; and when she had done he said, "They paid for the turnips."

"Paid for the turnips!" scolded the old woman. "A lot of children! What did they give you? Mushrooms? We can get them without losing our turnips."

"They gave me a tablecloth," said the old man; "it's a very good tablecloth."

He pulled it out of his shirt and spread it on the table; and as quickly as he could, before she began again, he said, "Tablecloth, turn inside out!"

The old woman stopped short, just when she was taking breath to scold with, when the tablecloth jumped up and danced in the air and settled on the table again, covered with things to eat and to drink. She smelt the meat, took a spoonful of the soup and tried all the other dishes.

"Look at all the washing up it will mean," says she.

"Tablecloth, turn outside in!" says the old man; and there was a whirl of white cloth and dishes and everything else, and then the tablecloth spread itself out on the table as clean as ever you could wish.

"That's not a bad tablecloth," says the old woman; "but, of course, they owed me something for stealing all those turnips."

The old man said nothing. He was very tired, and he just laid down and went to sleep.

As soon as he was asleep the old woman took the tablecloth and hid it away in an iron chest, and put a tablecloth of her own in its place. "They were my turnips," says she, "and I don't see why he should have a share in the tablecloth. He's had a meal from it once at my expense, and once is enough." Then she lay down and went to sleep, grumbling to herself even in her dreams.

Early in the morning the old woman woke the old man and told him to go up to the dovecot and see how those turnips were getting on.

He got up and rubbed his eyes. When he saw the tablecloth on the table, the wish came to him to have a bite of food to begin the day with. So he stopped in the middle of putting on his shirt, and called to the tablecloth, "Tablecloth, turn inside out!"

Nothing happened. Why should anything happen? It was not the same tablecloth.

The old man told the old woman. "You should have made a good feast yesterday," says he, "for the tablecloth is no good any more. That is, it's no good that way; it's like any ordinary tablecloth."

"Most tablecloths are," says the old woman. "But what are you dawdling about? Up you go and have a look at those turnips."

The old man went climbing up the narrow twisting stairs. He held on with both hands for fear of falling, because they were so steep. He climbed to the top of the house, to the top of the tower, to the top of the dovecot, and looked at the turnips. He looked at the turnips, and he counted the turnips, and then he came slowly down the stairs again wondering what the old woman would say to him.

"Well," says the old woman in her sharp voice, "are they doing nicely? Because if not, I know whose fault it is."

"They are doing finely," said the old man; "but some of them have gone. Indeed, quite a lot of them have been stolen away."

"Stolen away!" screamed the old woman. "How dare you stand there and tell me that? Didn't you find the thieves yesterday? Go and find those children again, and take a stick with you, and don't show yourself here till you can tell me that they won't steal again in a hurry."

"Let me have a bite to eat," begs the old man. "It's a long way to go on an empty stomach."

"Not a mouthful!" yells the old woman. "Off with you. Letting my turnips be stolen every night, and then talking to me about bites of food!"

So the old man went off again without his dinner, and hobbled away into the forest as quickly as he could to get out of earshot of the old woman's scolding tongue.

As soon as he was out of sight the old woman stopped screaming after him, and went into the house and opened the iron chest and took out the tablecloth the children had given the old man, and laid it on the table instead of her own. She told it to turn inside out, and up it flew and whirled about and flopped down flat again, all covered with good things. She ate as much as she could hold. Then she told the tablecloth to turn outside in, and folded it up and hid it away again in the iron chest.

Meanwhile the old man tightened his belt, because he was so hungry. He hobbled along through the green forest till he came to the little hut standing under the pine trees. There was no smoke coming from the chimney, but there was such a chattering you would have thought that all the Vanyas and Maroosias in Holy Russia were talking to each other inside.

He had no sooner come in sight of the hut than the dozens and dozens of little queer children came pouring out of the door to meet him. And every single one of them had a turnip, and showed it to the old man, and laughed and laughed as if it were the best joke in the world.

"I knew it was you," said the old man.

"Of course it was us," cried the children. "*We* stole the turnips."

"But how did you get to the top of the dovecot when the door into the house was bolted and fast?"

The children laughed and laughed and did not answer a word.

"Laugh you may," says the old man; "but it is I who get the scolding when the turnips fly away in the night."

"Never mind! never mind!" cried the children. "We'll pay for the turnips."

"All very well," says the old man; "but that tablecloth of yours — it was fine yesterday, but this morning it would not give me even a glass of tea and a hunk of black bread."

At that the faces of the little queer children were troubled and grave. For a moment or two they all chattered together, and took no notice of the old man. Then one of them said:

"Well, this time we'll give you something better. We'll give you a goat."

"A goat?" says the old man.

"A goat with a cold in its head," said the children; and they crowded round him and took him behind the hut where there was a grey goat with a long beard cropping the short grass.

"It's a good enough goat," says the old man; "I don't see anything wrong with him."

"It's better than that," cried the children. "You tell it to sneeze."

The old man thought the children might be laughing at him, but he did not care, and he remembered the tablecloth. So he took off his hat and bowed to the goat.

"Sneeze, goat," says he.

And instantly the goat started sneezing as if it would shake itself to pieces. And as it sneezed, good gold pieces flew from it in all directions, till the ground was thick with them.

"That's enough," said the children hurriedly; "tell him to stop for all this gold is no use to us, and it's such a bother having to sweep it away."

"Stop sneezing, goat," says the old man; and the goat stopped sneezing, and stood there panting and out of breath in the middle of the sea of gold pieces.

The children began kicking the gold pieces about, spreading them by walking through them as if they were dead leaves. My old father used to say that those gold pieces are lying about still for anybody to pick up; but I doubt if he knew just where to look for them, or he would have had better clothes on his back and a little more food on the table. But who knows? Some day we may come upon that little hut somewhere in the forest, and then we shall know what to look for.

The children laughed and chattered and kicked the gold pieces this way and that into the green bushes. Then they brought the old man into the hut and gave him a bowl of kasha to eat, because he had had no dinner. There was no magic about the kasha; but it was good enough kasha for all that, and hunger made it better. When the old man finished the kasha and drunk a glass of tea and smoked a little pipe, he got up and made a low bow and thanked the children. And the children tied a rope to the goat and sent the old man home with it. He hobbled away through the forest, and as he went he looked back, and there were the little queer children all dancing together, and he heard them chattering and shouting: "Who stole the turnips? *We* stole the turnips. Who paid for the turnips? *We* paid for the turnips. Who stole the tablecloth? Who will pay for the tablecloth? Who will steal turnips again? *We* will steal turnips again."

But the old man was too pleased with the goat to give much heed to what they said; and he hobbled home through the green forest as fast as he could, with the goat trotting and walking behind him, pulling leaves off the bushes to chew as they hurried along.

The old woman was waiting in the doorway of the house. She was still as angry as ever.

"Have you beaten the children?" she screamed. "Have you beaten the children for stealing my good turnips?"

"No," said the old man; "they paid for the turnips."

"What did they pay?"

"They gave me this goat."

"That skinny old goat! I have three already, and the worst of them is better than that."

"It has a cold in the head," says the old man.

"Worse than ever!" screams the old woman.

"Wait a minute," says the old man as quickly as he could, to stop her scolding. "Sneeze, goat."

And the goat began to shake itself almost to bits, sneezing and sneezing and sneezing. The good gold pieces flew all ways at once. And the old woman threw herself after the gold pieces, picking them up like an old hen picking up corn. As fast as she picked them up more gold pieces came showering down on her like heavy gold hail, beating her on her head and her hands as she grubbed after those that had fallen already.

"Stop sneezing, goat," says the old man; and the goat stood there tired and panting, trying to get its breath. But the old woman did not look up till she had gathered every one of the gold pieces. When she did look up, she said:

"There's no supper for you. I've had supper already."

The old man said nothing. He tied up the goat to the door-post of the house, where it could eat the green grass. Then he went into the house and lay down, and fell asleep at once, because he was an old man and had done a lot of walking.

As soon as he was asleep the old woman untied the goat and took it away and hid it in the bushes, and tied up one of her own goats instead. "They were my turnips," says she to herself, "and I don't see why he should have a share in the gold." Then she went in, and lay down grumbling to herself.

Early in the morning she woke the old man.

"Get up, you lazy fellow," says she, "you would lie all day and let all the thieves in the world come in and steal my turnips. Up with you to the dovecot and see how my turnips are getting on."

The old man got up and rubbed his eyes, and climbed up the rickety stairs, creak, creak, creak, holding on with both hands, till he came to the top of the house, to the top of the tower, to the top of the dovecot, and looked at the turnips.

He was afraid to come down, for there were hardly any turnips left at all.

And when he did come down, the scolding the old woman gave him was worse than the other two scoldings rolled into one. She was so angry that she shook like a rag in the high wind, and the old man put both hands to his ears and hobbled away into the forest.

He hobbled along as fast as he could hobble, until he came to the hut under the pine trees. This time the little queer children were not hiding under the blankets or in the stove, or chattering in the hut. They were all over the roof of the hut, dancing and crawling about. Some of them were even sitting on the chimney. And every one of the little queer children was playing with a turnip. As soon as they saw the old man they all came tumbling off the roof, one after another, head over heels, like a lot of peas rolling off a shovel.

"*We* stole the turnips!" they shouted, before the old man could say anything at all.

"I know you did," says the old man, "but that does not make it any better for me. And it is I who get the scolding when the turnips fly away in the night."

"Never again!" shouted the children.

"I'm glad to hear that," says the old man.

"And we'll pay for the turnips."

"Thank you kindly," says the old man. He hadn't the heart to be angry with those little queer children.

Three or four of them ran into the hut and came out again with a wooden whistle, a regular whistle-pipe, such as shepherds use. They gave it to the old man.

"I can never play that," says the old man. "I don't know one tune from another; and if I did, my old fingers are as stiff as oak twigs."

"Blow in it," cried the children; and all the others came crowding round, laughing and chattering and whispering to each other. "Is he going to blow in it?" they asked. "He *is* going to blow in it." How they laughed!

The old man took the whistle, and gathered his breath and puffed out his cheeks, and blew in the whistle-pipe as hard as he could. And before he could take the whistle from his lips, three lively whips had slipped out of it, and were beating him as hard as they could go, although there was nobody to hold them. Phew! phew! phew! The three whips came down on him one after the other.

"Blow again!" the children shouted, laughing as if they were mad. "Blow again — quick, quick, quick! — and tell the whips to get into the whistle."

The old man did not wait to be told twice. He blew for all he was worth, and instantly the three whips stopped beating him. "Into the whistle!" he cried; and the three lively whips shot up into the whistle, like three snakes going into a hole. He could hardly have believed they had been out at all if it had not been for the soreness of his back.

"You take that home," cried the children. "That'll pay for the turnips, and put everything right."

"Who knows?" said the old man; and he thanked the children, and set off home through the green forest.

"Good-bye," cried the little queer children. But as soon as he had started they forgot all about him. When he looked round to wave his hand to them, not one of them was thinking of him. They were up again on the roof of the hut, jumping over each other and dancing and crawling about, and rolling each other down the roof and climbing up again, as if they had been doing nothing else all day, and were going to do nothing else till the end of the world.

The old man hobbled home through the green forest with the whistle stuck safely away into his shirt. As soon as he came to the door of the hut, the old woman, who was sitting inside counting the gold pieces, jumped up and started her scolding.

"What have the children tricked you with this time?" she screamed at him.

"They gave me a whistle-pipe," says the old man, "and they are not going to steal the turnips any more."

"A whistle-pipe!" she screamed. "What's the good of that? It's worse than the tablecloth and the skinny old goat."

The old man said nothing.

"Give it to me!" screamed the old woman. "They were my turnips, so it is my whistle-pipe."

"Well, whatever you do, don't blow in it," says the old man, and he hands over the whistle-pipe.

She wouldn't listen to him.

"What?" says she; "I must not blow my own whistle-pipe?" And with that she put the whistle-pipe to her lips and blew.

Out jumped the three lively whips, flew up in the air, and began to beat her — phew phew! phew! — one after another. If they made the old man sore, it was nothing to what they did to the cross old woman.

"Stop them! Stop them!" she screamed, running this way and that in the hut, with the whips flying after her beating her all the time. "I'll never scold again. I am to blame. I stole the magic tablecloth, and put an old one instead of it. I hid it in the iron chest." She ran to the iron chest and opened it, and pulled out the tablecloth. "Stop them! Stop them!" she screamed, while the whips laid it on hard and fast, one after the other. "I am to blame. The goat that sneezes gold pieces is hidden in the bushes. The goat by the door is one of the old ones. I wanted all the gold for myself."

All this time the old man was trying to get hold of the whistle-pipe. But the old woman was running about the hut so fast, with the whips flying after her and beating her, that he could not get it out of her hands. At last he grabbed it. "Into the whistle," says he, and put it to his lips and blew.

In a moment the three lively whips had hidden themselves in the whistle. And there was the cross old woman, kissing his hand and promising never to scold any more.

"That's all right," says the old man; and he fetched the sneezing goat out of the bushes and made it sneeze a little gold, just to be sure that it was that goat and no other. Then he laid the tablecloth on the table and told it to turn inside out. Up it flew, and came down again with the best dinner that ever was cooked, only waiting to be eaten. And the old man and the old woman sat down and ate till they could eat no more. The old woman rubbed herself now and again. And the old man rubbed himself too. But there was never a cross word between them, and they went to bed singing like nightingales.

"Is that the end?" Maroosia always asked.

"Is that all?" asked Vanya, though he knew it was not.

"Not quite," said old Peter, "but the tale won't go any quicker than my old tongue."

In the morning the old woman had forgotten about her promise. And just from habit, she set about scolding the old man as if the whips had never jumped out of the whistle. She scolded him for sleeping too long, sent him upstairs, with a lot of cross words after him, to go to the top of the dovecot to see how those turnips were getting on.

After a little the old man came down.

"The turnips are coming on grandly," says he, "and not a single one has gone in the night. I told you the children said they would not steal any more."

"I don't believe you," said the old woman. "I'll see for myself. And if any are gone, you shall pay for it, and pay for it well."

Up she jumped, and tried to climb the stairs. But the stairs were narrow and steep and twisting. She tried and tried, and could not get up at all. So she gets angrier than ever, and starts scolding the old man again.

"You must carry me up," says she.

"I have to hold on with both hands, or I couldn't get up myself," says the old man.

"I'll get in the flour sack, and you must carry me up with your teeth," says she, "they're strong enough."

And the old woman got into the flour sack.

"Don't ask me any questions," says the old man; and he took the sack in his teeth and began slowly climbing up the stairs, holding on with both hands.

He climbed and climbed, but he did not climb fast enough for the old woman.

"Are we at the top?" says she.

The old man said nothing, but went on, climbing up and up, nearly dead with the weight of the old woman in the sack which he was holding in his teeth.

He climbed a little farther, and the old woman screamed out: "Are we at the top now? We must be at the top. Let me out, you old fool!'

The old man said nothing; he climbed on and on.

The old woman raged in the flour sack. She jumped about in the sack, and screamed at the old man:

"Are we near the top now? Answer me, can't you! Answer me at once, or you'll pay for it later. Are we near the top?"

"Very near," said the old man

And as he opened his mouth to say that the sack slipped from between his teeth, and bump, bump, bumpety bump, the old woman in the sack fell all the way to the very bottom, bumping on every step. That was the end of her.

After that the old man lived alone in the hut. When he wanted tobacco or clothes or a new axe, he made the goat sneeze some gold pieces, and off he went to the town with plenty of money in his pocket. When he wanted his dinner he had only to lay the tablecloth. He never had any washing-up to do, because the tablecloth did it for him. When he wanted to get rid of troublesome guests, he gave them the whistle to blow. And when he was lonely and wanted company, he went to the little hut under the pine trees and played with the little queer children.

Little Master Misery

Once upon a time there were two brothers, peasants, and one was kind and the other was cunning. And the cunning one made money and became rich — very rich — so rich that he thought himself far too good for the village. He went off to the town, and dressed in fine furs, and clothed his wife in rich brocades, and made friends among the merchants, and began to live as merchants live, eating all day long, no longer like a simple peasant who eats kasha one day, kasha the next day, and for a change kasha on the third day also. And always he grew richer and richer.

It was very different with the kind one. He lent money to a neighbour, and the neighbour never paid it back. He sowed before the last frost, and lost all his crops. His horse went lame. His cow gave no milk. If his hens laid eggs, they were stolen; and if he set a night-line in the river, someone else always pulled it out and stole the fish and the hooks. Everything went wrong with him, and each day saw him poorer than the day before. At last there came a time when he had not a crumb of bread in the house. He and his wife were thin as sticks because they had nothing to eat, and the children were crying all day long because of their little empty stomachs. From morning till night he dug and worked, struggling against poverty like a fish against the ice; but it was no good. Things went from bad to worse.

At last his wife said to him: "You must go to the town and see that rich brother of yours. He will surely not refuse to give you a little help."

And he said: "Truly, wife, there is nothing else to be done. I will go to the town, and perhaps my rich brother will help me. I am sure he would not let my children starve. After all, he is their uncle."

So he took his stick and tramped off to the town.

He came to the house of his rich brother. A fine house it was, with painted eaves and a doorway carved by a master. Many servants were there and food in plenty, and people coming and going. He went in and found his brother, and said:

"Dear brother of mine, I beg you help me, even if only a little. My wife and children are without bread. All day long they sit hungry and waiting, and I have no food to give them."

The rich brother looks at him, and hums and strokes his beard. Then says he: "I will help you. But, of course, you must do something in return. Stay here and work for me, and at the end of a week you shall have the help you have earned."

The poor brother thanked him, and bowed and kissed his hand, and praised God for the kindness of his brother's heart, and set instantly to work. For a whole week he slaved, and scarcely slept. He cleaned out the stables and cut the wood, swept the yard, drew water from the well, and ran errands for the cook. And at the end of the week his brother called him, and gave him a single loaf of bread.

"You must not forget," says the rich brother, "that I have fed you all the week you have been here, and all that food counts in the payment."

The poor brother thanked him, and was setting off to carry the loaf to his wife and children when the rich brother called him back.

"Stop a minute," said he, "I would like you to know that I am well disposed towards you. Tomorrow is my name-day. Come to the feast, and bring your wife with you."

"How can I do that, brother? Your friends are rich merchants, with fine clothes, and boots on their feet. And I have nothing but my old coat, and my legs are bound in rags and my feet shuffle along in birch-bark shoes. I do not want to shame you before your guests."

"Never mind about that," says the rich brother, "we will find a place for you."

"Very good, brother, and thank you kindly. God be praised for having given you a tender heart."

And the poor brother, though he was tired out after all the

work he had done, set off home as fast as he could to take the bread to his wife and children.

"He might have given you more than that," said his wife.

"But listen," said he, "what do you think of this? Tomorrow we are invited, you and I, as guests, to go to a great feast."

"What do you mean? A feast? Who has invited us?"

"My brother has invited us. Tomorrow is his name-day. I always told you he had a kind heart. We shall be well fed, and I dare say we shall be able to bring back something for the children."

"A pleasure like that does not often come our way," said his wife.

So early in the morning they got up, and walked all the way to the town, so as not to shame the rich brother by putting up their old cart in the yard beside the merchants' fine carriages. They came to the rich brother's house, and found the guests all assembled and making merry; rich merchants and their plump wives, all eating and laughing and drinking and talking.

They wished a long life to the rich brother, and the poor brother wanted to make a speech, congratulating him on his name-day. But the rich brother scarcely thanked him, because he was so busy entertaining the rich merchants and their plump, laughing wives. He was pressing food on his guests, now this, now that, and calling to the servants to keep their glasses filled and their plates full of all the tastiest kinds of food. As for the poor brother and his wife, the rich one forgot all about them, and they got nothing to eat and never a drop to drink. They just sat there with empty plates and empty glasses, watching how the others ate and drank. The poor brother laughed with the rest, because he did not wish to show that he had been forgotten.

The dinner came to an end. One by one the guests went up to the giver of the feast to thank him for his good cheer. And the poor brother too got up from the bench, and bowed low before his brother and thanked him.

The guests went home, drunken and joyful. A fine noise

they made, as people do on these occasions, shouting jokes to each other and singing songs at the top of their voices.

The poor brother and his wife went home empty and sad. All that long way they had walked, and now they had to walk it again, and the feast was over, and never a bite had they had in their mouths, nor a drop in their gullets.

"Come, wife," says the poor brother as he trudged along, "let us sing a song like the others."

"What a fool you are!" says his wife. Hungry and cross she was, as even Maroosia would be after a day like that watching other people stuff themselves. "What a fool you are!" says she. "People may very well sing when they have eaten tasty dishes and drunk good wine. But what reason have you got for making a merry noise in the night?"

"Why, my dear," says he, "we have been at my brother's name-day feast. I am ashamed to go home without a song. I'll sing. I'll sing so that everyone shall think he loaded us with good things like the rest."

"Well, sing if you like; but you'll sing by yourself."

So the peasant, the poor brother, started singing a song with his dry throat. He lifted his voice and sang like the rest, while his wife trudged silently beside him.

But as he sang it seemed to the peasant that he heard two voices singing — his own and another's. He stopped, and asked his wife:

"Is that you joining in my song with a little thin voice?"

"What's the matter with you? I never thought of singing with you. I never opened my mouth."

"Who is it then?"

"No one except yourself. Anyone would say you had had a drink of wine after all."

"But I heard someone . . . a little weak voice . . . a little sad voice . . . joining with mine."

"I heard nothing," said his wife; "but sing again, and I'll listen."

The poor man sang again. He sang alone. His wife listened, and it was clear that there were two voices singing — the dry voice of the poor man, and a little miserable voice that came from the shadows under the trees. The poor man stopped, and asked out loud:

"Who are you who are singing with me?"

And a little thin voice answered out of the shadows by the roadside, under the trees:

"I am Misery."

"So it was you, Misery, who were helping me?"

"Yes, master, I was helping you."

"Well, little Master Misery, come along with us and keep us company."

"I'll do that willingly," says little Master Misery, "and I'll never, never leave you at all — no, not if you have no other friend in the world."

And a wretched little man, with a miserable face and little thin legs and arms, came out of the shadows and went home with the peasant and his wife.

It was late when they got home, but little Master Misery asked the peasant to take him to the tavern. "After such a day as this has been," says he, "there's nothing else to be done."

"But I have no money," says the peasant.

"What of that?" says little Master Misery. "Spring has begun, and you have a winter jacket on. It will soon be summer, and whether you have it or not you won't wear it. Bring it along to the tavern, and change it for a drink."

The poor man went to the tavern with little Master Misery, and they sat there and drank the vodka that the tavern-keeper gave them in exchange for the coat.

Next day, early in the morning, little Master Misery began complaining. His head ached and he could not open his eyes, and he did not like the weather, and the children were crying, and there was no food in the house. He asked the peasant to come with him to the tavern again and forget all this wretchedness in a drink.

"But I've got no money," says the peasant.

"Rubbish!" says little Master Misery; "you have a sledge and a cart."

They took the cart and the sledge to the tavern, and stayed there drinking until the tavern-keeper said they had had all that the cart and the sledge were worth. Then the tavern-keeper took them and threw them out of doors into the night, and they picked themselves up and crawled home.

Next day Misery complained worse than before, and begged the peasant to come with him to the tavern. There was no getting rid of him, no keeping him quiet. The peasant sold his harrow and plough, so that he could no longer work his land. He went to the tavern with little Master Misery.

A month went by like that, and at the end of it the peasant had nothing left at all. He had even pledged the hut he lived in to a neighbour, and taken the money to the tavern.

And every day little Master Misery begged him to come. "There I am not wretched any longer," says Misery. "There I sing, and even dance, hitting the floor with my heels and making a merry noise."

"But now I have no money at all, and nothing left to sell," says the poor peasant. "I'd be willing enough to go with you, but I can't, and here is an end of it."

"Rubbish!" says Misery; "your wife has two dresses. Leave her one; she can't wear both at once. Leave her one, and buy a drink with the other. They are both ragged, but take the better of the two. The tavern-keeper is a just man, and will give us more drink for the better one."

The peasant took the dress and sold it; and Misery laughed and danced, while the peasant thought to himself, "Well, this is the end. I've nothing left to sell, and my wife has nothing either. We've the clothes on our backs, and nothing else in the world."

In the morning little Master Misery woke with a headache as usual, and a mouthful of groans and complaints. But he saw that the peasant had nothing left to sell, and he called out:

"Listen to me, master of the house."

"What is it, Misery?" says the peasant, who was master of nothing in the world.

"Go you to a neighbour and beg the loan of a cart and a pair of good oxen."

The poor peasant had no will of his own left. He did exactly as he was told. He went to his neighbour and begged the loan of the oxen and cart.

"But how will you repay me?" says the neighbour.

"I will do a week's work for you for nothing."

"Very well," says the neighbour, "take the oxen and cart, but be careful not to give them too heavy a load."

"Indeed I won't," says the peasant, thinking to himself that he had nothing to load them with. "And thank you very much," says he; and he goes back to Misery, taking with him the oxen and cart.

Misery looked at him and grumbled in his wretched little voice, "They are hardly strong enough."

"They are the best I could borrow," says the peasant, "and you and I have starved too long to be heavy."

And the peasant and little Master Misery sat together in the cart and drove off together, Misery holding his head in both hands and groaning at the jolt of the cart.

As soon as they had left the village, Misery sat up and asked the peasant:

"Do you know the big stone that stands alone in the middle of a field not far from here?"

"Of course I know it," says the peasant.

"Drive straight to it," says Misery, and went on rocking himself to and fro, and groaning and complaining in his wretched little voice.

They came to the stone, and got down from the cart and looked at the stone. It was very big and heavy, and was fixed in the ground.

"Heave it up," says Misery.

The poor peasant set to work to heave it up, and Misery helped him, groaning, and complaining that the peasant was nothing of a fellow because he could not do his work by himself. Well, they heaved it up, and there below it was a deep hole, and the hole was filled with gold pieces to the very top;

more gold pieces than ever you will see copper ones if you live to be a hundred and ten.

"Well, what are you staring at?" says Misery. "Stir yourself, and be quick about it, and load all this gold into the cart."

The peasant set to work, and piled all the gold into the cart down to the very last gold piece; while Misery sat on the stone and watched, groaning and chuckling in his weak, wretched little voice.

"Be quick," says Misery, "and then we can get back to the tavern."

The peasant looked into the pit to see that there was nothing left there, and then says he:

"Just take a look, little Master Misery, and see that we have left nothing behind. You are smaller than I, and can get right down into the pit . . ."

Misery slipped down from the stone, grumbling at the peasant, and bent over the pit.

"You've taken the lot," says he, "there's nothing to be seen."

122

"But what is that," says the peasant — "there, shining in the corner?"

"I don't see it."

"Jump down into the pit and you'll see it. It would be a pity to waste a gold piece."

Misery jumped down into the pit, and instantly the peasant rolled the stone over the hole and shut him in.

"Things will be better so," says the peasant. "If I were to let you out of that, sooner or later you would drink up all this money, just as you drank up everything I had."

Then the peasant drove home and hid the gold in the cellar; took the oxen and cart back to his neighbour, thanked him kindly, and began to think what he would do, now that Misery was his master no longer, and he with plenty of money.

"But he had to work for a week to pay for the loan of the oxen and cart," said Vanya.

"Well, during the week, while he was working, he was thinking all the time, in his head," said old Peter, a little grumpily. Then he went on with his tale.

As soon as the week was over, he bought a forest and built himself a fine house, and began to live twice as richly as his brother in the town. And his wife had two new dresses, perhaps more; with a lot of gold and silver braid, and necklaces of big yellow stones, and bracelets and sparkling rings. His children were well fed every day: rivers of milk between banks of kisel jelly, and mushrooms with sauce, and soup, and cakes with little balls of egg and meat hidden in the middle. And they had toys that squeaked, a little boy feeding a goose that poked its head into a dish, and a painted hen with a lot of chickens that all squeaked together.

Time went on, and when his name-day drew near he thought of his brother, the merchant, and drove off to the town to invite him to take part in the feast.

"I have not forgotten, brother, that you invited me to yours."

"What a fellow you are!" says his brother; "you have nothing to eat yourself, and here you are inviting other people for your name-day."

"Yes," said the peasant, "once upon a time, it is true, I had nothing to eat; but now, praise be to God, I am no poorer than yourself. Come to my name-day feast and you will see."

"Very well," says his brother, "I'll come; but don't think you can play any jokes on me."

On the morning of the peasant's name-day his brother, the merchant in the town, put on his best clothes, and his plump wife dressed in all her richest, and they got into their cart — a fine cart it was too, painted in the brightest colours — and off they drove together to the house of the brother who had once been poor. They took a basket of food with them, in case he had only been joking when he invited them to his name-day feast.

They drove to the village, and asked for him at the hut where he used to be.

An old man hobbling along the road answered them:

"Oh, you mean our Ivan Ilyitch. Well, he does not live here any longer. Where have you been that you have not heard? His is the big new house on the hill. You can see it through the trees over there, where all these people are walking. He has a kind heart, he has, and riches have not spoiled it. He has invited the whole village to feast with him, because today is his name-day."

"Riches!" thought the merchant; "a new house!" He was very much surprised, but as he drove along the road he was more surprised still. For he passed all the villagers on their way to the feast; and everyone was talking of his brother, and how kind he was and how generous, and what a feast there was going to be, and how many barrels of mead and wine had been taken up to the house. All the folk were hurrying along the road licking their lips, each one going faster than the other so as to be sure not to miss any of the good things.

The rich brother from the town drove with his wife into the courtyard of the fine new house. And there on the steps was the peasant brother, Ivan Ilyitch, and his wife, receiving their guests. And if the rich brother was well dressed, the peasant was better dressed; and if the rich brother's wife was in her fine clothes, the peasant's wife fairly glittered — what with the gold braid on her bosom and the shining silver in her hair.

And the peasant brother kissed his brother from the town on both cheeks, and gave him and his wife the best places at the table. He fed them — ah, how he fed them! — with little red slips of smoked salmon, and beetroot soup with cream, and slabs of sturgeon, and meats of three or four kinds, and game and sweet-meats of the best. There never was such a feast — no, not even at the wedding of a Tzar. And as for drink, there were red wine and white wine, and beer and mead in great barrels, and everywhere the peasant went about among his guests, filling glasses and seeing that their plates were kept piled with the foods each one liked best.

And the rich brother wondered and wondered, and at last he could wait no longer, and he took his brother aside and said:

"I am delighted to see you so rich. But tell me, I beg you, how it was that all this good fortune came to you."

The poor brother, never thinking, told him all — the whole truth about little Master Misery and the pit full of gold, and how Misery was shut in there under the big stone.

The merchant brother listened, and did not forget a word. He could hardly bear himself for envy, and as for his wife, she was worse. She looked at the peasant's wife with her beautiful head-dress, and she bit her lips till they bled.

As soon as they could, they said good-bye and drove off home.

The merchant brother could not bear the thought that his brother was richer than he. He said to himself, "I will go to the field, and move the stone, and let Master Misery out. Then he will go and tear my brother to pieces for shutting him in; and his riches will not be of much use to him then, even if Misery does not give them to me as a token of gratitude. Think of my brother daring to show off his riches to me!"

So he drove off to the field, and came at last to the big stone. He moved the stone on one side, and then bent over the pit to see what was in it.

He had scarcely put his head over the edge before Misery sprang up out of the pit, seated himself firmly on his shoulders, squeezed his neck between his little wiry legs, and pulled out handfuls of his hair.

"Scream away!" cried little Master Misery. "You tried to kill me, shutting me up in there, while you went off and bought fine clothes. You tried to kill me, and came to feast your eyes on my corpse. Now, whatever happens, I'll never leave you again."

"Listen, Misery!" screamed the merchant. "Ai, ai! stop pulling my hair. You are choking me. Ai! Listen. It was not I who shut you in under the stone. . . ."

"Who was it, if it was not you?" asked Misery, tugging out his hair, and digging his knees into the merchant's throat.

"It was my brother. I came here on purpose to let you out. I came out of pity."

Misery tugged the merchant's hair, and twisted the merchant's ears till they nearly came off.

"Liar, liar!" he shouted in his little, wretched angry voice. "You tricked me once. Do you think you'll get the better of me again by a clumsy lie of that kind? Now then. Gee up! Home we go."

And so the rich brother went trotting home, crying with pain; while little Master Misery sat firmly on his shoulders, pulling at his hair.

Instantly Misery was at his old tricks.

"You seem to have bought a good deal with the gold," he said, looking at the merchant's house. "We'll see how far it will go." And every day he rode the rich merchant to the tavern, and made him drink up all his money, and his house, his clothes, his horses and carts and sledges — everything he had — until he was as poor as his brother had been in the beginning.

The merchant thought and thought, and puzzled his brain to find a way to get rid of him. And at last one night, when Misery had groaned himself to sleep, the merchant went out into the yard and took a big cart wheel and made two stout wedges of wood, just big enough to fit into the hub of the wheel. He drove one wedge firmly in at one end of the hub, and left the wheel in the yard with the other wedge, and a big hammer lying handy close to it.

In the morning Misery wakes as usual, and cries out to be taken to the tavern.

"We've sold everything I've got," says the merchant.

"Well, what are you going to do to amuse me?" says Misery.

"Let's play hide-and-seek in the yard," says the merchant.

"Right," says Misery, "but you'll never find me, for I can make myself so small I can hide in a mouse-hole in the floor."

"We'll see," says the merchant.

The merchant hid first, and Misery found him at once.

"Now it's my turn," says Misery, "but what's the good? You'll never find me. Why, I could get inside the hub of that wheel if I had a mind to."

"What a liar you are!" says the merchant; "you never could get into that little hole."

"Look," says Misery, and he made himself little, little, little, and sat on the hub of the wheel.

"Look," says he, making himself smaller again; and then, pouf! in he pops into the hole of the hub.

Instantly the merchant took the other wedge and the hammer, and drove the wedge into the hole. The first wedge had closed up the other end, and so there was Misery shut up inside the hub of the cart wheel.

The merchant set the wheel on his shoulders, and took it to the river and threw it out as far as he could, and it went floating away down to the sea.

Then he went home and set to work to make money again, and earn his daily bread; for Misery had made him so poor that he had nothing left, and had to hire himself out to make a living, just as his peasant brother used to do.

But what happened to Misery when he went floating away?

He floated away down the river, shut up in the hub of the wheel. He ought to have starved there. But I am afraid some silly, greedy fellow thought to get a new wheel for nothing, and pulled the wedges out and let him go; for, by all I hear, Misery is still wandering about the world and making people wretched — bad luck to him!

A Chapter of Fish

Sometimes in spring, when the big river flooded its banks and made lakes of the meadows, and the little rivers flowed deep, old Peter spent a few days netting fish. Also in summer he set night-lines in the little river not far from where it left the forest. And so it happened that one day he sat in the warm sunshine outside his hut, mending his nets and making floats for them; not cork floats like ours, but little rolls of the silver bark of the birch tree.

And while he sat there Vanya and Maroosia watched him, and sometimes even helped, holding a piece of the net between them, while old Peter fastened on the little glistening rolls of bark that were to keep it up in the water. And all the time old Peter worked he smoked, and told them stories about fish.

First he told them what happened when the first pike was born, and how it is that all the little fish are not eaten by the great pike with his huge greedy mouth and his sharp teeth.

*****

On the eve of Ivanov Day (that is the day of Saint John, which is Midsummer) there was born the pike, a huge fish, with such teeth as never were. And when the pike was born the waters of the river foamed and raged, so that the ships in the river were all but swamped, and the pretty young girls who were playing on the banks ran away as fast as they could, frightened, they were, by the roaring of the waves, and the black wind and the white foam on the water. Terrible was the birth of the sharp-toothed pike.

And when the pike was born he did not grow up by months or by days, but by hours. Every day it was two inches longer than the day before. In a month it was two yards long; in two months it was twelve feet long; in three months it was raging up and down the river like a tempest, eating the bream and the perch, and all the small fish that came in its way. There was a bream or a perch swimming lazily in the stream. The pike saw it as it raged by, caught it in its great white mouth, and instantly the bream or the perch was gone, torn to pieces by the pike's teeth, and swallowed as you would swallow a sunflower seed. And bream and perch are big fish. It was worse for the little ones.

What was to be done? The bream and the perch put their heads together in a quiet pool. It was clear enough that the

great pike would eat every one of them. So they called a meeting of all the little fish, and set to thinking what could be done by way of dealing with the great pike, which had such sharp teeth and was making so free with their lives.

They all came to the meeting — bream, and perch, and roach, and dace, and gudgeon; yes, and the little yersh with his spiny back.

The silly roach said, "Let us kill the pike."

But the gudgeon looked at him with his great eyes, and asked, "Have you got good teeth?"

"No," says the roach, "I haven't any teeth."

"You'd swallow the pike, I suppose?" says the perch.

"My mouth is too small."

"Then do not use it to talk foolishness," said the gudgeon; and the roach's fins blushed scarlet, and are red to this day.

"I will set my prickles on end," says the perch, who has a row of sharp prickles in the fin on his back. "The pike won't find them too comfortable in his throat."

"Yes," said the bream, "but you will have to go into his throat to put them there, and he'll swallow you all the same. Besides, we have not all got prickles."

There was a lot more foolishness talked. Even the minnows had something to say, until they were made to be quiet by the dace.

Now the little yersh had come to the meeting, with his spiny back, and his big front fins, and his head all shining in blue and gold and green. And when he had heard all they had to say, he began to talk.

"Think away," says he, "and break your heads, and spoil your brains, if ever you had any; but listen for a moment to what I have to say."

And all the fish turned to listen to the yersh, who is the cleverest of all the little fish, because he has a big head and a small body.

"Listen," says the yersh. "It is clear enough that the pike lives in this big river, and that he does not give the little fish a chance, crunches them all with his sharp teeth, and swallows them ten at a time. I quite agree that it would be much better for everybody if he could be killed; but not one of us is strong enough for that. We are not strong enough to kill him; but we can starve him, and save ourselves at the same time. There's no living in the big river while he is here. Let all us little fish clear out, and go and live in the little rivers that flow into the big. There the waters are shallow, and we can hide among the weeds. No one will touch us there, and we can live and bring up our children in peace, and only be in danger when we go visiting from one little river to another. And as for the great

131

pike, we will leave him alone in the big river to rage hungrily up and down. His teeth will soon grow blunt, for there will be nothing for him to eat."

All the little fish waved their fins and danced in the water when they heard the wisdom of the yersh's speech. And the yersh and the roach, and the bream and the perch, and the dace and the gudgeon left the big river and swam up the little rivers between the green meadows. And there they began again to live in peace and bring up their little ones, though the cunning fishermen set nets in the little rivers and caught many of them on their way. From that time on there have never been many little fish in the big river.

And as for the monstrous pike, he swam up and down the great river, lashing the waters, and driving his nose through the waves, but found no food for his sharp teeth. He had to take to worms, and was caught in the end on a fisherman's hook. Yes, and the fisherman made soup of him — the best fish soup that ever was made. He was a friend of mine when I was a boy, and he gave me a taste in my wooden spoon.

*****

Then he told them the story of other pike, and particularly of the pike that was king of a river, and made the little fish come together on the top of the water so that the young hunter could cross over with dry feet. And he told them of the pike that hid the lover of the princess by swallowing him and lying at the bottom of a deep pool, and how the princess saw her lover sitting in the pike, when the big fish opened his mouth to snap up a little perch that swam too near his nose. Then he told them of the big trial in the river, when the fishes chose judges, and made a case at law against the yersh, and found him guilty, and how the yersh spat in the faces of the judges and swam merrily away.

Finally, he told them the story of the Golden Fish. But that is a long story, and a chapter all by itself, and begins on the next page.

132

The Golden Fish

"This," said old Peter, "is a story against wanting more than enough."

Long ago, near the shore of the blue sea, an old man lived with his old woman in a little old hut made of earth and moss and logs. They never had a rouble to spend. A rouble! they never had a kopeck. They just lived there in the little hut, and the old man caught fish out of the sea in his old net, and the old woman cooked the fish; and so they lived, poorly enough in summer and worse in winter. Sometimes they had a few fish to sell, but not often. In the summer evenings they sat outside their hut on a broken old bench, and the old man mended the holes in his ragged old net. There were holes in it a hare could jump through with his ears standing, let alone one of those little fishes that live in the sea. The old woman sat on the bench beside him, and patched his trousers and complained.

Well, one day the old man went fishing, as he always did. All day long he fished, and caught nothing. And then in the evening, when he was thinking he might as well give up and go home, he threw his net for the last time, and when he came to pull it in he began to think he had caught an island instead of a haul of fish, and a strong and lively island at that — the net was so heavy and pulled so hard against his feeble old arms.

"This time," says he, "I have caught a hundred fish at least."

Not a bit of it. The net came in as heavy as if it were full of fighting fish, but empty —

"Empty?" said Maroosia.

"Well, not quite empty," said old Peter, and went on with his tale.

Not quite empty, for when the last of the net came ashore there was something glittering in it — a golden fish, not very

133

big and not very little, caught in the meshes. And it was this single golden fish which had made the net so heavy.

The old fisherman took the golden fish in his hands.

"At least it will be enough for supper," said he.

But the golden fish lay still in his hands, and looked at him with eyes, and spoke — yes, my dears, it spoke, just as if it were you or I.

"Old man," says the fish, "do not kill me. I beg you throw me back into the blue waters. Some day I may be able to be of use to you."

"What?" says the old fisherman; "and do you talk with a human voice?"

"I do," says the fish. "And my fish's heart feels pain like yours. It would be as bitter to me to die as it would be to yourself."

"And is that so?" says the old fisherman. "Well, you shall not die this time." And he threw the golden fish back into the sea.

You would have thought the golden fish would have splashed with his tail, and turned head downwards, and swum away into the blue depths of the sea. Not a bit of it. It stayed there with its tail slowly flapping in the water so as to keep its head up, and it looked at the fisherman with its wise eyes, and it spoke again.

"You have given me my life," says the golden fish. "Now ask anything you wish from me, and you shall have it."

The old fisherman stood there on the shore, combing his beard with his old fingers, and thinking. Think as he would, he could not call to mind a single thing he wanted.

"No, fish," he said at last; "I think I have everything I need."

"Well, if ever you do want anything, come and ask for it," says the fish, and turns over, flashing gold, and goes down into the blue sea.

The old fisherman went back to his hut, where his wife was waiting for him.

"What!" she screamed out; "you haven't caught so much as one little fish for our supper?"

"I caught one fish, mother," says the old man: "a golden fish it was, and it spoke to me; and I let it go, and it told me to ask for anything I wanted."

"And what did you ask for? Show me."

"I couldn't think of anything to ask for; so I did not ask for anything at all."

"Fool," says his wife, "and dolt, and us with no food to put in our mouths. Go back at once, and ask for some bread."

Well, the poor old fisherman got down his net, and tramped back to the seashore. And he stood on the shore of the wide blue sea, and he called out:

> "Head in air and tail in sea,
> Fish, fish, listen to me."

And in a moment there was the golden fish with his head out of the water, flapping his tail below him in the water, and looking at the fisherman with his wise eyes.

"What is it?" said the fish.

"Be so kind," says the fisherman, "be so kind. We have no bread in the house."

"Go home," says the fish, and turned over and went down into the sea.

"God be good to me," says the old fisherman, "but what shall I say to my wife, going home like this without the bread?" And he went home very wretchedly, and slower than he came.

As soon as he came within sight of his hut he saw his wife, and she was waving her arms and shouting.

"Stir your old bones," she screamed out. "It's as fine a loaf as ever I've seen."

And he hurried along, and found his old wife cutting up a huge loaf of white bread, mind you, not black — a huge loaf of white bread, nearly as big as Maroosia.

"You did not do so badly after all," said his old wife as they sat there with the samovar on the table between them, dipping their bread in the hot tea.

But that night, as they lay sleeping on the stove, the old

woman poked the old man in the ribs with her bony elbow. He groaned and woke up.

"I've been thinking," says his wife, "your fish might have given us a trough to keep the bread in while he was about it. There is a lot left over, and without a trough it will go bad, and not be fit for anything. And our old trough is broken; besides, it's too small. First thing in the morning off you go, and ask your fish to give us a new trough to put the bread in."

Early in the morning she woke the old man again, and he had to get up and go down to the seashore. He was very much afraid, because he thought the fish would not take it kindly. But at dawn, just as the red sun was rising out of the sea, he stood on the shore, and called out in his windy old voice:

> "Head in air and tail in sea,
> Fish, fish, listen to me."

And there in the morning sunlight was the golden fish, looking at him with its wise eyes.

"I beg your pardon," says the old man, "but could you, just to oblige my wife, give us some sort of trough to put the bread in?"

"Go home," says the fish; and down it goes into the blue sea.

The old man went home, and there, outside the hut, was the old woman, looking at the handsomest bread trough that ever was seen on earth. Painted it was, with little flowers, in three colours, and there were strips of gilding about its handles.

"Look at this," grumbled the old woman. "This is far too fine a trough for a tumble-down hut like ours. Why, there is scarcely a place in the roof where the rain does not come through. If we were to keep this trough in such a hut, it would be spoiled in a month. You must go back to your fish and ask it for a new hut."

"I hardly like to do that," says the old man.

"Get along with you," says his wife. "If the fish can make a trough like this, a hut will be no trouble to him. And, after all, you must not forget he owes his life to you."

"I suppose that is true," says the old man; but he went back to the shore with a heavy heart. He stood on the edge of the sea and called out, doubtfully:

> "Head in air and tail in sea,
> Fish, fish, listen to me."

Instantly there was a ripple in the water, and the golden fish was looking at him with its wise eyes.

"Well?" says the fish.

"My old woman is so pleased with the trough that she wants a new hut to keep it in, because ours, if you could only see it, is really falling to pieces, and the rain comes in and —"

"Go home," says the fish.

The old fisherman went home, but he could not find his old hut at all. At first he thought he had lost his way. But then he saw his wife. And she was walking about, first one way and then the other, looking at the finest hut that God ever gave a poor moujik to keep him from the rain and the cold, and the too great heat of the sun. It was built of sound logs, neatly finished at the ends and carved. And the overhanging of the roof was cut in patterns, so neat, so pretty, you could never think how they had been done. The old woman looked at it from all sides. And the old man stood, wondering. Then they went in together. And everything within the hut was new and clean. There were a fine big stove, and strong wooden benches, and a good table, and a fire lit in the stove, and logs ready to put in, and a samovar already on the boil — a fine new samovar of glittering brass.

You would have thought the old woman would have been satisfied with that. Not a bit of it.

"You don't know how to lift your eyes from the ground," says she. "You don't know what to ask. I am tired of being a peasant woman and a moujik's wife. I was made for something better. I want to be a lady, and have good people to do the

137

work, and see folk bow and curtsy to me when I meet them walking abroad. Go back at once to the fish, you old fool, and ask him for that, instead of bothering him for little trifles like bread troughs and moujiks' huts. Off with you."

The old fisherman went back to the shore with a sad heart; but he was afraid of his wife, and he dared not disobey her. He stood on the shore, and called out in his windy old voice:

> "Head in air and tail in sea,
> Fish, fish, listen to me."

Instantly there was the golden fish looking at him with its wise eyes.

"Well?" says the fish.

"My old woman won't give me a moment's peace," says the old man, "and since she has the new hut — which is a fine one, I must say; as good a hut as ever I saw — she won't be content at all. She is tired of being a peasant's wife, and wants to be a lady with a house and servants, and to see the good folk curtsy to her when she meets them walking abroad."

"Go home," says the fish.

The old man went home, thinking about the hut, and how pleasant it would be to live in it, even if his wife were a lady.

But when he got home the hut had gone, and in its place there was a fine brick house, three stories high. There were servants running this way and that in the courtyard. There was a cook in the kitchen, and there was his old woman, in a dress of rich brocade, sitting idle in a tall carved chair, and giving orders right and left.

"Good health to you, wife," says the old man.

"Ah, you clown that you are, how dare you call me your wife! Can't you see that I'm a lady? Here! Off with this fellow to the stables, and see that he gets a beating he won't forget in a hurry."

Instantly the servants seized the old man by the collar and lugged him along to the stables. There the grooms treated him to such a whipping that he could hardly stand on his feet.

After that the old woman made him doorkeeper. She ordered that a besom should be given him to clean up the courtyard, and said that he was to have his meals in the kitchen. A wretched life the old man lived. All day long he was sweeping up the courtyard, and if there was a speck of dirt to be seen in it anywhere, he paid for it at once in the stable under the whips of the grooms.

Time went on, and the old woman grew tired of being only a lady. And at last there came a day when she sent into the yard to tell the old man to come before her. The poor old man combed his hair and cleaned his boots, and came into the house, and bowed low before the old woman.

"Be off with you, you old good-for-nothing!" says she. "Go and find your golden fish, and tell him from me that I am tired of being a lady. I want to be Tzaritza, with generals and courtiers and men of state to do whatever I tell them."

The old man went along to the seashore, glad enough to be out of the courtyard and out of reach of the stablemen with their whips. He came to the shore, and cried out in his windy old voice:

> "Head in air and tail in sea,
> Fish, fish, listen to me."

And there was the golden fish looking at him with its wise eyes.

"What's the matter now, old man?" says the fish.

"My old woman is going on worse than ever," says the old fisherman. "My back is sore with the whips of her grooms. And now she says it isn't enough for her to be a lady; she wants to be a Tzaritza."

"Never you worry about it," says the fish. "Go home and praise God"; and with that the fish turned over and went down into the sea.

The old man went home slowly, for he did not know what his wife would do to him if the golden fish did not make her into a Tzaritza.

But as soon as he came near he heard the noise of trumpets and the beating of drums, and there where the fine stone house had been was now a great palace with a golden roof. Behind it was a big garden of flowers, that are fair to look at but have no fruit, and before it was a meadow of fine green grass. And on the meadow was an army of soldiers drawn up in squares and all dressed alike. And suddenly the fisherman saw his old woman in the gold and silver dress of a Tzaritza come stalking out on the balcony with her generals and boyars to hold a review of her troops. And the drums beat and the trumpets sounded, and the soldiers cried "Hurrah!" And the poor old fisherman found a dark corner in one of the barns, and lay down in the straw.

Time went on, and at last the old woman was tired of being Tzaritza. She thought she was made for something better. And one day she said to her chamberlain:

"Find me that ragged old beggar who is always hanging about in the courtyard. Find him, and bring him here."

The chamberlain told his officers, and the officers told the servants, and the servants looked for the old man, and found him at last asleep on the straw in the corner of one of the barns. They took some of the dirt off him, and brought him before the Tzaritza, sitting proudly on her golden throne.

"Listen, old fool!" says she. "Be off to your golden fish, and tell it I am tired of being Tzaritza. Anybody can be Tzaritza. I want to be the ruler of the seas, so that all the waters shall obey me, and all the fishes shall be my servants."

"I don't like to ask that," said the old man, trembling.

"What's that?" she screamed at him. "Do you dare to answer the Tzaritza? If you do not set off this minute, I'll have your head cut off and your body thrown to the dogs."

Unwillingly the old man hobbled off. He came to the shore, and cried out with a windy, quavering old voice:

> "Head in air and tail in sea,
> Fish, fish, listen to me."

Nothing happened.

The old man thought of his wife, and what would happen to him if she were still Tzaritza when he came home. Again he called out:

> "Head in air and tail in sea,
> Fish, fish, listen to me."

Nothing happened, nothing at all.

A third time, with the tears running down his face, he called out in his windy, creaky, quavering old voice:

> "Head in air and tail in sea,
> Fish, fish, listen to me."

Suddenly there was a loud noise, louder and louder over the sea. The sun hid itself. The sea broke into waves, and the waves piled themselves one upon another. The sky and the sea turned black, and there was a great roaring wind that lifted the white crests of the waves and tossed them abroad over the waters. The golden fish came up out of the storm and spoke out of the sea.

"What is it now?" says he, in a voice more terrible than the voice of the storm itself.

"O fish," says the old man, trembling like a reed shaken by the storm, "my old woman is worse than before. She is tired of being Tzaritza. She wants to be the ruler of the seas, so that all the waters shall obey her and all the fishes be her servants."

The golden fish said nothing, nothing at all. He turned over and went down into the deep seas. And the wind from the sea was so strong that the old man could hardly stand against it. For a long time he waited, afraid to go home; but at last the storm calmed, and it grew towards evening, and he hobbled back, thinking to creep in and hide amongst the straw.

As he came near, he listened for the trumpets and the drums. He heard nothing except the wind from the sea rustling the little leaves of birch trees. He looked for the palace.

It was gone, and where it had been was a little tumble-down hut of earth and logs. It seemed to the old fisherman that he knew the little hut, and he looked at it with joy. And he went to the door of the hut, and there was sitting his old woman in a ragged dress, cleaning out a saucepan, and singing in a creaky old voice. And this time she was glad to see him, and they sat down together on the bench and drank tea without sugar, because they had not any money.

They began to live again as they used to live, and the old man grew happier every day. He fished and fished, and many were the fish that he caught, and of many kinds; but never again did he catch another golden fish that could talk like a human being. I doubt whether he would have said anything to his wife about it, even if he had caught one every day.

*****

"What a horrid old woman!" said Maroosia.

"I wonder the old fisherman forgave her," said Vanya.

"I think he might have beaten her a little," said Maroosia. "She deserved it."

"Well," said old Peter, "supposing we could have everything we wanted for the asking, I wonder how it would be. Perhaps God knew what He was doing when He made those golden fishes rare."

"Are there really any of them?" asked Vanya.

"Well, there was once one, anyhow," said old Peter; and then he rolled his nets neatly together, hung them on the fence, and went into the hut to make the dinner. And Vanya and Maroosia went in with him to help him as much as they could: though Vanya was wondering all the time whether he could make a net, and throw it in the little river where old Peter fished, and perhaps pull out a golden fish that would speak to him with the voice of a human being.

Who Lived in the Skull?

Once upon a time a horse's skull lay on the open plain. It had been picked clean by the ants, and shone white in the sunlight.

Little Burrowing Mouse came along, twirling his whiskers and looking at the world. He saw the white skull, and thought it was as good as a palace. He stood up in front of it and called out:

"Little house, little house! Who lives in the little house?"

No one answered, for there was no one inside.

"I will live there myself," says little Burrowing Mouse, and in he went, and set up house in the horse's skull.

Croaking Frog came along, a jump, three long strides, and a jump again.

"Little house, little house! Who lives in the little house?"

"I am Burrowing Mouse; who are you?"

"I am Croaking Frog."

"Come in and make yourself at home."

So the frog went in, and they began to live, the two of them together.

Hare Hide-in-the-Hill came running by.

"Little house, little house! Who lives in the little house?"

"Burrowing Mouse and Croaking Frog. Who are you?"

"I am Hare Hide-in-the-Hill."

"Come along in."

So the hare put his ears down and went in, and they began to live, the three of them together.

Then the fox came running by.

"Little house, little house! Who lives in the little house?"

"Burrowing Mouse and Croaking Frog and Hare Hide-in-the-Hill. Who are you?"

"I am Fox Run-about-Everywhere."

"Come along in; we've room for you."

So the fox went in, and they began to live, the four of them together.

Then the wolf came prowling by, and saw the skull.

"Little house, little house! Who lives in the little house?"

"Burrowing Mouse, and Croaking Frog, and Hare Hide-in-the-Hill, and Fox Run-about-Everywhere. Who are you?"

"I am Wolf Leap-out-of-the-Bushes."

"Come in then."

So the wolf went in, and they began to live, the five of them together.

And then there came along the Bear. He was very slow and very heavy.

"Little house, little house! Who lives in the little house?"

"Burrowing Mouse, and Croaking Frog, and Hare Hide-in-the-Hill, and Fox Run-about-Everywhere, and Wolf Leap-out-of-the-Bushes. Who are you?"

"I am Bear Squash-the-Lot."

And the Bear sat down on the horse's skull, and squashed the whole lot of them.

*****

The way to tell that story is to make one hand the skull, and the fingers and thumb of the other hand the animals that go in one by one. At least that was the way old Peter told it; and when it came to the end, and the Bear came along, why, the Bear was old Peter himself, who squashed both little hands, and Vanya or Maroosia, whichever it was, all together in one big hug.

Alenoushka and her Brother

Once upon a time there were two orphan children, a little boy and a little girl. Their father and mother were dead, and they had not even an old grandfather to spend his time in telling them stories. They were alone. The little boy was called Ivanoushka,* and the little girl's name was Alenoushka.*

They set out together to walk through the whole of the great wide world. It was a long journey they set out on, and they did not think of any end to it, but only of moving on and on, and never stopping long enough in one place to be unhappy there.

They were travelling one day over a broad plain, padding along on their little bare feet. There were no trees on the plain, no bushes; open flat country as far as you could see, and the great sun up in the sky burning the grass and making their throats dry, and the sandy ground so hot that they could scarcely bear to set their feet on it. All day from early morning they had been walking, and the heat grew greater and greater towards noon.

"Oh," said little Ivanoushka, "my throat is so dry. I want a drink. I must have a drink — just a little drink of cool water."

"We must go on," said Alenoushka, "till we come to a well. Then we will drink."

They went on along the track, with their eyes burning and their throats as dry as sand on a stove.

But presently Ivanoushka cried out joyfully. He saw a horse's hoofmark in the ground. And it was full of water, like a little well.

"Sister, sister," says he, "the horse has made a little well for me with his great hoof, and now we can have a drink; and oh, but I am thirsty!"

"Not yet, brother," says Alenoushka. "If you drink from the

* That means that they were called Ivan and Elena. Ivanoushka and Alenoushka are affectionate forms of these names.

147

hoofmark of a horse, you will turn into a little foal, and that would never do."

"I am so very thirsty," says Ivanoushka; but he did as his sister told him, and they walked on together under the burning sun.

A little farther on Ivanoushka saw the hoofmark of a cow, and there was water in it glittering in the sun.

"Sister, sister," says Ivanoushka, "the cow has made a little well for me, and now I can have a drink."

"Not yet, brother," says Alenoushka. "If you drink from the hoofmark of a cow, you will turn into a little calf, and that would never do. We must go on till we come to a well. There we will drink and rest ourselves. There will be trees by the well, and shadows, and we will lie down there by the quiet water and cool our hands and feet, and perhaps our eyes will stop burning."

So they went on farther along the track that scorched the bare soles of their feet, and under the sun that burned their heads and their little bare necks. The sun was high in the sky above them, and it seemed to Ivanoushka that they would never come to the well.

But when they had walked on and on, and he was nearly crying with thirst, only that the sun had dried up all his tears and burnt them before they had time to come into his eyes, he saw another footprint. It was quite a tiny footprint, divided in the middle — the footprint of a sheep; and in it was a little drop of clear water, sparkling in the sun. He said nothing to his sister, nothing at all. But he went down on his hands and knees and drank that water, that little drop of clear water, to cool his burning throat. And he had no sooner drunk it than he had turned into a little lamb. . . .

"A little white lamb," said Maroosia.

"With a black nose," said Vanya.

A little lamb, said old Peter, a little lamb who ran round and round Alenoushka, frisking and leaping, with its little tail tossing in the air.

Alenoushka looked round for her brother, but could not see

him. But there was the little lamb, leaping round her, trying to lick her face, and there in the ground was the print left by the sheep's foot.

She guessed at once what had happened, and burst into tears. There was a hayrick close by, and under the hayrick Alenoushka sat down and wept. The little lamb, seeing her so sad, stood gravely in front of her; but not for long, for he was a little lamb, and he could not help himself. However sad he felt, he had to leap and frisk in the sun, and toss his little white tail.

Presently a fine gentleman came riding by on his big black horse. He stopped when he came to the hayrick. He was very much surprised at seeing a beautiful little girl sitting there, crying her eyes out, while a white lamb frisked this way and that, and played before her, and now and then ran up to her and licked the tears from her face with its little pink tongue.

"What is your name," says the fine gentleman, "and why are you in trouble? Perhaps I may be able to help you."

"My name is Alenoushka, and this is my little brother Ivanoushka, whom I love." And she told him the whole story.

"Well, I can hardly believe all that," says the fine gentleman. "But come with me, and I will dress you in fine clothes, and set silver ornaments in your hair, and bracelets of gold on your little brown wrists. And as for the lamb, he shall come too, if you love him. Wherever you are there he shall be, and you shall never be parted from him."

And so Alenoushka took her little brother in her arms, and the fine gentleman lifted them up before him on the big black horse, and galloped home with them across the plain to his big house not far from the river. And when he got home he made a feast and married Alenoushka, and they lived together so happily that good people rejoiced to see them, and bad ones were jealous. And the little lamb lived in the house, and never grew any bigger, but always frisked and played, and followed Alenoushka wherever she went.

And then one day, when the fine gentleman had ridden far away to the town to buy a new bracelet for Alenoushka, there came an old witch. Ugly she was, with only one tooth in her head, and wicked as ever went about the world doing evil to decent folk. She begged from Alenoushka, and said she was hungry, and Alenoushka begged her to share her dinner. And she put a spell in the wine that Alenoushka drank, so that Alenoushka fell ill, and before evening, when the fine gentleman came riding back, had become pale, pale as snow, and as thin as an old stick.

"My dear," says the fine gentleman, "what is the matter with you?"

"Perhaps I shall be better tomorrow," says Alenoushka.

Well, the next day the gentleman rode into the fields, and the old hag came again while he was out.

"Would you like me to cure you?" says she. "I know a way to make you as well as ever you were. Plump you will be, and pretty again, before your husband comes riding home."

"And what must I do?" says Alenoushka, crying to think herself so ugly.

"You must go to the river and bathe this afternoon," says the old witch. "I will be there and put a spell on the water. Secretly you must go, for if anyone knows whither you have gone my spell will not work."

So Alenoushka wrapped a shawl about her head, and slipped out of the house and went to the river. Only the little lamb, Ivanoushka, knew where she had gone. He followed her, leaping about, and tossing his little white tail. The old witch was waiting for her. She sprang out of the bushes by the riverside, and seized Alenoushka, and tore off her pretty white dress, and fastened a heavy stone about her neck, and threw her from the bank into a deep place, so that she sank to the bottom of the river. Then the old witch, the wicked hag, put on Alenoushka's pretty white dress, and cast a spell, and made herself so like Alenoushka to look at that nobody could tell the difference. Only the little lamb had seen everything that had happened.

The fine gentleman came riding home in the evening, and he rejoiced when he saw his dear Alenoushka well again, with plump pink cheeks, and a smile on her rosy lips.

But the little lamb knew everything. He was sad and melancholy, and would not eat, and went every morning and every evening to the river, and there wandered about the banks, and cried, "Baa, baa," and was answered by the sighing of the wind in the long reeds.

The witch saw that the lamb went off by himself every morning and every evening. She watched where he went, and when she knew she began to hate the lamb; and she gave orders for the sticks to be cut, and the iron cauldron to be heated, and the steel knives made sharp. She sent a servant to catch the lamb; and she said to the fine gentleman, who thought all the time that she was Alenoushka, "It is time for the lamb to be killed, and made into a tasty stew."

The fine gentleman was astonished.

"What," says he, "you want to have the lamb killed? Why,

you called it your brother when first I found you by the hayrick in the plain. You were always giving it caresses and sweet words. You loved it so much that I was sick of the sight of it, and now you give orders for its throat to be cut. Truly," says he, "the mind of woman is like the wind in summer."

The lamb ran away when he saw that the servant had come to catch him. He heard the sharpening of the knives, and had seen the cutting of the wood, and the great cauldron taken from its place. He was frightened, and he ran away, and came to the river bank, where the wind was sighing through the tall reeds. And there he sang a farewell song to his sister, thinking he had not long to live. The servant followed the lamb cunningly, and crept near to catch him, and heard his little song. This is what he sang:

> "Alenoushka, little sister,
> They are going to slaughter me;
> They are cutting wooden faggots,
> They are heating iron cauldrons,
> They are sharpening knives of steel."

And Alenoushka, lamenting, answered the lamb from the bottom of the river:

> "O my brother Ivanoushka,
> A heavy stone is round my throat,
> Silken grass grows through my fingers,
> Yellow sand lies on my breast."

The servant listened, and marvelled at the miracle of the lamb singing, and the sweet voice answering him from the river. He crept away quietly, and came to the fine gentleman, and told him what he had heard; and they set out together to the river, to watch the lamb, and listen, and see what was happening.

The little white lamb stood on the bank of the river weeping, so that his tears fell into the water. And presently he sang again:

> "Alenoushka, little sister,
> They are going to slaughter me;
> They are cutting wooden faggots,
> They are heating iron cauldrons,
> They are sharpening knives of steel."

And Alenoushka answered him, lamenting, from the bottom of the river:

> "O my brother Ivanoushka,
> A heavy stone is round my throat,
> Silken grass grows through my fingers,
> Yellow sand lies on my breast."

The fine gentleman heard, and he was sure that the voice was the voice of his own dear wife, and he remembered how she had loved the lamb. He sent his servant to fetch men, and fishing nets and nets of silk. The men came running, and they dragged the river with fishing nets, and brought their nets empty to land. Then they tried with nets of fine silk, and, as they drew them in, there was Alenoushka lying in the nets as if she were asleep.

They brought her to the bank and untied the stone from her white neck, and washed her in fresh water and clothed her in white clothes. But they had no sooner done all this than she woke up, more beautiful than ever she had been before, though then she was pretty enough, God knows. She woke, and sprang up, and threw her arms round the neck of the little white lamb, who suddenly became once more her little brother Ivanoushka, who had been so thirsty as to drink water from the hoofmark of a sheep. And Ivanoushka laughed and shouted in the sunshine, and the fine gentleman wept tears of joy. And they all praised God and kissed each other, and went home together, and began to live as happily as before, even more happily, because Ivanoushka was no longer a lamb. But as soon as they got home the fine gentleman turned the old witch out of the house. And she became an ugly old hag, and went away to the deep woods, shrieking as she went.

"And did she ever come back again?" asked Vanya.

"No, she never came back again," said old Peter. "Once was enough."

"And what happened to Ivanoushka when he grew up?"

"He grew up as handsome as Alenoushka was pretty. And he became a great hunter. And he married the sister of the fine gentleman. And they all lived happily together, and ate honey every day, with white bread and new milk."

The Fire-bird, the Horse of Power
and the Princess Vasilissa

Once upon a time a strong and powerful Tzar ruled in a country far away. And among his servants was a young archer, and this archer had a horse — a horse of power — such a horse as belonged to the wonderful men of long ago — a great horse with a broad chest, eyes like fire, and hoofs of iron. There are no such horses nowadays. They sleep with the strong men who rode them, the bogatirs, until the time comes when Russia has need of them. Then the great horses will thunder up from under the ground, and the valiant men leap from the graves in the armour they have worn so long. The strong men will sit on those horses of power, and there will be swinging of clubs and thunder of hoofs, and the earth will be swept clean from the enemies of God and the Tzar. So my grandfather used to say, and he was as much older than I as I am older than you, little ones, and so he should know.

Well, one day long ago, in the green time of the year, the young archer rode through the forest on his horse of power. The trees were green; there were little blue flowers on the ground under the trees; the squirrels ran in the branches, and the hares in the undergrowth; but no birds sang. The young archer rode along the forest path and listened for the singing of the birds, but there was no singing. The forest was silent, and the only noises in it were the scratching of four-footed beasts, the dropping of fir cones, and the heavy stamping of the horse of power in the soft path.

"What has come to the birds?" said the young archer.

He had scarcely said this before he saw a big curving feather lying in the path before him. The feather was larger than a swan's, larger than an eagle's. It lay in the path, glittering like a flame; for the sun was on it, and it was a feather of pure gold. Then he knew why there was no singing in the forest. For he knew that the fire-bird had flown that

155

way, and that the feather in the path before him was a feather from its burning breast.

The horse of power spoke and said:

"Leave the golden feather where it lies. If you take it you will be sorry for it, and know the meaning of fear."

But the brave young archer sat on the horse of power and looked at the golden feather, and wondered whether to take it or not. He had no wish to learn what it was to be afraid, but he thought, "If I take it and bring it to the Tzar my master, he will be pleased; and he will not send me away with empty hands, for no tzar in the world has a feather from the burning breast of the fire-bird." And the more he thought, the more he wanted to carry the feather to the Tzar. And in the end he did not listen to the words of the horse of power. He leapt from the saddle, picked up the golden feather of the fire-bird, mounted his horse again, and galloped back through the green forest till he came to the palace of the Tzar.

He went into the palace, and bowed before the Tzar and said:

"O Tzar, I have brought you a feather of the fire-bird." The Tzar looked gladly at the feather, and then at the young archer.

"Thank you," says he; "but if you have brought me a feather of the fire-bird, you will be able to bring me the bird itself. I should like to see it. A feather is not a fit gift to bring to the Tzar. Bring the bird itself, or, I swear by my sword, your head shall no longer sit between your shoulders!"

The young archer bowed his head and went out. Bitterly he wept, for he knew now what it was to be afraid. He went out into the courtyard, where the horse of power was waiting for him, tossing its head and stamping on the ground.

"Master," says the horse of power, "why do you weep?"

"The Tzar has told me to bring him the fire-bird, and no man on earth can do that," says the young archer, and he bowed his head on his breast.

"I told you," says the horse of power, "that if you took the feather you would learn the meaning of fear. Well, do not be

156

frightened yet, and do not weep. The trouble is not now; the trouble lies before you. Go to the Tzar and ask him to have a hundred sacks of maize scattered over the open field, and let this be done at midnight."

The young archer went back into the palace and begged the Tzar for this, and the Tzar ordered that at midnight a hundred sacks of maize should be scattered in the open field.

Next morning, at the first redness in the sky, the young archer rode out on the horse of power, and came to the open field. The ground was scattered all over with maize. In the middle of the field stood a great oak with spreading boughs. The young archer leapt to the ground, took off the saddle, and let the horse of power loose to wander as he pleased about the field. Then he climbed up into the oak and hid himself among the green boughs.

The sky grew red and gold, and the sun rose. Suddenly there was a noise in the forest round the field. The trees shook and swayed, and almost fell. There was a mighty wind. The sea piled itself into waves with crests of foam, and the fire-bird came flying from the other side of the world. Huge and golden and flaming in the sun, it flew, dropped down with open wings into the field, and began to eat the maize.

The horse of power wandered in the field. This way he went, and that, but always he came a little nearer to the fire-bird. Nearer and nearer came the horse. He came close up to the fire-bird, and then suddenly stepped on one of its spreading fiery wings and pressed it heavily to the ground. The bird struggled, flapping mightily with its fiery wings, but it could not get away. The young archer slipped down from the tree, bound the fire-bird with three strong ropes, swung it on his back, saddled the horse, and rode to the palace of the Tzar.

The young archer stood before the Tzar, and his back was bent under the great weight of the fire-bird, and the broad wings of the bird hung on either side of him like fiery shields, and there was a trail of golden feathers on the floor. The young archer swung the magic bird to the foot of the throne before the Tzar; and the Tzar was glad, because since the beginning of the world no tzar had seen the fire-bird flung before him like a wild duck caught in a snare.

The Tzar looked at the fire-bird and laughed with pride. Then he lifted his eyes and looked at the young archer, and says he:

"As you have known how to take the fire-bird, you will know how to bring me my bride, for whom I have long been waiting. In the land of Never, on the very edge of the world, where the red sun rises in flame from behind the sea, lives the Princess Vasilissa. I will marry none but her. Bring her to me, and I will reward you with silver and gold. But if you do not bring her, then, by my sword, your head will no longer sit between your shoulders!"

The young archer wept bitter tears, and went out into the

courtyard where the horse of power was stamping the ground with its hoofs of iron and tossing its thick mane.

"Master, why do you weep?" asked the horse of power.

"The Tzar has ordered me to go to the land of Never, and to bring back the Princess Vasilissa."

"Do not weep — do not grieve. The trouble is not yet; the trouble is to come. Go to the Tzar and ask him for a silver tent with a golden roof, and for all kinds of food and drink to take with us on the journey."

The young archer went in and asked the Tzar for this, and the Tzar gave him a silver tent with silver hangings and a gold-embroidered roof, and every kind of rich wine and the tastiest of foods.

Then the young archer mounted the horse of power and rode off to the land of Never. On and on he rode, many days and nights, and came at last to the edge of the world, where the red sun rises in flame from behind the deep blue sea.

On the shore of the sea the young archer reined in the horse of power, and the heavy hoofs of the horse sank in the sand. He shaded his eyes and looked out over the blue water, and there was the Princess Vasilissa in a little silver boat, rowing with golden oars.

The young archer rode back a little way to where the sand ended and the green world began. There he loosed the horse to wander where he pleased, and to feed on the green grass. Then on the edge of the shore, where the green grass ended and grew thin and the sand began, he set up the shining tent, with its silver hangings and its gold-embroidered roof. In the tent he set out the tasty dishes and the rich flagons of wine which the Tzar had given him, and he sat himself down in the tent and began to regale himself, while he waited for the Princess Vasilissa.

The Princess Vasilissa dipped her golden oars in the blue water, and the little silver boat moved lightly through the dancing waves. She sat in the little boat and looked over the blue sea to the edge of world, and there, between the golden sand and the green earth, she saw the tent standing,

159

silver and gold in the sun. She dipped her oars, and came nearer to see it better. The nearer she came the fairer seemed the tent, and at last she rowed to the shore and grounded her little boat on the golden sand, and stepped out daintily and came up to the tent. She was a little frightened, and now and again she stopped and looked back to where the silver boat lay on the sand with the blue sea beyond it. The young archer said not a word, but went on regaling himself on the pleasant dishes he had set out there in the tent.

At last the Princess Vasilissa came up to the tent and looked in.

The young archer rose and bowed before her. Says he:

"Good day to you, Princess! Be so kind as to come in and take bread and salt with me, and taste my foreign wines."

And the Princess Vasilissa came into the tent and sat down with the young archer, and ate sweetmeats with him, and drank his health in a golden goblet of the wine the Tzar had given him. Now this wine was heavy, and the last drop from the goblet had no sooner trickled down her little slender throat than her eyes closed against her will, once, twice, and again.

"Ah me!" says the Princess, "it is as if the night itself had perched on my eyelids, and yet it is but noon."

And the golden goblet dropped to the ground from her little fingers, and she leant back on a cushion and fell instantly asleep. If she had been beautiful before, she was lovelier still when she lay in that deep sleep in the shadow of the tent.

Quickly the young archer called to the horse of power. Lightly he lifted the Princess in his strong young arms. Swiftly he leapt with her into the saddle. Like a feather she lay in the hollow of his left arm, and slept while the iron hoofs of the great horse thundered over the ground.

They came to the Tzar's palace, and the young archer leapt from the horse of power and carried the Princess into the palace. Great was the joy of the Tzar; but it did not last for long.

"Go, sound the trumpets for our wedding," he said to his servants, "let all the bells be rung."

The bells rang out and the trumpets sounded, and at the noise of the horns and the ringing of the bells the Princess Vasilissa woke up and looked about her.

"What is this ringing of bells," says she, "and this noise of trumpets? And where, oh, where is the blue sea, and my little silver boat with its golden oars?" And the Princess put her hand to her eyes.

"The blue sea is far away," says the Tzar, "and for your little silver boat I give you a golden throne. The trumpets sound for our wedding, and the bells are ringing for our joy."

But the Princess turned her face away from the Tzar; and there was no wonder in that, for he was old, and his eyes were not kind.

And she looked with love at the young archer; and there was no wonder in that either, for he was a young man fit to ride the horse of power.

The Tzar was angry with the Princess Vasilissa, but his anger was as useless as his joy.

"Why, Princess," says he, "will you not marry me, and forget your blue sea and your silver boat?"

"In the middle of the deep blue sea lies a great stone," says the Princess, "and under that stone is hidden my wedding-dress. If I cannot wear that dress I will marry nobody at all."

Instantly the Tzar turned to the young archer, who was waiting before the throne.

"Ride swiftly back," says he, "to the land of Never, where the red sun rises in flame. There — do you hear what the Princess says? — a great stone lies in the middle of the sea. Under that stone is hidden her wedding-dress. Ride swiftly. Bring back that dress, or, by my sword, your head shall no longer sit between your shoulders!"

The young archer wept bitter tears, and went out into the courtyard, where the horse of power was waiting for him, champing its golden bit.

"There is no way of escaping death this time," he said.

"Master, why do you weep?" asked the horse of power.

"The Tzar has ordered me to ride to the land of Never, to

fetch the wedding-dress of the Princess Vasilissa from the bottom of the deep blue sea. Besides, the dress is wanted for the Tzar's wedding, and I love the Princess myself."

"What did I tell you?" says the horse of power. "I told you that there would be trouble if you picked up the golden feather from the fire-bird's burning breast. Well, do not be afraid. The trouble is not yet; the trouble is to come. Up! into the saddle with you, and away for the wedding-dress of the Princess Vasilissa!"

The young archer leapt into the saddle, and the horse of power, with his thundering hoofs, carried him swiftly through the green forests and over the bare plains, till they came to the edge of the world, to the land of Never, where the red sun rises in flame from behind the deep blue sea. There they rested, at the very edge of the sea.

The young archer looked sadly over the wide waters, but the horse of power tossed its mane and did not look at the sea, but on the shore. This way and that it looked, and saw at last a huge lobster moving slowly, sideways, along the golden sand.

Nearer and nearer came the lobster, and it was a giant among lobsters, the tzar of all the lobsters; and it moved slowly along the shore, while the horse of power moved carefully and as if by accident, until it stood between the lobster and the sea. Then when the lobster came close by, the horse of power lifted an iron hoof and set it firmly on the lobster's tail.

"You will be the death of me!" screamed the lobster — as well he might, with the heavy foot of the horse of power pressing his tail into the sand. "Let me live, and I will do whatever you ask of me."

"Very well," says the horse of power, "we will let you live," and he slowly lifted his foot. "But this is what you shall do for us. In the middle of the blue sea lies a great stone, and under that stone is hidden the wedding-dress of the Princess Vasilissa. Bring it here."

The lobster groaned with the pain in his tail. Then he cried out in a voice that could be heard all over the deep blue sea.

And the sea was disturbed, and from all sides lobsters in thousands made their way towards the bank. And the huge lobster that was the oldest of them all and the tzar of all the lobsters that live between the rising and the setting of the sun, gave them the order and sent them back into the sea. And the young archer sat on the horse of power and waited.

After a little time the sea was disturbed again, and the lobsters in their thousands came to the shore, and with them they brought a golden casket in which was the wedding-dress of the Princess Vasilissa. They had taken it from under the great stone that lay in the middle of the sea.

The tzar of all the lobsters raised himself painfully on his bruised tail and gave the casket into the hands of the young archer, and instantly the horse of power turned himself about and galloped back to the palace of the Tzar, far, far away, at the other side of the green forests and beyond the treeless plains.

The young archer went into the palace and gave the casket into the hands of the Princess, and looked at her with sadness in his eyes, and she looked at him with love. Then she went away into an inner chamber, and came back in her wedding-dress, fairer than the spring itself. Great was the joy of the Tzar. The wedding feast was made ready, and the bells rang, and flags waved above the palace.

The Tzar held out his hand to the Princess, and looked at her with his old eyes. But she would not take his hand.

"No," says she, "I will marry nobody until the man who brought me here has done penance in boiling water."

Instantly the Tzar turned to his servants and ordered them to make a great fire, and to fill a great cauldron with water and set it on the fire, and, when the water should be at its hottest, to take the young archer and throw him into it, to do penance for having taken the Princess Vasilissa away from the land of Never.

There was no gratitude in the mind of that Tzar.

Swiftly the servants brought wood and made a mighty fire, and on it they laid a huge cauldron of water, and built the fire round the walls of the cauldron. The fire burned hot and the water steamed. The fire burned hotter, and the water bubbled and seethed. They made ready to take the young archer, to throw him into the cauldron.

"Oh, misery!" thought the young archer. "Why did I ever take the golden feather that had fallen from the fire-bird's burning breast? Why did I not listen to the wise words of the horse of power?" And he remembered the horse of power, and he begged the Tzar:

"O lord Tzar, I do not complain. I shall presently die in the heat of the water on the fire. Suffer me, before I die, once more to see my horse."

"Let him see his horse," says the Princess.

"Very well," says the Tzar. "Say good-bye to your horse, for you will not ride him again. But let your farewells be short, for we are waiting."

The young archer crossed the courtyard and came to the horse of power, who was scraping the ground with his iron hoofs.

"Farewell, my horse of power," says the young archer. "I should have listened to your words of wisdom, for now the end is come, and we shall never more see the green trees pass above us and the ground disappear beneath us, as we race the wind between the earth and the sky."

"Why so?" says the horse of power.

"The Tzar has ordered that I am to be boiled to death — thrown into that cauldron that is seething on the great fire."

"Fear not," says the horse of power, "for the Princess Vasilissa has made him do this, and the end of these things is better than I thought. Go back, and when they are ready to throw you in the cauldron, do you run boldly and leap yourself into the boiling water."

The young archer went back across the courtyard, and the servants made ready to throw him into the cauldron.

"Are you sure that the water is boiling?" says the Princess Vasilissa.

"It bubbles and seethes," said the servants.

"Let me see for myself," says the Princess, and she went to the fire and waved her hand above the cauldron. And some say there was something in her hand, and some say there was not.

"It is boiling," says she, and the servants laid hands on the young archer; but he threw them from him, and ran and leapt boldly before them all into the very middle of the cauldron.

Twice he sank below the surface, borne round with the bubbles and foam of the boiling water. Then he leapt from the cauldron and stood before the Tzar and the Princess. He had become so beautiful a youth that all who saw cried aloud in wonder.

"This is a miracle," says the Tzar. And the Tzar looked at the beautiful young archer, and thought of himself — of his age, of his bent back, and his grey beard, and his toothless gums. "I too will become beautiful," thinks he, and he rose from his throne and clambered into the cauldron, and was boiled to death in a moment.

And the end of the story? They buried the Tzar, and made the young archer Tzar in his place. He married the Princess Vasilissa, and lived many years with her in love and good fellowship. And he built a golden stable for the horse of power, and never forgot what he owed to him.

The Hunter and his Wife

It sometimes happened that the two children asked too many questions even for old Peter, though he was the kindest old Russian peasant who ever was a grandfather. Sometimes he was busy; sometimes he was tired, and really could not think of the right answer; sometimes he did not know the right answer. And once, when Vanya asked him why the sun was hot, and his sister Maroosia went on and on asking if the sun was a fire, who lit it? and if it was burning, why didn't it burn out? old Peter grumbled that he would not answer any more.

For a moment the two children were quiet, and then Maroosia asked one more question.

Old Peter looked up from the net he was mending. "Maroosia, my dear," he said, "you had better watch the tip of your tongue, or perhaps, when you are grown up and have a husband, the same thing will happen to you that happened to the wife of the huntsman who saw a snake in a burning wood-pile."

"Oh, tell us what happened to her!" said Maroosia.

"That is another question," said old Peter; "but I'll tell you, and then perhaps you won't ask any more, and will give my old head a rest."

And then he told them the story of the hunter and his wife.

Once upon a time there was a hunter who went out into the forest to shoot game. He had a wife and two dogs. His wife was for ever asking questions, so that he was glad to get away from her into the forest. And she did not like dogs, and said they were always bringing dirt into the house with their muddy paws. So that the dogs were glad to get away into the forest with the hunter.

One day the hunter and the two dogs wandered all day through the deep woods, and never got a sight of a bird; no, they never even saw a hare. All day long they wandered on and saw nothing. The hunter had not fired a cartridge. He did not want to go home and have to answer his wife's questions about why he had an empty bag, so he went deeper and deeper into the thick forest. And suddenly, as it grew towards evening, the sharp smell of burning wood floated through the trees, and the hunter, looking about him, saw the flickering of a fire. He made his way towards it, and found a clearing in the forest, and a wood-pile in the middle of it, and it was burning so fiercely that he could scarcely come near it.

And this was the marvel, that in the middle of the blazing timbers was sitting a great snake, curled round and round upon itself and waving its head above the flames.

As soon as it saw the hunter it called out, in a loud hissing voice, to come near.

He went as near as he could, shading his face from the heat.

"My good man," says the snake, "pull me out of the fire, and you shall understand the talk of the beasts and the songs of the birds."

"I'll be happy to help you," says the hunter, "but how? for the flames are so hot that I cannot reach you."

"Put the barrel of your gun into the fire, and I'll crawl out along it."

The hunter put the barrel of his long gun into the flames, and instantly the snake wound itself about it, and so escaped out of the fire.

"Thank you, my good man," says the snake; "you shall know henceforward the language of all living things. But one thing you must remember. You must not tell anyone of this, for if you tell you will die the death; and man only dies once, and that will be an end of your life and your knowledge."

Then the snake slipped off along the ground, and almost before the hunter knew it was going, it was gone, and he never saw it again.

Well, he went on with the two dogs, looking for something to shoot at; and when the dark night fell he was still far from home, away in the deep forest.

"I am tired," he thought, "and perhaps there will be birds stirring in the early morning. I will sleep the night here, and try my luck at sunrise."

He made a fire of twigs and broken branches, and lay down beside it, together with his dogs. He had scarcely lain down to sleep when he heard the dogs talking together and calling each other "Brother". He understood every word they said.

"Well, brother," says the first, "you sleep here and look after our master, while I run home to look after the house and yard. It will soon be one o'clock, and when the master is away that is the time for thieves."

"Off with you, brother, and God be with you," says the second.

And the hunter heard the first dog go bounding away through the undergrowth, while the second lay still, with its head between its paws, watching its master blinking at the fire.

Early in the morning the hunter was awakened by the noise of the dog pushing through the brushwood on its way back. He heard how the dogs greeted each other.

"Well, and how are you, brother?" says the first.

"Finely," says the second; "and how's yourself?"

"Finely too. Did the night pass well?"

"Well enough, thanks be to God. But with you, brother? How was it at home?"

"Oh, badly. I ran home, and the mistress, when she sees me, sings out, 'What the devil are you doing here without your master? Well, there's your supper'; and she threw me a crust of bread, burnt to a black cinder. I snuffed it and snuffed it, but as for eating it, it was burnt through. No dog alive could have made a meal of it. And with that she ups with a poker and beats me. Brother, she counted all my ribs and nearly broke each one of them. But at night, later on — just as I thought — thieves came into the yard, and were going to clear out the barn and the larder. But I let loose such a howl, and leapt upon them so vicious and angry, that they had little thought to spare for other people's goods, and had all they could do to get away whole themselves. And so I spent the night."

The hunter heard all that the dogs said, and kept it in mind. "Wait a bit, my good woman," says he, "and see what I have to say to you when I get home."

That morning his luck was good, and he came home with a couple of hares and three or four woodcock.

"Good day, mistress," says he to his wife, who was standing in the doorway.

"Good day, master," says she.

"Last night one of the dogs came home."

"It did," says she.

"And how did you feed it?"

"Feed it, my love?" says she. "I gave it a whole basin of milk, and crumbled a loaf of bread for it."

"You lie, you old witch," says the hunter; "you gave it nothing but a burnt crust, and you beat it with the poker."

The old woman was so surprised that she let the truth out of her mouth before she knew. She says to her husband, "How on earth did you know all that?"

"I won't tell you," says the hunter.

"Tell me, tell me," begs the old woman, just like Maroosia when she wants to know too much.

"I can't tell you," says the hunter; "it's forbidden me to tell."

"Tell me, dear one," says she.

"Truly, I can't."

"Tell me, my little pigeon."

"If I tell you I shall die the death."

"Rubbish, my dearest; only tell me."

"But I shall die."

"Just tell me that one little thing. You won't die for that."

And so she bothered him and bothered him, until he thought, "There's nothing to be done if a woman sets her mind on a thing. I'd better die and get it over at once."

So he put on a clean white shirt, and lay down on the bench in the corner, under the sacred images, and made all ready for his death; and was just going to tell his wife the whole truth about the snake and the wood-pile, and how he knew the language of all living things. But just then there was a great clucking in the yard, and some of the hens ran into the cottage, and after them came the cock, scolding first one and then another, and boasting:

"That's the way to deal with you," says the cock; and the hunter, lying there in his white shirt, ready to die, heard and understood every word. "Yes," says the cock, as he drove the hens about the room, "you see I am not such a fool as our master here, who does not know how to keep a single wife in order. Why, I have thirty of you and more, and the whole lot hear from me sharp enough if they do not do as I say."

As soon as the hunter heard this he made up his mind to be a fool no longer. He jumped up from the bench, and took his whip and gave his wife such a beating that she never asked him another question to this day. And she has never yet learnt how it was that he knew what she did in the hut while he was away in the forest.

*****

"Yes," said Maroosia, "but then she was a bad woman; and besides, my husband would never call me an old witch."

"Old witch!" said Vanya and bolted out of the hut with Maroosia after him; and so old Peter was left in peace.

The Three Men of Power –
Evening, Midnight and Sunrise

Long ago there lived a King, and he had three daughters, the loveliest in all the world. He loved them so well that he built a palace for them underground, lest the rough winds should blow on them or the red sun scorch their delicate faces. A wonderful palace it was, down there underground, with fountains and courts, and lamps burning, and precious stones glittering in the light of the lamps. And the three lovely princesses grew up in that palace underground, and knew no other light but that of the coloured lanterns, and had never seen the broad world that lies open under the sun by day and under the stars by night. Indeed, they did not know that there was a world outside those glittering walls, above that shining ceiling, carved and gilded and set with precious stones.

But it so happened that among the books that were given them to read was one in which was written of the world: how the sun shines in the sky; how trees grow green; how the grass waves in the wind and the leaves whisper together; how the rivers flow between their green banks and through the flowery meadows, until they come to the blue sea that joins the earth and the sky. They read in that book of white-walled towns, of churches with gilded and painted domes, of the brown wooden huts of the peasants, of the great forests, of the ships on the rivers, and of the long roads with the folk moving on them, this way and that, about the world.

And when the King came to see them, as he was used to do, they asked him:

"Father, is it true that there is a garden in the world?"

"Yes," said the King.

"And green grass?"

"Yes," said the King.

"And little shining flowers?"

"Why, yes," said the King, wondering and stroking his silver beard.

And the three lovely princesses all begged him at once:

"Oh, your Majesty, our own little father, whom we love, let us out to see this world. Let us out just so that we may see this garden, and walk in it on the green grass, and see the shining flowers."

The King turned his head away and tried not to listen to them. But what could he do? They were the loveliest princesses in the world, and when they begged him just to let them walk in the garden he could see the tears in their eyes. And after all, he thought, there were high walls to the garden.

So he called up his army, and set soldiers all round the garden, and a hundred soldiers to each gate, so that no one should come in. And then he let the princesses come up from their underground palace, and step out into the sunshine in the garden, with ten nurses and maids to each princess to see that no harm came to her.

The princesses stepped out into the garden, under the blue sky, shading their eyes at first because they had never before been in the golden sunlight. Soon they were taking hands, and running this way and that along the garden paths and over the green grass, and gathering posies of shining flowers to set in their girdles and to shame their golden crowns. And the King sat and watched them with love in his eyes, and was glad to see how happy they were. And after all, he thought, what with the high walls and the soldiers standing to arms, nothing could get in to hurt them.

But just as he had quieted his old heart a strong whirlwind came down out of the blue sky, tearing up trees and throwing them aside, and lifting the roofs from the houses. But it did not touch the palace roofs, shining green in the sunlight, and it plucked no trees from the garden. It raged this way and that, and then with its swift whirling arms it caught up the three lovely princesses, and carried them up into the air, over the high walls and over the heads of the guarding soldiers. For a moment the King saw them, his daughters, the three lovely princesses, spinning round and round, as if they were dancing in the sky. A moment later they were no more than little whirling specks, like dust in the sunlight. And then they were out of sight, and the King and all the maids and nurses were alone in the empty garden. The noise of the wind had gone. The soldiers did not dare to speak. The only sound in the King's ears was the sobbing and weeping of the maids and nurses.

The King called his generals, and made them send the soldiers in all directions over the country to bring back the princesses, if the whirlwind should tire and set them again upon the ground. The soldiers went to the very boundaries of the kingdom, but they came back as they went. Not one of them had seen the three lovely princesses.

Then the King called together all his faithful servants, and promised a great reward to anyone who should bring news of the three princesses. It was the same with the servants as with the soldiers. Far and wide they galloped out. Slowly, one by one, they rode back, with bent heads, on tired horses. Not one of them had seen the King's daughters.

Then the King called a grand council of his wise boyars and men of state. They all sat round and listened as the King told his tale and asked if one of them would not undertake the task of finding and rescuing the three princesses. "The wind has not set them down within the boundaries of my kingdom; and now, God knows, they may be in the power of wicked men or worse." He said he would give one of the princesses in marriage to anyone who could follow where the wind went and bring his daughters back: yes, and besides, he would make him the richest man in the kingdom. But the boyars and the wise men of state sat round in silence. He asked them one by one. They were all silent and afraid. For they were boyars and wise men of state, and not one of them would undertake to follow the whirlwind and rescue the three princesses.

The King wept bitter tears.

"I see," he said, "I have no friends about me in the palace. My soldiers cannot, my servants cannot, and my boyars and wise men will not, bring back my three sweet maids, whom I love better than my kingdom."

And with that he sent heralds throughout the kingdom to announce the news, and to ask if there were none among the common folk, the moujiks, the simple folk like us, who would put his hand to the work of rescuing the three lovely princesses, since not one of the boyars and wise men was willing to do it.

Now, at that time in a certain village lived a poor widow, and she had three sons, strong men, true bogatirs and men of power. All three had been born in a single night: the eldest at evening, the middle one at midnight, and the youngest just as the sky was lightening with the dawn. For this reason they were called Evening, Midnight, and Sunrise. Evening was dusky, with brown eyes and hair; Midnight was dark, with eyes and hair as black as charcoal; while Sunrise had hair golden as the sun, and eyes blue as morning sky. And all three were as strong as any of the strong men and mighty bogatirs who have shaken this land of Russia with their tread.

As soon as the King's word had been proclaimed in the village, the three brothers asked for their mother's blessing, which she gave them, kissing them on the forehead and on both cheeks. Then they made ready for the journey and rode off to the capital — Evening on his horse of dusky brown, Midnight on his black horse, and Sunrise on his horse that was as white as clouds in summer. They came to the capital, and as they rode through the streets everybody stopped to look at them, and all the pretty young women waved handkerchiefs at the windows. But the three brothers looked neither to right nor left but straight before them, and they rode to the palace of the King.

They came to the King, bowed low before him, and said:

"May you live for many years, O King. We have come to you not for feasting but for service. Let us, O King, ride out to rescue your three princesses."

"God give you success, my good young men," says the King. "What are your names ?"

"We are three brothers — Evening, Midnight, and Sunrise."

"What will you have to take with you on the road?"

"For ourselves, O King, we want nothing. Only, do not leave our mother in poverty, for she is old."

The King sent for the old woman, their mother, and gave her a home in his palace, and made her eat and drink at his table, and gave her new boots made by his own cobblers, and new clothes sewn by the very sempstresses who were used to make dresses for the three daughters of the King, who were the loveliest princesses in the world, and had been carried away by the whirlwind. No old woman in Russia was better looked after than the mother of the three young bogatirs and men of power, Evening, Midnight, and Sunrise, while they were away on their adventure seeking the King's daughters.

The young men rode out on their journey. A month they rode together, two months, and in the third month they came to a broad desert plain, where there were no towns, no villages, no farms, and not a human being to be seen. They rode on over the sand, through the rank grass, over the stony wastes. At last, on the other side of that desolate plain, they came to a thick forest. They found a path through the thick under-growth, and rode along that path together into the very heart of the forest, And there, alone in the heart of the forest, they came to a hut with a railed yard and a shed full of cattle and sheep. They called out with their strong young voices, and were answered by the lowing of the cattle, the bleating of the sheep, and the strong wind in the tops of the great trees.

They rode through the railed yard and came to the hut. Evening leant from his brown horse and knocked on the window. There was no answer. They forced open the door, and found no one at all.

"Well, brothers," says Evening, "let us make ourselves at home. Let us stay here awhile. We have been riding three months. Let us rest, and then ride farther. We shall deal better with our adventure if we come to it as fresh men, and not dusty and weary from the long road."

The others agreed. They tied up their horses, fed them, drew water from the well, and gave them to drink; and then, tired out, they went into the hut, said their prayers to God, and lay down to sleep with their weapons close to their hands, like true bogatirs and men of power.

In the morning the youngest brother, Sunrise, said to the eldest brother, Evening:

"Midnight and I are going hunting today, and you shall rest here, and see what sort of dinner you can give us when we come back."

"Very well," says Evening; "but tomorrow I shall go hunting, and one of you shall stay here and cook the dinner."

Nobody made bones about that, and so Evening stood at the door of the hut while the others rode off — Midnight on his black horse, and Sunrise on his horse, white as a summer cloud. They rode off into the forest, and disappeared among the green trees.

Evening watched them out of sight, and then, without

thinking twice about what he was doing, went out into the yard, picked out the finest sheep he could see, caught it, killed it, skinned it, cleaned it, and set it in a cauldron on the stove so as to be ready and hot whenever his brothers should come riding back from the forest. As soon as that was done, Evening lay down on the broad bench to rest himself.

He had scarcely lain down before there were a knocking and a rattling and a stumbling, and the door opened, and in walked a little man a yard high, with a beard seven yards long* flowing out behind him over both his shoulders. He looked round angrily, and saw Evening, who yawned, and sat up on the bench, and began chuckling at the sight of him. The little man screamed out:

"What are you chuckling about? How dare you play the master in my house? How dare you kill my best sheep?"

Evening answered him, laughing:

"Grow a little bigger, and it won't be so hard to see you down there. Till then it will be better for you to keep a civil tongue in your head."

The little man was angry before, but now he was angrier.

"What?" he screamed. "I am little, am I? Well, see what little does!"

And with that he grabbed an old crust of bread, leapt on Evening's shoulders, and began beating him over the head. Yes, and the little fellow was so strong he beat Evening till he was half dead, and was blind in one eye and could not see out of the other. Then, when he was tired, he threw Evening under the bench, took the sheep out of the cauldron, gobbled it up in a few mouthfuls, and, when he had done, went off again into the forest.

When Evening came to his senses again, he bound up his head with a dishcloth, and lay on the ground and groaned.

Midnight and Sunrise rode back, on the black horse and the white, and came to the hut, where they found their brother

---

* The little man was really one arshin high, and his beard was seven arshins long. An arshin is 0•77 of a yard, so anyone who knows decimals can tell exactly how high the little man was and the precise length of his beard.

groaning on the ground, unable to see out of his eyes, and with a dishcloth round his head.

"What are you tied up like that for?" they asked; "and where is our dinner?"

Evening was ashamed to tell them the truth — how he had been thumped about with a crust of bread by a little fellow only a yard high. He moaned and said:

"O my brothers, I made a fire in the stove, and fell ill from the great heat in this little hut. My head ached. All day I lay senseless, and could neither boil nor roast. I thought my head would burst with the heat, and my brains fly beyond the seventh world."

Next day Sunrise went hunting with Evening, whose head was still bound up in a dishcloth, and hurting so sorely that he could hardly see. Midnight stayed at home. It was his turn to see to the dinner. Sunrise rode out on his cloud-white horse, and Evening on his dusky brown. Midnight stood in the doorway of the hut, watched them disappear among the green trees, and then set about getting the dinner.

He lit the fire, but was careful not to make it too hot. Then he went into the yard, caught the very fattest of the sheep, killed it, skinned it, cleaned it, cut it up, and set it on the stove. Then, when all was ready, he lay down on the bench and rested himself.

But before he had lain there long there were a knocking, a stamping, a rattling, a grumbling, and in came the little old man, one yard high, with a beard seven yards long, and without wasting words the little fellow leapt on the shoulders of the bogatir, and set to beating him and thumping him, first on one side of his head and then on the other. He gave him such a banging that he very nearly made an end of him altogether. Then the little fellow ate up the whole of the sheep in a few mouthfuls, and went off angrily into the forest, with his long white beard flowing behind him.

Midnight tied up his head with a handkerchief, and lay down under the bench, groaning and groaning, unable to put his head to the ground, or even to lay it in the crook of his arm, it was so bruised by the beating given it by the little old man.

In the evening the brothers rode back, and found Midnight groaning under the bench, with his head bound up in a handkerchief.

Evening looked at him and said nothing. Perhaps he was thinking of his own bruised head, which was still tied up in a dishcloth.

"What's the matter with you?" says Sunrise.

"There never was such another stove as this," says Midnight. "I'd no sooner lit it than it seemed as if the whole hut were on fire. My head nearly burst. It's aching now; and as for your dinner, why, I've not been able to put a hand to anything all day."

Evening chuckled to himself, but Sunrise only said, "That's bad, brother; but you shall go hunting tomorrow, and I'll stay at home, and see what I can do with the stove."

And so on the third day the two elder brothers went hunting — Midnight on his black horse, and Evening on his horse of dusky brown. Sunrise stood in the doorway of the hut, and saw them disappear under the green trees. The sun shone on his golden curls, and his blue eyes were like the sky itself. There never was such another bogatir as he.

He went into the hut and lit the stove. Then he went out into the yard, chose the best sheep he could find, killed it, skinned it, cleaned it, cut it up, and set it on the stove. He made everything ready, and then lay down on the bench.

Before he had lain there very long he heard a stumping, a thumping, a knocking, a rattling, a grumbling, a rumbling. Sunrise leaped up from the bench and looked out through the window of the hut. There in the yard was the little old man, one yard high, with a beard seven yards long. He was carrying a whole haystack on his head and a great tub of water in his arms. He came into the middle of the yard, and set down his tub to water all the beasts. He set down the haystack and scattered the hay about. All the cattle and the sheep came together to eat and to drink, and the little man stood and counted them. He counted the oxen, he counted the goats, and then he counted the sheep. He counted them once, and his eyes began to flash. He counted them twice, and he began to grind his teeth. He counted them a third time, made sure that one was missing, and then he flew into a violent rage, rushed across the yard and into the hut, and gave Sunrise a terrific blow on the head.

Sunrise shook his head as if a fly had settled on it. Then he jumped suddenly and caught the end of the long beard of the little old man, and set to pulling him this way and that, round and round the hut, as if his beard was a rope. Phew! how the little man roared.

Sunrise laughed, and tugged him this way and that, and mocked him, crying out, "If you do not know the ford, it is better not to go into the water," meaning that the little fellow had begun to beat him without finding out who was the stronger.

The little old man, one yard high, with a beard seven yards long, began to pray and to beg:

"O man of power, O great and mighty bogatir, have mercy upon me. Do not kill me. Leave me my soul to repent with."

Sunrise laughed, and dragged the little fellow out into the yard, whirled him round at the end of his beard, and brought him to a great oak trunk that lay on the ground. Then with a heavy iron wedge he fixed the end of the little man's beard firmly in the oaken trunk, and, leaving the little man howling and lamenting, went back to the hut, set it in order again, saw that the sheep was cooking as it should, and then lay down in peace to wait for the coming of his brothers.

Evening and Midnight rode home, leapt from their horses, and came into the hut to see how the little man had dealt with their brother. They could hardly believe their eyes when they saw him alive and well, without a bruise, lying comfortably on the bench.

He sat up and laughed in their faces.

"Well, brothers," says he, "come along with me into the yard, and I think I can show you that headache of yours. It's a good deal stronger than it is big, but for the time being you need not be afraid of it, for it's fastened to an oak timber that all three of us together could not lift."

He got up and went into the yard. Evening and Midnight followed him with shamed faces. But when they came to the oaken timber the little man was not there. Long ago he had torn himself free and run away into the forest. But half his beard was left, wedged in the trunk, and Sunrise pointed to that and said:

"Tell me, brothers, was it the heat of the stove that gave you your headaches? Or had this long beard something to do with it?"

The brothers grew red, and laughed, and told him the whole truth.

Meanwhile Sunrise had been looking at the end of the beard, the end of the half beard that was left, and he saw that it had been torn out by the roots, and that drops of blood from the little man's chin showed the way he had gone.

Quickly the brothers went back to the hut and ate up the sheep. Then they leapt on their horses, and rode off into the green forest, following the drops of blood that had fallen from the little man's chin. For three days they rode through the green forest, until at last the red drops of the trail led them to a deep pit, a black hole in the earth, hidden by thick bushes and going far down into the underworld.

Sunrise left his brothers to guard the hole, while he went off into the forest and gathered bast, and twisted it, and made a strong rope, and brought it to the mouth of the pit, and asked his brothers to lower him down.

He made a loop in the rope. His brothers kissed him on both cheeks, and he kissed them back. Then he sat in the loop, and Evening and Midnight lowered him down into the darkness. Down and down he went, swinging in the dark, till he came into a world under the world, with a light that was neither that of the sun, nor of the moon, nor of the stars. He stepped from the loop in the rope of twisted bast, and set out walking through the underworld, going whither his eyes led him, for he found no more drops of blood, nor any other traces of the little old man.

He walked and walked, and came at last to a palace of copper, green and ruddy in the strange light. He went into that palace, and there came to meet him in the copper halls a maiden whose cheeks were redder than the aloe and whiter than the snow. She was the youngest daughter of the King, and the loveliest of the three princesses, who were the loveliest in all the world. Sweetly she curtsied to Sunrise, as he stood there with his golden hair and his eyes blue as the sky at morning, and sweetly she asked him:

"How have you come hither, my brave young man — of your own will or against it?"

"Your father has sent to rescue you and your sisters."

She bade him sit at the table, and gave him food and brought him a little flask of the water of strength.

"Strong you are," says she, "but not strong enough for what is before you. Drink this, and your strength will be greater than it is; for you will need all the strength you have and can win, if you are to rescue us and live."

Sunrise looked in her sweet eyes, and drank the water of strength in a single draught, and felt gigantic power forcing its way throughout his body.

"Now," thought he, "let come what may."

Instantly a violent wind rushed through the copper palace, and the Princess trembled.

"The snake that holds me here is coming," says she. "He is flying hither on his strong wings."

She took the great hand of the bogatir in her little fingers, and drew him to another room, and hid him there.

The copper palace rocked in the wind, and there flew into the great hall a huge snake with three heads. The snake hissed loudly, and called out in a whistling voice:

"I smell the smell of a Russian soul. What visitor have you here?"

"How could anyone come here?" said the Princess. "You have been flying over Russia. There you smelt Russian souls, and the smell is still in your nostrils, so that you think you smell them here."

"It is true," said the snake: "I have been flying over Russia. I have flown far. Let me eat and drink, for I am both hungry and thirsty."

All this time Sunrise was watching from the other room. The Princess brought meat and drink to the snake, and in the drink she put a philtre of sleep.

The snake ate and drank, and began to feel sleepy. He coiled himself up in rings, laid his three heads in the lap of the Princess, told her to scratch them for him, and dropped into a deep sleep.

The Princess called Sunrise, and the bogatir rushed in, swung his glittering sword three times round his golden head, and cut off all three heads of the snake. It was like felling three oak trees at a single blow. Then he made a great fire of wood, and threw upon it the body of the snake, and, when it was burnt up, scattered the ashes over the open country.

"And now fare you well," says Sunrise to the Princess; but she threw her arms about his neck.

"Fare you well," says he. "I go to seek your sisters. As soon as I have found them I will come back."

And at that she let him go.

He walked on farther through the underworld, and came at last to a palace of silver, gleaming in the strange light.

He went in there, and was met with sweet words and kindness by the second of the three lovely princesses. In that palace he killed a snake with six heads. The Princess begged him to stay; but he told her he had yet to find her eldest sister. At that she wished him the help of God, and he left her, and went on farther.

He walked and walked, and came at last to a palace of gold, glittering in the light of the underworld. All happened as in the other palaces. The eldest of the three daughters of the King met him with courtesy and kindness. And he killed a snake with twelve heads and freed the Princess from her imprisonment. The Princess rejoiced, and thanked Sunrise, and set about her packing to go home.

And this was the way of her packing. She went out into the broad courtyard and waved a scarlet handkerchief, and instantly the whole palace, golden and glittering, and the kingdom belonging to it, became little, little, little, till it went into a little golden egg. The Princess tied the egg in a corner of her handkerchief, and set out with Sunrise to join her sisters and go home to her father.

Her sisters did their packing in the same way. The silver palace and its kingdom were packed by the second sister into a little silver egg. And when they came to the copper palace, the youngest of the three lovely princesses clapped her hands and kissed Sunrise on both his cheeks, and waved a scarlet handkerchief, and instantly the copper palace and its kingdom were packed into a little copper egg, shining ruddy and green.

And so Sunrise and the three daughters of the King came to the foot of the deep hole down which he had come into the underworld. And there was the rope hanging with the loop at

185

its end. And they sat in the loop, and Evening and Midnight pulled them up one by one, rejoicing together. Then the three brothers took, each of them, a princess with him on his horse, and they all rode together back to the old King, telling tales and singing songs as they went. The Princess from the golden palace rode with Evening on his horse of dusky brown; the Princess from the silver palace rode with Midnight on his horse as black as charcoal; but the Princess from the copper palace, the youngest of them all, rode with Sunrise on his horse, white as a summer cloud. Merry was the journey through the green forest, and gladly they rode over the open plain, till they came at last to the palace of her father.

There was the old King, sitting melancholy alone, when the three brothers with the princesses rode into the courtyard of the palace. The old King was so glad that he laughed and cried at the same time, and his tears ran down his beard.

"Ah me!" says the old King, "I am old, and you young men have brought my daughters back from the very world under the world. Safer they will be if they have you to guard them, even than they were in the palace I had built for them underground. But I have only one kingdom and three daughters."

"Do not trouble about that," laughed the three princesses, and they all rode out together into the open country, and there the princesses broke their eggs, one after the other, and there were the palaces of silver, copper, and gold, with the kingdoms belonging to them, and the cattle and the sheep and the goats. There was a kingdom for each of the brothers. Then they made a great feast, and had three weddings all together, and the old King sat with the mother of the three strong men, and men of power, the noble bogatirs, Evening, Midnight, and Sunrise, sitting at his side. Great was the feasting, loud were the songs, and the King made Sunrise his heir, so that some day he would wear his crown. But little did Sunrise think of that. He thought of nothing but the youngest Princess. And little she thought of it, for she had no eyes but for Sunrise. And merrily they lived together in the copper palace. And happily they rode together on the horse that was as white as clouds in summer.

Salt

One evening, when they were sitting round the table after their supper, old Peter asked the children what story they would like to hear. Vanya asked whether there were any stories left which they had not already heard.

"Why," said old Peter, "you have heard scarcely any of the stories, for there is a story to be told about everything in the world."

"About everything, grandfather?" asked Vanya.

"About everything," said old Peter.

"About the sky, and the thunder, and the dogs, and the flies, and the birds, and the trees, and the milk?"

"There is a story about every one of those things."

"I know something there isn't a story about," said Vanya.

"And what's that?" asked old Peter, smiling in his beard.

"Salt," said Vanya. "There can't be a story about salt." He put the tip of his finger into the little box of salt on the table, and then he touched his tongue with his finger to taste.

"But of course there is a story about salt," said old Peter.

"Tell it us," said Maroosia; and presently, when his pipe had been lit twice and gone out, old Peter began.

*****

Once upon a time there were three brothers, and their father was a great merchant who sent his ships far over the sea, and traded here and there in countries the names of which I, being an old man, can never rightly call to mind. Well, the names of the two elder brothers do not matter, but the youngest was called Ivan the Ninny, because he was always playing and never working; and if there was a silly thing to do, why, off he went and did it. And so, when the brothers grew up, the father sent the two elder ones off, each in a fine ship laden with gold and jewels, and rings and bracelets, and laces and silks, and sticks with little bits of silver hammered into their handles, and spoons with patterns of blue and red, and everything else you can think of that costs too much to buy. But he made Ivan the Ninny stay at home, and did not give him a ship at all. Ivan saw his brothers go sailing off over the sea on a summer morning, to make their fortunes and come back rich men; and then, for the first time in his life, he wanted to work and do something useful. He went to his father and kissed his hand, and he kissed the hand of his little old mother, and he begged his father to give him a ship so that he could try his fortune like his brothers.

"But you have never done a wise thing in your life, and no one could count all the silly things you've done if he spent a hundred days in counting," said his father.

"True," said Ivan; "but now I am going to be wise, and sail the sea and come back with something in my pockets to show that I am not a ninny any longer. Give me just a little ship, father mine — just a little ship for myself."

"Give him a little ship," said the mother. "He may not be a ninny after all."

"Very well," said his father. "I will give him a little ship; but I am not going to waste good roubles by giving him a rich cargo."

"Give me any cargo you like," said Ivan.

So his father gave him a little ship, a little old ship, and a cargo of rags and scraps and things that were not fit for anything but to be thrown away. And he gave him a crew of ancient old sailormen who were past work; and Ivan went on board and sailed away at sunset, like the ninny he was. And the feeble, ancient old sailormen pulled up the ragged, dirty sails, and away they went over the sea to learn what fortune, good or bad, God had in mind for a crew of old men with a ninny for a master.

The fourth day after they set sail there came a great wind over the sea. The feeble old men did the best they could with the ship; but the old, torn sails tore from the masts, and the wind did what it pleased, and threw the little ship on an unknown island away in the middle of the sea. Then the wind dropped, and left the little ship on the beach, and Ivan the Ninny and his ancient old men, like good Russians, praising God that they were still alive.

"Well, children," said Ivan, for he knew how to talk to sailors, "do you stay here and mend the sails, and make new ones out of the rags we carry as cargo, while I go inland and see if there is anything that could be of use to us."

So the ancient old sailormen sat on deck with their legs crossed, and made sails out of rags, of torn scraps of old brocades, of soiled embroidered shawls, of all the rubbish that they had with them for a cargo. You never saw such sails. The tide came up and floated the ship, and they threw out anchors at bow and stern, and sat there in the sunlight, making sails and patching them and talking of the days when they were young. All this while Ivan the Ninny went walking off into the island.

Now in the middle of that island was a high mountain, a high mountain it was, and so white that when he came near it Ivan the Ninny began thinking of sheepskin coats, although it was midsummer and the sun was hot in the sky. The trees were green round about, but there was nothing growing on the mountain at all. It was just a great white mountain piled up into the sky in the middle of a green island. Ivan walked a little way up the white slopes of the mountain, and then, because he felt thirsty, he thought he would let a little snow melt in his mouth. He took some in his fingers and stuffed it in. Quickly enough it came out again, I can tell you, for the mountain was not made of snow but of good Russian salt. And if you want to try what a mouthful of salt is like, you may.

"No, thank you, grandfather," the children said hurriedly together.

Old Peter went on with his tale.

Ivan the Ninny did not stop to think twice. The salt was so clean and shone so brightly in the sunlight. He just turned round and ran back to the shore, and called out to his ancient old sailormen and told them to empty everything they had on board over into the sea. Over it all went, rags and tags and rotten timbers, till the little ship was as empty as a soup bowl after supper. And then those ancient old men were set to work carrying salt from the mountain and taking it on board the little ship, and stowing it away below deck till there was not room for another grain. Ivan the Ninny would have liked to take the whole mountain, but there was not room in the little ship. And for that the ancient old sailormen thanked God, because their backs ached and their old legs were weak, and they said they would have died if they had had to carry any more.

Then they hoisted up the new sails they had patched together out of the rags and scraps of shawls and old brocades, and they sailed away once more over the blue sea. And the wind stood fair, and they sailed before it, and the ancient old sailors rested their backs, and told old tales, and took turn and turn about at the rudder.

And after many days' sailing they came to a town, with towers and churches and painted roofs, all set on the side of a hill that sloped down into the sea. At the foot of the hill was a quiet harbour, and they sailed in there and moored the ship and hauled down their patchwork sails.

Ivan the Ninny went ashore, and took with him a little bag of clean white salt to show what kind of goods he had for sale, and he asked his way to the palace of the Tzar of that town. He came to the palace, and went in and bowed to the ground before the Tzar.

"Who are you?" says the Tzar.

"I, great lord, am a Russian merchant, and here in a bag is some of my merchandise, and I beg your leave to trade with your subjects in this town."

"Let me see what is in the bag," says the Tzar.

Ivan the Ninny took a handful from the bag and showed it to the Tzar.

"What is it?" says the Tzar.

"Good Russian salt," says Ivan the Ninny.

Now in that country they had never heard of salt, and the Tzar looked at the salt, and he looked at Ivan and he laughed.

"Why, this," says he, "is nothing but white dust, and that we can pick up for nothing. The men of my town have no need to trade with you. You must be a ninny."

Ivan grew very red, for he knew what his father used to call him. He was ashamed to say anything. So he bowed to the ground, and went away out of the palace.

But when he was outside he thought to himself, "I wonder what sort of salt they use in these parts if they do not know good Russian salt when they see it. I will go to the kitchen."

So he went round to the back door of the palace, and put his head into the kitchen, and said, "I am very tired. May I sit down here and rest a little while?"

"Come in," says one of the cooks. "But you must sit just there, and not put even your little finger in the way of us; for we are the Tzar's cooks, and we are in the middle of making ready his dinner." And the cook put a stool in a corner out of the way, and Ivan slipped in round the door, and sat down in the corner and looked about him. There were seven cooks at least, boiling and baking, and stewing and toasting, and roasting and frying. And as for scullions, they were as thick as cockroaches, dozens of them, running to and fro, tumbling over each other, and helping the cooks.

Ivan the Ninny sat on his stool, with his legs tucked under him and the bag of salt on his knees. He watched the cooks and the scullions, but he did not see them put anything in the dishes which he thought could take the place of salt. No; the meat was without salt, the kasha was without salt, and there was no salt in the potatoes. Ivan nearly turned sick at the thought of the tastelessness of all that food.

There came the moment when all the cooks and scullions ran out of the kitchen to fetch the silver platters on which to lay the dishes. Ivan slipped down from his stool, and running from stove to stove, from saucepan to frying pan, he dropped a pinch of salt, just what was wanted, no more no less, in every one of the dishes. Then he ran back to the stool in the corner, and sat there, and watched the dishes being put on the silver platters and carried off in gold-embroidered napkins to be the dinner of the Tzar.

The Tzar sat at table and took his first spoonful of soup. "The soup is very good today," says he, and he finishes the soup to the last drop.

"I've never known the soup so good," says the Tzaritza, and she finishes hers.

"This is the best soup I ever tasted," says the Princess, and down goes hers, and she, you know, was the prettiest princess who ever had dinner in this world.

It was the same with the kasha and the same with the meat. The Tzar and the Tzaritza and the Princess wondered why they had never had so good a dinner in all their lives before.

"Call the cooks," says the Tzar. And they called the cooks, and the cooks all came in, and bowed to the ground, and stood in a row before the Tzar.

"What did you put in the dishes today that you never put before?" says the Tzar.

"We put nothing unusual, your greatness," say the cooks, and bowed to the ground again.

"Then why do the dishes taste better?"

"We do not know, your greatness," say the cooks.

"Call the scullions," says the Tzar. And the scullions were called, and they too bowed to the ground, and stood in a row before the Tzar.

"What was done in the kitchen today that has not been done there before?" says the Tzar.

"Nothing, your greatness," say all the scullions except one.

And that one scullion bowed again, and kept on bowing, and then he said, "Please, your greatness, please, great lord, there is usually none in the kitchen but ourselves; but today there was a young Russian merchant, who sat on a stool in the corner and said he was tired."

"Call the merchant," says the Tzar.

So they brought in Ivan the Ninny, and he bowed before the Tzar, and stood there with his little bag of salt in his hand.

"Did you do anything to my dinner?" says the Tzar.

"I did, your greatness," says Ivan.

"What did you do?"

"I put a pinch of Russian salt in every dish."

"That white dust?" says the Tzar.

"Nothing but that."

"Have you got any more of it?"

"I have a little ship in the harbour laden with nothing else," says Ivan.

"It is the most wonderful dust in the world," says the Tzar, "and I will buy every grain of it you have. What do you want for it?"

Ivan the Ninny scratched his head and thought. He thought that if the Tzar liked it as much as all that it must be worth a fair price, so he said, "We will put the salt into bags, and for every bag of salt you must give me three bags of the same weight — one of gold, one of silver, and one of precious stones. Cheaper than that, your greatness, I could not possibly sell."

"Agreed," says the Tzar. "And a cheap price, too, for a dust so full of magic that it makes dull dishes tasty, and tasty dishes so good that there is no looking away from them."

So all the day long, and far into the night, the ancient old sailormen bent their backs under sacks of salt, and bent them again under sacks of gold and silver and precious stones. When all the salt had been put in the Tzar's treasury — yes, with twenty soldiers guarding it with great swords shining in the moonlight — and when the little ship was loaded with riches, so that even the deck was piled high with precious stones, the ancient old men lay down among the jewels and slept till morning, when Ivan the Ninny went to bid good-bye to the Tzar.

"And whither shall you sail now?" asked the Tzar.

"I shall sail away to Russia in my little ship," says Ivan.

And the Princess, who was very beautiful, said, "A little Russian ship?"

"Yes," says Ivan.

"I have never seen a Russian ship," says the Princess, and she begs her father to let her go to the harbour with her nurses and maids, to see the little Russian ship before Ivan set sail.

She came with Ivan to the harbour, and the ancient old sailormen took them on board.

She ran all over the ship, looking now at this and now at that, and Ivan told her the names of everything — deck, mast, and rudder.

"May I see the sails?" she asked. And the ancient old men hoisted the ragged sails, and the wind filled the sails and tugged.

"Why doesn't the ship move when the sails are up?" asked the Princess.

"The anchor holds her," said Ivan.

"Please let me see the anchor," says the Princess.

"Haul up the anchor, my children, and show it to the Princess," says Ivan to the ancient old sailormen.

And the old men hauled up the anchor, and showed it to the Princess; and she said it was a very good little anchor. But, of course, as soon as the anchor was up the ship began to move. One of the ancient old men bent over the tiller, and, with a fair wind behind her, the little ship slipped out of the harbour and away to the blue sea. When the Princess looked round, thinking it was time to go home, the little ship was far from land, and away in the distance she could only see the gold towers of her father's palace, glittering like pin points in the sunlight. Her nurses and maids wrung their hands and made an outcry, and the Princess sat down on a heap of jewels, and put a handkerchief to her eyes, and cried and cried and cried.

Ivan the Ninny took her hands and comforted her, and told her of the wonders of the sea that he would show her, and the wonders of the land. And she looked up at him while he talked, and his eyes were kind and hers were sweet; and the end of it was that they were both very well content, and agreed to have a marriage feast as soon as the little ship should bring them to the home of Ivan's father. Merry was that voyage. All day long Ivan and the Princess sat on deck and said sweet things to each other, and at twilight they sang songs, and drank tea, and told stories. As for the nurses and maids, the Princess told them to be glad; and so they danced and clapped their hands, and ran about the ship, and teased the ancient old sailormen.

When they had been sailing many days, the Princess was looking out over the sea, and she cried out to Ivan, "See, over there, far away, are two big ships with white sails, not like our sails of brocade and bits of silk."

Ivan looked, shading his eyes with his hands.

"Why, those are the ships of my elder brothers," said he. "We shall all sail home together."

And he made the ancient old sailormen give a hail in their

cracked old voices. And the brothers heard them, and came on board to greet Ivan and his bride. And when they saw that she was a Tzar's daughter, and that the very decks were heaped with precious stones, because there was no room below, they said one thing to Ivan and something else to each other.

To Ivan they said, "Thanks be to God, He has given you good trading."

But to each other, "How can this be?" says one. "Ivan the Ninny bringing back such a cargo, while we in our fine ships have only a bag or two of gold."

"And what is Ivan the Ninny doing with a princess?" says the other.

And they ground their teeth, and waited their time, and came up suddenly, when Ivan was alone in the twilight, and picked him up by his head and his heels, and hove him overboard into the dark blue sea.

Not one of the old men had seen them, and the Princess was not on deck. In the morning they said that Ivan the Ninny must have walked overboard in his sleep. And they drew lots. The eldest brother took the Princess, and the second brother took the little ship laden with gold and silver and precious stones. And so the brothers sailed home very well content. But the Princess sat and wept all day long, looking down into the blue water. The elder brother could not comfort her, and the second brother did not try. And the ancient old sailormen muttered in their beards, and were sorry, and prayed to God to give rest to Ivan's soul; for although he had been a ninny, and although he had made them carry a lot of salt and other things, yet they loved him, because he knew how to talk to ancient old sailormen.

But Ivan was not dead. As soon as he splashed into the water, he crammed his fur hat a little tighter on his head, and began swimming in the sea. He swam about until the sun rose, and then, not far away, he saw a floating timber log, and he swam to the log, and got astride of it, and thanked God. And he sat there on the log in the middle of the sea, twiddling his thumbs for want of something to do.

There was a strong current in the sea that carried him along, and at last, after floating for many days without ever a bite for his teeth or a drop for his gullet, his feet touched land. Now that was at night, and he left the log and walked up out of the sea, and lay down on the shore and waited for morning.

When the sun rose he stood up, and saw that he was on a bare island, and he saw nothing at all on the island except a huge house as big as a mountain; and as he was looking at the house the great door creaked with a noise like that of a hurricane among the pine forests, and opened; and a giant came walking out, and came to the shore, and stood there, looking down at Ivan.

"What are you doing here, little one?" says the giant.

Ivan told him the whole story, just as I have told it to you.

The giant listened to the very end, pulling at his monstrous whiskers. Then he said, "Listen, little one. I know more of the story than you, for I can tell you that tomorrow morning your eldest brother is going to marry your Princess. But there is no need for you to take on about it. If you want to be there, I will carry you and set you down before the house in time for the wedding. And a fine wedding it is like to be, for your father thinks well of those brothers of yours bringing back all those precious stones, and silver and gold enough to buy a kingdom."

And with that he picked up Ivan the Ninny and set him on his great shoulders, and set off striding through the sea.

He went so fast that the wind of his going blew off Ivan's hat.

"Stop a moment," shouts Ivan, "my hat has blown off."

"We can't turn back for that," says the giant, "we have already left your hat five hundred versts behind us." And he rushed on, splashing through the sea. The sea was up to his armpits. He rushed on, and the sea was up to his waist. He rushed on, and before the sun had climbed to the top of the blue sky he was splashing up out of the sea with the water about his ankles. He lifted Ivan from his shoulders and set him on the ground.

"Now," says he, "little man, off you run, and you'll be in time for the feast. But don't you dare to boast about riding on my shoulders. If you open your mouth about that you'll smart for it, if I have to come ten thousand thousand versts."

Ivan the Ninny thanked the giant for carrying him through the sea, promised that he would not boast, and then ran off to his father's house. Long before he got there he heard the musicians in the courtyard playing as if they wanted to wear out their instruments before night. The wedding feast had begun, and when Ivan ran in, there, at the high board, was sitting the Princess, and beside her his eldest brother. And there were his father and mother, his second brother, and all the guests. And every one of them was as merry as could be, except the Princess, and she was as white as the salt he had sold to her father.

Suddenly the blood flushed into her cheeks. She saw Ivan in the doorway. Up she jumped at the high board, and cried out, "There, there is my true love, and not this man who sits beside me at the table."

"What is this?" says Ivan's father, and in a few minutes knew the whole story.

He turned the two elder brothers out of doors, gave their ships to Ivan, married him to the Princess, and made him his heir. And the wedding feast began again, and they sent for the ancient old sailormen to take part in it. And the ancient old sailormen wept with joy when they saw Ivan and the Princess, like two sweet pigeons, sitting side by side; yes, and they lifted their flagons with their old shaking hands, and cheered with their old cracked voices, and poured the wine down their dry old throats.

There was wine enough and to spare, beer too, and mead — enough to drown a herd of cattle. And as the guests drank and grew merry and proud they set to boasting. This one bragged of his riches, that one of his wife. Another boasted of his cunning, another of his new house, another of his strength, and this one was angry because they would not let him show how he could lift the table on one hand. They all drank Ivan's health, and he drank theirs, and in the end he could not bear to listen to their proud boasts.

"That's all very well," says he, "but I am the only man in the world who rode on the shoulders of a giant to come to his wedding feast."

The words were scarcely out of his mouth before there were a tremendous trampling and a roar of a great wind. The house shook with the footsteps of the giant as he strode up. The giant bent down over the courtyard and looked in at the feast.

"Little man, little man," says he, "you promised not to boast of me. I told you what would come if you did, and here you are and have boasted already."

"Forgive me," says Ivan; "it was the drink that boasted, not I."

"What sort of drink is it that knows how to boast?" says the giant.

"You shall taste it," says Ivan.

And he made his ancient old sailormen roll a great barrel of wine into the yard, more than enough for a hundred men, and after that a barrel of beer that was as big, and then a barrel of mead that was no smaller.

"Try the taste of that," says Ivan the Ninny.

Well, the giant did not wait to be asked twice. He lifted the barrel of wine as if it had been a little glass, and emptied it down his throat. He lifted the barrel of beer as if it had been an acorn, and emptied it after the wine. Then he lifted the barrel of mead as if it had been a very small pea, and swallowed every drop of mead that was in it. And after that he began stamping about and breaking things. Houses fell to pieces this way and that, and trees were swept flat like grass. Every step the giant took was followed by the crash of breaking timbers. Then suddenly he fell flat on his back and slept. For three days and nights he slept without waking. At last he opened his eyes.

"Just look about you," says Ivan, "and see the damage that you've done."

"And did that little drop of drink make me do all that?" says the giant. "Well, well, I can well understand that a drink like that can do a bit of bragging. And after that," says he, looking at the wrecks of houses, and all the broken things scattered about — "after that," says he, "you can boast of me for a thousand years, and I'll have nothing against you."

And he tugged at his great whiskers, and wrinkled his eyes, and went striding off into the sea.

That is the story about salt, and how it made a rich man of Ivan the Ninny, and besides, gave him the prettiest wife in the world, and she a Tzar's daughter.

The Christening in the Village

This chapter is not one of old Peter's stories, though there are, doubtless, some stories in it. It tells how Vanya and Maroosia drove to the village to see a new baby.

Old Peter had a sister who lived in the village not so very far away from the forest. And she had a plump daughter, and the daughter was called Nastasia, and she was married to a handsome peasant called Sergie, who had three cows, a lot of pigs, and a flock of fat geese. And one day when old Peter had gone to the village to buy tobacco and sugar and sunflower seeds, he came back in the evening, and said to the children:

"There's something new in the village."

"What sort of a something?" asked Vanya.

"Alive," said old Peter.

"Is there a lot of it?" asked Vanya.

"No, only one."

"Then it can't be pigs," said Vanya, in a melancholy voice. "I thought it was pigs."

"Perhaps it is a little calf," said Maroosia.

"I know what it is," said Vanya.

"Well?"

"It's a foal. It's brown all over with white on its nose, and a lot of white hairs in its tail."

"No"

"What is it then, grandfather?"

"I'll tell you, little pigeons. It's small and red, and it's got a bumpy head with hair on it like the fluff of a duckling. It has blue eyes, and ten fingers to its fore paws, and ten toes to its hind feet — five to each."

"It's a baby," said Maroosia.

"Yes. Nastasia has got a little son, Aunt Sofia has got a grandson, you have got a new cousin, and I have got a new great-nephew. Think of that! Already it's a son, and a cousin, and a grandson, and a great-nephew, and he's only been alive twelve hours. He lost no time in taking a position for himself. He'll be a great man one of these days if he goes on as fast as that."

The children had jumped up as soon as they knew it was a baby.

"When is the christening?"

"The day after tomorrow."

"O grandfather!"

"Well?"

"Who is going to the christening?"

"The baby, of course."

"Yes; but other people?"

"All the village."

"And us?"

"I have to go, and I suppose there'll be room in the cart for two little bear cubs like you."

And so it was settled that Vanya and Maroosia were to go to the christening of their new cousin, who was only twelve hours old. All the next day they could think of nothing else, and early on the morning of the christening they were up and about, Maroosia seeing that Vanya had on a clean shirt, and herself putting a green ribbon in her hair. The sun shone, and the leaves on the trees were all new and bright, and the sky was pale blue through the flickering green leaves.

Old Peter was up early too, harnessing the little yellow horse into the old cart. The cart was of rough wood, without springs, like a big box fixed on long larch poles between two pairs of wheels. The larch poles did instead of springs, bending and creaking, as the cart moved over the forest track. The shafts came from the front wheels upwards to the horse's shoulders, and between the ends of them there was a tall strong hoop of wood, called a douga, which rose high over the shoulders of the horse, above his collar, and had two little bells hanging from it at the top. The wooden hoop was painted green with little red flowers. The harness was mostly of ropes, but that did not matter so long as it held together. The horse had a long tail and mane, and looked as untidy as a little boy; but he had a green ribbon in his forelock in honour of the christening, and he could go like anything, and never got tired.

When all was ready, old Peter arranged a lot of soft fresh hay in the cart for the children to sit in. Hay is the best thing in the world to sit in when you drive in a jolting Russian cart. Old Peter put in a tremendous lot, so that the horse could eat some of it while waiting in the village, and yet leave them enough to make them comfortable on the journey back. Finally, old Peter took a gun that he had spent all the evening before in cleaning, and laid it carefully in the hay.

"What is the gun for?" asked Vanya.

"I am to be a godparent," said old Peter, "and I want to give him a present. I could not give him a better present than a gun, for he shall be a forester, and a good shot, and you cannot begin too early."

Presently Vanya and Maroosia were tucked into the hay, and old Peter climbed in with the plaited reins, and away they went along the narrow forest track, where the wheels followed the ruts and splashed through the deep holes; for the spring was young, and the roads had not yet dried. Some of the deepest holes had a few pine branches laid in them, but that was the only road-mending that ever was done. Overhead were the tall firs and silver birches with their little pale round leaves; and somewhere, not far away, a cuckoo was calling, while the murmur of the wild pigeons never stopped for a moment.

They drove on and on through the forest, and at last came out from among the trees into the open country, a broad, flat plain stretching to the river. Far away they could see the big square sail of a boat, swelled out in the light wind, and they knew that there was the river, on the banks of which stood the village. They could see a small clump of trees, and, as they came nearer, the pale green cupolas of the white village church rising above the tops of the birches.

Presently they came to a rough wooden bridge, and crossed over a little stream that was on its way to join the big river.

Vanya looked at it.

"Grandfather," he asked, "when the frost went, which was water first — the big river or the little river?"

"Why, the little river, of course," said old Peter. "It's always the little streams that wake first in the spring, and running down to the big river make it swell and flood and break up the ice. It's always been so ever since the quarrel between the Vazouza and the Volga."

"What was that?" said Vanya.

"It was like this," said old Peter.

*****

The Vazouza and the Volga flow for a long way side by side, and then they join and flow together. And the Vazouza is a little river; but the Volga is the mother of all Russia, and the greatest river in the world.

And the little Vazouza was jealous of the Volga.

"You are big and noisy," she says to the Volga, "and terribly strong; but as for brains," says she, "why, I have more brains in a single ripple than you in all that lump of water."

Of course the Volga told her not to be so rude, and said that little rivers should know their place and not argue with the great.

But the Vazouza would not keep quiet, and at last she said to the Volga: "Look here, we will lie down and sleep, and we will agree that the one of us who wakes first and comes first to the sea is the wiser of the two."

And the Volga said, "Very well, if only you will stop talking."

So the little Vazouza and the big Volga lay and slept, white and still, all through the winter. And when the spring came, the little Vazouza woke first, brisk and laughing and hurrying and rushed away as hard as she could go towards the sea. When the Volga woke the little Vazouza was already far ahead. But the Volga did not hurry. She woke slowly and shook the ice from herself, and then came roaring after the Vazouza, a huge foaming flood of angry water.

And the little Vazouza listened as she ran, and she heard the Volga coming after her; and when the Volga caught her up — a tremendous foaming river, whirling along trees and blocks of ice — she was frightened, and she said:

"O Volga, let me be your little sister. I will never argue with you any more. You are wiser than I and stronger than I. Only take me by the hand and bring me with you to the sea."

And the Volga forgave the little Vazouza, and took her by the hand and brought her safely to the sea. And they have never quarrelled again. But all the same, it is always the little Vazouza that gets up first in the spring, and tugs at the white blankets of ice and snow, and wakes her big sister from her winter sleep.

*****

They drove on over the flat open country, with no hedges, but only ditches to drain off the floods, and very often not even ditches to divide one field from another. And huge crows, with grey hoods and shawls, pecked about in the grass at the roadside or flew heavily in the sunshine. They passed a little girl with a flock of geese, and another little girl lying in the grass holding a long rope which was fastened to the horns of a brown cow. And the little girl lay on her face and slept among the flowers, while the cow walked slowly round her, step by step, chewing the grass and thinking about nothing at all.

And at last they came to the village, where the road was wider; and instead of one pair of ruts there were dozens, and the cart bumped worse than ever. The broad earthy road had no stones in it; and in places where the puddles would have been deeper than the axles of the wheels, it had been mended by laying down fir logs and small branches in the puddles, and putting a few spadefuls of earth on the top of them.

The road ran right through the village. On either side of it were little wooden huts. The ends of the timbers crossed outside at the four corners of the huts. They fitted neatly into each other, and some of them were carved. And there were no slates or tiles on the roofs, but little thin slips of wood overlapping each other. There was not a single stone hut or cottage in the village. Only the church was partly brick, whitewashed, with bright green cupolas up in the air, and thin gold crosses on the tops of the cupolas, shining in the clear sky.

Outside the church were rows of short posts, with long rough fir timbers nailed on the top of them, to which the country people tied their horses when they came to church. There were several carts there already, with bright-coloured rugs lying on the hay in them; and the horses were eating hay or biting the logs. Always, except when the logs are quite new, you can tell the favourite places for tying up horses to them, because the timbers will have deep holes in them, where they have been gnawed away by the horses' teeth. They bite the timbers, while their masters eat sunflower seeds, not for food, but to pass the time.

"Now then," said old Peter, as he got down from the cart, tied the horse, gave him an armful of hay from the cart, and lifted the children out. "Be quick. We shall be late if we don't take care. I believe we are late already. Good health to you, Fedor," he said to an old peasant, "and has the baby gone in?"

"He has, Peter. And my health is not so bad; and how is yours?"

"Good also, Fedor, thanks be to God. And will you see to these two? for I am a god-parent, and must be near the priest."

"Willingly," said the old peasant Fedor. "How they do grow, to be sure, like young birch trees. Come along then, little pigeons."

Old Peter hurried into the church, followed by Fedor with Vanya and Maroosia. They all crossed themselves and said a prayer as they went in.

The ceremony was just beginning.

The priest, in his silk robes, was standing before the gold and painted screen at the end of the church, and there were the basin of holy water, and old Peter's sister, and the nurse Babka Tanya, very proud, holding the baby in a roll of white linen, and rocking it to and fro. There were coloured pictures of saints all over the screen, which stretches from one side of the church to the other. Some of the pictures were framed in gilt frames under glass, and were partly painted and partly metal. The faces and hands of the saints were painted, and their clothes were glittering silver or gold. Little lamps were burning in front of them, and candles.

A Russian christening is very different from an English one. For one thing, the baby goes right into the water, not once, but three times. Babka Tanya unrolled the baby, and the priest covered its face with his hand, and down it went under the water, once, twice, and again. Then he took some of the sacred ointment on his finger and anointed the baby's forehead, and feet, and hands, and little round stomach. Then, with a pair of scissors, he cut a little pinch of fluff from the baby's head, and rolled it into a pellet with the ointment, and threw the pellet into the holy water. And after that the baby was carried solemnly three times round the holy water. The priest blessed it and prayed for it; and there it was, a little true Russian, ready to be carried back to its mother, Nastasia, who lay at home in her cottage waiting for it.

When they got outside the church, they all went to Nastasia's cottage to congratulate her on her baby, and to tell her what good lungs it had, and what a handsome face, and how it was exactly like its father.

Nastasia smiled at Vanya and Maroosia; but they had no eyes except for the baby, and for all that belonged to it, especially its cradle. Now a Russian baby has a very much finer cradle than an English baby. A long fir pole is fastened in the middle and at one end to the beams in the ceiling of the hut, so that the other end swings free, just below the rafters. From this end is hung a big basket, and on the ropes by which the basket hangs are fastened shawls of bright colours. The baby is tucked in the basket, the shawls closed round it; and as the mother or the nurse sits at her spinning, she just kicks the basket gently now and again, and it swings up and down from the end of the pole, as if it were hung from the branch of a tree.

This baby had a fine new basket and a larch pole, newly fixed, white and shining, under the dark beams of the ceiling. It had presents besides old Peter's gun. It had a fine wooden spoon with a picture on it of a cottage and a fish. It had a wooden bowl and a painted mug, bought from one of the peddling barges that go up and down the rivers selling chairs and crockery, just like the caravans that travel our English roads. And also, although it was so young, it had a little sacred picture, made of metal, a picture of St Nikolai; because this was St Nikolai's day, and the baby was called Nikolai.

There was a samovar already steaming in the cottage, and a great cake of pastry, and cabbage and egg and fish. And there were cabbage soup with sour cream, and black bread and a little white bread, and red kisel jelly and a huge jug of milk.

And everybody ate and drank and talked as if they were never going to stop. The sun was warm, and presently the men went outside and sat on a log, leaning their backs against the wall of the hut and making cigarettes and smoking, or eating sunflower seeds, cracking the husks with their teeth, taking out the white kernels, and blowing the husks away. And the women sat in the hut, and now and then brought out glasses of hot tea to the men, and then went back again to talk of what a fine man the baby would be, and to remember other babies. And the old women looked at the young mothers and laughed, and said that they could remember the days when they were christened — when they were babies themselves, no bigger than the little Nikolai who swung in the basket and squalled, or slept proudly, just as if he knew that all the world belonged to him because he was so very young. And Vanya and Maroosia ate sunflower seeds too, and sometimes played outside the cottage and sometimes inside; but mostly stood very quiet close to the swinging cradle, waiting till old Babka Tanya, the nurse, should pull the shawls a little way aside and let them see the pink, crumpled face of the little Nikolai, and the yellow fluff, just like a duckling's, which covered his bumpy pink head.

At last, towards evening, old Peter packed what was left of the hay into the cart, and packed Vanya and Maroosia in with the hay. Everybody said good-byes all round, and Peter climbed in and took up the rope reins.

"He'll be a fine man," he shouted through the door to Nastasia, "a fine man; and God grant he'll be as healthy as he is good. Till we meet again," he cried out merrily to the villagers; and Vanya and Maroosia waved their hands, and off they drove, back again to the hut in the forest.

They were very much quieter on the way back than they had been when they drove to the village in the morning. And the early summer day was quiet as it came to its end. There was a corn-crake rattling in the fields, and more than once they saw frogs hop out of the road as they drove by in the twilight. A hare ran before them through the dusk and disappeared. And when they came to the wooden bridge over the stream, a tall grey bird with a long beak rose up from the bank and flew slowly away, carrying his long legs, like a thin pair of crutches, straight out behind him.

"Who is that?" asked Vanya sleepily from his nest in the hay. "That is Mr Crane," said old Peter. "Perhaps he is on his way to visit Miss Heron and tell her that this time he has really made up his mind, and to ask her to let bygones be bygones."

"What bygones?" said Vanya.

Old Peter watched the crane's slow, steady flight above the low marshy ground on either side of the stream, and then he said:

"Why, surely you know all about that. It is an old story, little one, and I must have told it you a dozen times."

"No, never, grandfather," said Maroosia. She was nearly as sleepy as Vanya after the day in the village, and the fuss and pleasure of the christening.

"Oh, well," said old Peter; and he told the tale of Mr Crane and Miss Heron as the cart bumped slowly along the rough road, while Vanya and Maroosia looked out with sleepy eyes from their nest of hay and listened, and the sky turned green, and the trees grew dim, and the frogs croaked in the ditches.

*****

Mr Crane and Miss Heron lived in a marsh five miles across from end to end. They lived there, and fed on the frogs which they caught in their long bills, and held up in the air for a moment, and then swallowed, standing on one leg. The marsh was always damp, and there were always plenty of frogs, and life went well for them, except that they saw very little company. They had no one to pass the time of day with. For Mr Crane had built his little hut on one side of the marsh, and Miss Heron had built hers on the other.

So it came into the head of Mr Crane that it was dull work living alone. If only I were married, he thought, there would be two of us to drink our tea beside the samovar at night, and I should not spend my evenings in melancholy, thinking only of frogs. I will go to see Miss Heron, and I will offer to marry her.

210

So off he flew to the other side of the marsh, flap, flap, with his legs hanging out behind, just as we saw him tonight. He came to the other side of the marsh, and flew down to the hut of Miss Heron. He tapped on the door with his long beak.

"Is Miss Heron at home?"

"At home," said Miss Heron.

"Will you marry me?" said Mr Crane.

"Of course I won't," said Miss Heron; "your legs are long and ill-shaped, and your coat is short, and you fly awkwardly, and you are not even rich. You would have no dainties to feed me with. Off with you, long-bodied one, and don't come bothering me."

She shut the door in his face.

Mr Crane looked the fool he thought himself, and went off home, wishing he had never made the journey.

But as soon as he was gone, Miss Heron, sitting alone in her hut, began to think things over and to be sorry she had spoken in such a hurry.

"After all," thinks she, "it is poor work living alone. And Mr Crane, in spite of what I said about his looks, is really a handsome enough young fellow. Indeed at evening, when he stands on one leg, he is very handsome indeed. Yes, I will go and marry him."

So off flew Miss Heron, flap, flap, over five miles of marsh, and came to the hut of Mr Crane.

"Is the master at home?"

"At home," said Mr Crane.

"Ah, Mr Crane," said Miss Heron, "I was chaffing you just now. When shall we be married?"

"No, Miss Heron," said Mr Crane, "I have no need of you at all. I do not wish to marry, and I would not take you for my wife even if I did. Clear out, and let me see the last of you." He shut the door.

Miss Heron wept tears of shame, that ran from her eyes down her long bill and dropped one by one to the ground. Then she flew away home, wishing she had not come.

As soon as she was gone Mr Crane began to think, and he

211

said to himself, "What a fool I was to be so short with Miss Heron! It's dull living alone. Since she wants it, I will marry her." And he flew off after Miss Heron. He came to her hut, and told her:

"Miss Heron, I have thought things over. I have decided to marry you."

"Mr Crane," said Miss Heron, "I, too, have thought things over. I would not marry you, not for ten thousand young frogs."

Off flew Mr Crane.

As soon as he was gone Miss Heron thought, "Why didn't I agree to marry Mr Crane? It's dull alone. I will go at once and tell him I have changed my mind."

She flew off to betroth herself; but Mr Crane would have none of her, and she flew back again.

And so they go on to this day — first one and then the other flying across the marsh with an offer of marriage, and flying back with shame. They have never married, and never will.

*****

"Grandfather," whispered Maroosia, tugging at old Peter's sleeve, "Vanya is asleep."

They drove on through the forest silently, except for the creaking of the cart and the loud singing of the nightingales in the tops of the tall firs. They came at last to their hut.

"Ah!" said old Peter, as he lifted them out, first one and then the other; "it isn't only Vanya who's asleep." And he carried them in, and put them to bed without waking them.

THE BATTLE OF THE BIRDS AND THE BEASTS

The Battle of the Birds and the Beasts

There was a boy called Ivan who lived in a hut in the forest. And outside the hut, close by, a mouse and a sparrow lived in a nest together.

This was in the days before it had been settled who was to live on earth and who in trees. Birds and beasts and men all lived on the ground together. Only the fish kept to themselves, because they were in the water.

The mouse and the sparrow lived in a nest in the ground, very warm and happy, and ate berries and grain side by side. The sparrow brought berries from the trees, and the mouse brought the berries that grow near the ground, and grains of corn, and all the other things that a mouse can get without wings.

All went well until one day when they were having their dinner. It was like this. They had a pile of berries and grain between them, and every time the mouse took a berry, so did the sparrow. And when the sparrow took a grain, the mouse took one also. In this way no one got more than his share. But it so happened that when they had done sharing there was one little shining grain of corn left over.

"That should be mine," said the mouse.

"It should be mine," said the sparrow.

"But," says the mouse, "I fetched it."

"You did, did you," says the sparrow, "but who fetched the berries?"

"Let's share it," says the mouse.

"I'll bite it in half," says the sparrow, "and so we shall not quarrel."

So the sparrow took the grain of corn in his beak. It was very hard and very slippery. He tossed up his head, to get it to one side of his beak, and before he could stop it, it had slipped down his throat.

And there was the mouse watching him and waiting for his share.

"Where is it?" says the mouse.

"I've swallowed it," says the sparrow.

"You have, have you?" says the mouse ruffling his fur.

"It was a mistake," says the sparrow.

"Easy to say that, with a good grain of corn already in your greedy gullet," says the mouse.

And with that the mouse ran at the sparrow and bit him in the leg. And the sparrow hopped on one foot and beat the mouse with his wings. From the noise they made, they might have been a hundred times as big.

And Ivan heard the noise and came out of his hut, and there they were, fighting like anything, and calling each other names.

He was not the only one who heard them.

The rabbit heard them, and ran to help the mouse. The blackbird heard them and flew to help the sparrow. They fought too, and the noise was louder than ever, and was heard by the pigeon and the hare. They took a hand. Then came the dog and the cock, the cat and the owl, the fox and the hawk, the rat and the robin, the bull and the swan. The mouse fought the sparrow. The rat fought the robin. The rabbit fought the blackbird. The hare fought the pigeon. The dog fought the hen. The fox fought the hawk. The cat fought the owl. The bull fought the swan. And other beasts fought other birds. They pranced and flapped and bit and pecked and screamed and barked and squealed and bellowed together.

And Ivan stood behind a tree, where he could see well, and be safe out of the way.

The noise they made brought bigger beasts to the battle. And bigger birds came flying from far away to fight the bigger beasts. The nest of the mouse and the sparrow was trodden under foot by the wild boar as it fought with the solan goose. But neither the mouse nor the sparrow noticed that, for they were fighting, blinded in a little whirlwind of flying feathers and fur.

But suddenly a dreadful stillness fell upon the forest.

The beasts stopped fighting, and bent their heads to the ground, and put their tails between their legs, and waited, trembling. For the earth was shaking with the coming of the Bear, the Tzar of all the beasts. And the birds stopped fighting and stood there, trembling, and ruffling out their feathers, such feathers as they had left, and waited, for the air was shaken with the coming of the Fire-Bird, the Tzar of all the birds.

There was such silence in the forest that Ivan heard a leaf hit the ground as it dropped from a tree.

Then the Bear swung heavily through the undergrowth, and stood there, looking at all the beasts and birds. And the beasts crawled with their bellies on the ground, and got behind the Bear, and waited, panting after the fight, and looking with red frightened eyes to see what would happen to the birds.

Then the Fire-Bird flew through the tall trees, like a great torch flung through the green dusk of the forest. And the birds fluttered away behind the Fire-Bird, and put their heads under their wings, and shivered the feathers on their trembling bodies. And the Fire-Bird, golden and scarlet, with burning breast, and gleaming wings, was alone before the Bear.

Then began the fight.

The Bear raised himself on his hindlegs, and growled terribly, and lifted his black lips so that his white teeth shone red in the firelight that fell upon them from the burning breast of the Fire-Bird. The Fire-Bird spread wide his gleaming wings and rose into the air and came down upon the head of the Bear. The Bear yelled in pain from the scorching of his eyes, and beat off the Bird with slow heavy blows of his great paws. The claws of the Bear were claws of steel, and the ground was red and gold with the feathers of the Bird.

Long they fought.

The hair of the Bear was singed to his skin and as he fought, he groaned in his pain. The Fire-Bird fought silently, beating the Bear with his golden wings, and scorching him with the burning feathers of his breast. And the beasts whimpered as they watched and heard the groaning of their Tzar. And the birds trembled where they stood. And the earth of the forest shook with the trampling of the Bear, and the roots of the trees were loosened in the ground. A wild wind drove through the forest, now this way now that, from the beating of the Fire-Bird's wings, and the tall trees waved before it like fine grass.

At last the Fire-Bird pressed his burning breast on the head of the Bear and blinded him. The Bear in his great pain rolled on the ground taking the Fire-Bird with him. One of the golden wings was broken in that rolling. The Fire-Bird could fight no more. The Bear, blinded and scorched, could fight no more. He stood there, groaning, while the beasts whimpered about him. Then he lumbered heavily away into the forest. The bull shook his great head and went off among the trees, swinging his angry tail. The wolf and the fox and the hare and the rabbit and the rat and the wild boar went their ways. The wild goose and the swan rose in the air and flew back to the marshlands. The hawk and the owl flew off, the hawk high above the forest, the owl still keeping in the shadow of the great trees. One by one the Beasts and the Birds were gone, and at last none was left but the mouse and the sparrow, and the Fire-Bird with his broken golden wing.

The boy, Ivan, stepped from behind his tree, and came to the Fire-Bird lying there on the ground. The mouse and the sparrow huddled together. Their nest had been trodden under foot by the wild boar, and they had nowhere to live.

"And all for a grain of corn," chirped the sparrow.

"And the Bear, the great Tzar of the Beasts, is blinded and burned," squeaked the mouse.

"And the Fire-Bird, before whose coming the forest itself is silent, has a broken wing," says the sparrow.

"And our home is gone," says the mouse.

"If only I had not lived with you," says the sparrow.

"You shall not live with me again," says the mouse.

218

And with that the mouse burrowed a hole for himself under Ivan's hut. And the sparrow made a nest for himself in a hole in the wall.

But Ivan cut the bough of a tree, and took ropes of bast, and bound the broken wing of the Fire-Bird to the bough, so that the wing should mend.

Says he: "If you lie quiet for a day or two, you'll be flying as well as ever, and in the meantime we can keep each other company."

The sparrow was taking a beakful of moss to his nest. "Do you hear that?" he says to the mouse, who was sitting at the mouth of his hole cleaning his whiskers. "That boy is not afraid even of the Fire-Bird."

"Why should he be afraid of him?" squeaks the mouse. "The Bear broke his wing."

"Aye, and went off with blind eyes and no hair," says the sparrow.

They would have fought again. But, just as they were going to fight, the mouse looks at the sparrow, and says he: "If we fight, the others will come and fight too, and this time, who knows? they may trample the hut itself to pieces."

"True," says the sparrow, and flew to his nest in the wall, while the mouse ran back to his hole.

The Fire-Bird lay in Ivan's hut. A week he lay there, and covered his breast with his good wing, lest the heat of his burning breast should turn the hut to cinders. His broken wing mended. And on the eighth day the Fire-Bird struts gloriously out of the hut into the sunlight, and the mouse looks from his hole, and the sparrow from his nest, to see the sunlight on the Fire-Bird's gleaming feathers.

"Do you think you can fly now?" says Ivan, and the Fire-Bird did not answer but shook his mighty wings. He looked round at the broken trees and trampled earth where the Beasts had fought with the Birds. And the flames in his eyes twinkled, and says he to Ivan: "Up on my back, Ivan, and we will find something to put on this open ground."

Ivan sat on the back of the Fire-Bird between his golden

wings, and the Fire-Bird flew up out of the clearing in the forest, and over the tops of the tall trees. And down below in the forest the beasts grumbled silently to themselves as they heard the flapping of his wings, and blinked when they looked up through the leaves and saw him pass far overhead like a blazing bit out of the sun. The blind Bear growled under his breath and lifted his scorched head, and a ray of heat from the burning breast of the Bird fell on the Bear's head, and the Bear put his head between his paws, and whimpered wretchedly.

But Ivan, sitting up there between the wings of the Fire-Bird, sang aloud as they flew through the blue air, beyond the forest, beyond the plains, beyond the blue hills, and the marshlands and the sea that lie behind the hills.

And the Fire-Bird says to Ivan: "Look down, and tell me what you see."

And Ivan looks, and says: "There is a palace by the sea-shore."

"It is the palace of my eldest sister," says the Fire-Bird. "We will rest there, and drink tea with my eldest sister."

The Fire-Bird dropped from the sky like a falling star, while Ivan caught his breath.

In the doorway of the palace stood a Princess, as straight as a fir and as slender as a birch tree. She moved like a woman, but she was made of fine gold, and her bare arms shone in the sunlight, like the feathers of the Bird, her brother.

"Welcome, brother," says the Princess of gold, and went before them into the palace, and called for a samovar and two glasses, one for herself and the other for the Fire-Bird.

"And a third glass for Ivan," says the Fire-Bird.

The Princess stiffened like a gold statue.

"I will not drink with him," says she, and stands there scornful, because she was a Princess, and her brother was the Fire-Bird, and Ivan was a poor peasant lad.

The golden feathers of the Fire-Bird rustled with anger, and he went back into the courtyard. "Away," says he, and Ivan climbed up and sat again between his wings.

Then the Fire-Bird rose like a flaming eagle, up, up, into the sky above the palace.

"Watch now," says he to Ivan, when he was high in the sky, hovering like a blazing hawk.

With that he bent his head and thrust his beak deep into his burning breast and plucked a feather and let it go. Ivan watched it falling, scarlet and gold, like a feather of blood and flame. It fell, and almost before it touched the palace roof, the whole palace took fire and burned up in a single monstrous flame. The flame died as swiftly as it rose, and left nothing but a dark place of ashes on the gold shore of the sea.

They flew on. Evening fell. The sun went down and the moon rose. Once more the Fire-Bird asked Ivan what he saw.

And Ivan, leaning forward, looked down between the neck of the Bird and his great golden shoulder, and saw another palace, carven and glittering pale in the moonlight, in the middle of a great plain.

"That is the palace of my second sister," says the Fire-Bird. "We will rest there and drink tea."

Again they flew down, and alighted in the courtyard of the palace. The moonlight fell on its carven roofs, and in its doorway stood a Princess, of silver, with her silver arms clasped behind her head, as she was looking at the moon.

"Welcome, brother," says she, and went before them to call for the samovar.

"Two glasses," says she.

"Three," says the Fire-Bird.

"There is no third here who may drink with you and me," says the Princess in her slow proud voice.

And with that the Fire-Bird turned from her, saying not a word. And Ivan sat between his wings as he flew up again high in the air between the earth and the moon. Once more the Fire-Bird plucked a feather from his breast, and it fell, blazing, through the night, and that palace, like the first, was burned up in a single sudden flame.

They flew on through the night. The moon went down, the stars paled and flickered out, and the dawn spread over the

sky. Once more the Fire-Bird told Ivan to look down. Ivan leaned forward over the great golden shoulder of the Bird, and shielded his face from the heat of his burning breast, and saw mountains far below, and lakes, and in the heart of the mountains, a palace. The palace was of bronze with green roofs just touched with the first rays of the sun. And in the doorway of the palace was a little Princess of fine copper, lifting her metal arms to the dawn.

"That is the palace of my little youngest sister," says the Fire-Bird as he flew down out of the sunlight.

"Welcome, brother," says the little Princess, "and who is your guest?"

"This is Ivan who healed my wing when it was broken in fighting with the Bear."

"He is welcome," says the little Princess, and threw her copper arms about Ivan's neck and kissed him on both cheeks. And her kiss was the kiss of a young girl, and her arms were soft about his neck.

The sun rose higher. The samovar was brought out into the courtyard, and they drank tea there in the sunshine, Ivan, the Fire-Bird and the little Princess. All day long they drank tea and feasted together.

At evening the Fire-Bird stretched his golden wings. "Up on my back, Ivan," says he. "And you, little sister, pack him a palace in a wooden box, for we have some open ground to cover, where the trees were trodden under in the fight."

"I will give you my own," says the little Princess, and with that she clapped her hands. The palace grew littler and littler. When it was small enough, she picked it up and put it in a wooden box and gave it to Ivan.

"But where will you live?" says Ivan.

"I shall have to come with you," says the Princess.

So they climbed up on the back of the Fire-Bird, and sat there with their arms about each other's waists, holding the box with the palace on their knees.

As the sun set, the Fire-Bird flapped his great gold wings, and flew up into the dusky sky, and so through the night, like a flying fire. They flew through the moonlight and the dark and next day in the sunlight flew down to the forest and the trampled open ground where the Beasts had fought with the Birds.

There was silence in the forest as the Fire-Bird flew above the trees. There was silence when he flew down to Ivan's hut. The sparrow sat silent in his nest in the wall, and the mouse trembled in his hole under the hut.

Ivan and the Princess opened the box, and took out the palace. One of its towers had been chipped on the journey, but they soon mended that. Then the Princess clapped her hands, and the little palace grew bigger and bigger and bigger until it was as big as it had been when Ivan and the Fire-Bird came flying down to it in the dawn. Then it stopped growing. Ivan and the Princess were just going to walk in, when they looked round for the Fire-Bird.

He was gone. While the palace was growing he had flapped his great golden wings, and flown away over the tops of the tall trees.

Just then, as the Fire-Bird was gone, all the birds in the forest began to sing. The beasts moved again in the undergrowth. The sparrow flew chirping from the wall of the hut and began to build a nest for himself under the roof of the palace. The mouse ran out squeaking, and ran into the palace in front of Ivan and the little Princess, and found a snug hole for himself near the larder.

Ivan and the Princess went into the palace, and drank tea and ate cakes and told stories to each other. They settled down and lived there very happily. The Fire-Bird never came again, nor will he until there is another war between the Birds and the Beasts. And that is not likely, because since that time the Birds and Beasts no longer live together. The birds live in trees and under the roofs of palaces and huts and windmills, while all the four-footed ones live on the ground. The sparrow lives in the roof of Ivan's palace, and the mouse close by the larder. They no longer share their food together. And so there are no more battles between the Birds and the Beasts.

The Swan Princess

Once upon a time there was a Tzar and his son was Prince Ivan who grew tired of palaces and went out into the open country.

On the mountains, in the wide valleys he lived, and on the shores of the blue sea. But most of all he lived in the marshlands where there are many birds. He lived in a gold and silver tent that glittered like frost in sunlight. He slept in gold embroidered blankets and in the daytime went shooting with his bow and arrows and set snares for the grey geese and the wild swans.

One day he caught a young swan, wearing her first white feathers, as white as clouds in summer. And Prince Ivan, looking at her beauty, could not kill her, but took her back at night to his tent and set her in a wicker basket, to take as a gift to his father, the Tzar. "There shall be no blood on those white feathers," he said. "She shall swim in my father's lake, and my little sisters shall feed her with crumbs from golden plates." And he lay down to sleep under his gold embroidered blankets.

In the morning he got up, brushed the sleep from his eyes, and went again to his hunting.

But as soon as he was gone, the white swan came out of the wicker basket, and shook herself, and stood there as a sweet young girl, as pretty as a birch tree, and watched from the doorway of the tent until Prince Ivan was out of sight. Then she busied herself in the tent like a good housewife, and made dishes ready of all kinds, and laid them on the table at evening, a dinner for Prince Ivan when he should come home. And, as she heard him coming, singing across the marshlands, as he came from the sea-shore, she shook herself once more, and turned again into a young white swan, and went back into the wicker basket.

Prince Ivan came into the tent, sniffing with his nostrils because of the good smell of food. He saw the table laid and a dinner smoking on the table. "Who is this?" says he. "Who has been in my tent? One of my little sisters must have been here today. I shall take her the skin of a white fox to make winter boots for her little feet." Then he thought no more about it, for he was very hungry. And he sat down and ate as a man will who has been hunting all day. Then he covered what was left of the food with a napkin, and lay down under his gold embroidered blankets, and slept.

As soon as he slept, the swan turned again into a young girl, cleared the table, was a swan once more, and went back into the wicker basket, where she slept like a lump of snow.

In the morning, when he found the table cleared, Prince Ivan thought he had dreamed his dinner of the day before. He made himself tea, and hot porridge, and went out again to his hunting.

And as soon as he was gone, the young swan came out of the basket, shook herself, turned into a sweet young girl, and watched him until he was out of sight. Then she made him a better dinner than the day before, and, when she heard him coming, shook herself, was a swan once more, and lay in the basket with her head under her wing.

Prince Ivan came in, laden with hares and geese and fat duck. He dropped them in a corner of the tent, and looked round and saw the table, with the steam rising from the dinner.

"Who has done this?" says he. "Come out and show yourself, whoever you are. Who is there here?"

None answered. He listened. There was silence in the tent. He went outside. There was silence in the open country, but for the croaking of the frogs in the marshlands, and the crying of the wild birds.

He sat down and ate up the dinner. Then he covered what was left with a napkin, lay down under his embroidered blankets, and slept. And again the swan made herself a young girl, and cleared the table, turned once more into a swan, and slept in the wicker basket.

On the third day, when Prince Ivan saw the table cleared he knew well that he had left it covered at night. Thinks he to himself, "Today I shall know who plays housewife for me." And he took his bow and arrow and went out as if he were going to his hunting. And as soon as he was gone, the white swan came out of the basket, shook herself and was a young girl, and watched from the door of the tent until Prince Ivan was out of sight. Then she set about making a dinner for him that should be even better than the other two.

But Ivan the Prince, as soon as he was out of sight, went no further. He waited a little, and then came back quickly and quietly, like a hunter after wild goats, making no noise with his feet, and keeping close in the hollows of the ground, so that even if the swan girl had been looking for him, she would not have seen him. And Ivan the Prince crept up to the door of his tent, and listened, and he could hear the clatter of dishes, and the swan girl, singing a little bird-song as she went about her work.

He waited till he heard that she was near the doorway of the tent, and then leapt through the doorway and caught her in his arms. And she looked at him with frightened eyes, and cried like a lost bird, and struggled in his arms.

She twisted and twisted in his arms, and twisted into a strip of gold cloth. And Ivan the Prince stood there startled with nothing in his hands but a strip of gold cloth. "Where is she?" he cried, and tore the gold cloth in half. "Where is she?" he cried again, with a bit of gold cloth in each hand. "Oh, that she would be here again, as I saw her here just now."

And with that the gold cloth was gone, and there stood the swan maiden, as pretty as a birch tree, and on the floor about his feet were white swan feathers blowing hither and thither in the light wind that blew through the door of the tent.

And so Ivan the Prince never went back to his father the Tzar. He married the swan maiden, and cut trees with his axe, while she gathered moss, and they built a house together, there in the open country not far from the marshlands and the shore of the blue sea. And the house had a yard and a hut in the yard, and there came an old woman out of the marshes, and lived in the hut and guarded the house when Prince Ivan and the swan maiden went walking together.

And near the end of the winter a little son was born to them, and Ivan the Prince had never been so happy, as when he came home from his day's hunting, stamping the snow from his boots, and then going in quietly to find his swan maiden singing to her baby, rocking the cradle with her foot while the old hag minded the fire.

But as the winter wore away, the swan maiden no longer sang to her baby. At night she sat and looked into the fire and in the daytime she used to go to the door of the little house, and look far away, above the bare trees and the windy clouds into the blue sky.

At last, one morning, the old hag who lived in the yard caught Ivan the Prince by his sleeve, as he was going out hunting. "Listen," says she. "The spring has come. You must watch your young wife or lose her. Do not go far from the house."

And Prince Ivan looked back to the little house, and there at the door was his swan maiden, looking up and far away into the blue sky, as if she could see the stars in daylight. And on the birch trees near by was the first green of the young leaves.

Ivan waited, wondering.

The old woman left him and went back to the house. The swan maiden stood in the doorway, and it was as if she did not see the old hag as she went in because her eyes were for nothing but the sky.

And Ivan went slowly back to the house and waited close by the doorway. The swan maiden did not see him or hear him, for she was looking beyond the clouds and had no eyes for anything on earth. She did not hear him for she was listening to the sound of wings so far away that even the hunter Prince Ivan could not hear them.

For a long time Prince Ivan heard and saw nothing as he stood there watching his young wife. But at last he too heard the beating of wings. Then far away he could see them coming, a flock of wild swans. They flew nearer and nearer and over the little house. And as they flew an old wild swan that flew at the head of the flock cried out to the swan maiden:

> "Ti! ho! ho! my little daughter!
> Ti! ho! ho! my own!
> Let me give you wings
> And strong tail feathers.
> Fly with us beyond the sea.
> Fly with us beyond the blue."

And that was her father flying by. And Prince Ivan heard how his young wife at the house door cried back to him:

> "Ti! ho! ho! my little father!
> Ti! ho! ho! my own!
> Do not give me wings,
> Nor yet tail feathers.
> I'll not fly with you over the sea.
> I'll not fly with you over the blue.
> For I have a little baby,
> And I have my dear."

And the wild swans flew on, over the marshlands and over the blue sea.

And then again Prince Ivan heard the beating of wings. Another flock of wild swans flew down out of the clouds and over the little house. And as they flew a wild swan cried to the swan maiden who stood in the doorway:

> "Ti! ho! ho! my little daughter!
> Ti! ho! ho! my own!
> Let me give you wings
> And strong tail feathers.

> Fly with us over the sea.
> Fly with us beyond the blue."

And that was her mother flying by. And Prince Ivan heard how his young wife at the house door cried back to her:

> "Ti! ho! ho! my little mother!
> Ti! ho! ho! my own!
> Do not give me wings
> Nor yet tail feathers.
> I'll not fly with you over the sea.
> I'll not fly with you over the blue.
> For I have a little baby,
> And I have my dear,"

And the second flock of wild swans flew on, and away, over the blue sea.

Prince Ivan moved nearer, and then a third time he heard the beating of wings. A third flock of wild swans flew over the house. And again a wild swan cried down to the swan maiden who stood in the doorway:

> "Ti! ho! ho! my little sister!
> Ti! ho! ho! my own!
> Let me give you wings
> And strong tail feathers.
> Fly with us across the sea.
> Fly with us beyond the blue."

And that was her brother flying by. And Ivan the Prince heard how his young wife at the house door called back into the sky:

> "Ti! ho! ho! my little brother!
> Ti! ho! ho! my own!
> Do not give me wings,
> Nor yet tail feathers.
> I'll not fly with you over the sea.

I'll not fly with you over the blue.
For I have a little baby,
And I have my dear."

And the third flock of wild swans flew on and away over the marshlands and over the blue sea.

Prince Ivan moved nearer and nearer till he stood close by the swan maiden, there in the doorway of their little house. And his heart was glad, for she had said that she would not leave him, But just then he heard the beating of wings a fourth time. A fourth flock of wild swans flew over the little house. And again a wild swan called down to the swan maiden:

"Ti! ho! ho! my little sweetheart!
Ti! ho! ho! my love!
Let me give you wings
And strong tail feathers.
Fly with me over the sea.
Fly with me beyond the blue."

And the swan maiden lifted her arms, and her eyes shone. For that was the voice of her swan sweetheart. And she called out to him:

"Ti! ho! ho! my own dear sweetheart!
Ti! ho! ho! my love!
Give me broad wings
And strong tail feathers.
I'll fly with you over the sea.
I'll fly with you over the blue."

And the flock of wild swans flew down towards the house. The swan maiden was on tiptoe just going to fly up and away with them when Prince Ivan caught her in his arms.

And the wild swans wailed in the air, and beat the air with their strong wings, and flew on and away over the blue sea.

But the swan maiden wept in Prince Ivan's arms. She

sobbed and said to him: "If you had not caught me I should have flown away with my swan sweetheart to the swan kingdom beyond the sea. But now I must stay with you for ever. Who will give me wings? Who will give me tail feathers? For my dear swan sweetheart has flown away."

But Prince Ivan kissed away her tears, and they went into the little house to play with their baby, and they have been living happily ever since, for the wild swans never came again.

Omelya and the Pike

An old man and an old woman had three sons. Two of them went to trade in the bazaar, and they left Omelya, the youngest son, behind, and said to him: "You obey the old woman here, and we will bring you a red kaftan, red boots and a red hat."

Omelya lay down on the stove. And the old woman said to him: "Omelya, go and get water."

And says he: "But I am so warm here."

"Take care," says the old woman, "for they won't buy you a red kaftan, red boots and a red hat if you don't do as you are told."

So Omelya took the buckets and ran off to get water. He came to the river, threw in the buckets, pulled them out again on the end of their rope, and there in one of them he had caught a little pike. "Omelya," says the pike, "let me go in the river, and I will do you a lot of good."

"And what will you do for me?"

"Whenever you want anything, call upon me, and you shall have it."

He let the pike go, and, says he, "At my request, and at the pike's command, you, bucket, get along home by yourself." And off goes a bucket with never a one to carry it.

And the folk said, "Hi! Look at this, children. What's this that Omelya is up to?" And the buckets came along and set themselves on the bench.

Then the old woman was for sending him off again. "Off with you, Omelya, cut wood, and bring it to keep up the fire."

Omelya lay still on the stove, and says he, "It's warm for me here."

"Take care or they will not buy you a red kaftan, red boots and a red hat."

Says Omelya: "At my request, and at the pike's command,

off with you, hatchet, and cut wood, and you, faggots, when you are cut, come along here by yourselves to the hut." The hatchet went off and cut wood, and the wood came by itself to the hut.

They spent the night, and the wood was all used up in the stove. More was wanted from the forest. "Omelya, off with you to the forest."

"But it is warmer here."

"Take care, or they will not buy you a red kaftan, red boots and a red hat."

He went out in the road, and got out his sledge, sat down on it instead of pulling it, and says he: "At my request, and at the pike's command, you, sledge, get along to the forest where there is wood." Off they went. The sledge went through the town. Oi, how the folk stared. They came to the forest. Says he: "At my request, and at the pike's command, hatchet, cut wood, wood pile yourself on the sledge, and, sledge, carry the lot." The hatchet cut the wood, and the wood piled itself on the sledge, and, says Omelya, "Hatchet, cut now a green oak club." It was done, he sat himself on the wood with the club, and off he went home again. In the town there were crowds of folk waiting for him. They wanted to take him. They wanted to beat him to a jelly. They wanted to haul him before the judge. What business had Omelya to go riding about in a sledge when they had to pull their own? And who ever heard of a lad like him with a hatchet that cut wood by itself? Omelya slipped along in his sledge, and when the people tried to stop him, he says, "At my request, and at the pike's command, have at them, oak club, and break their arms and legs." Up jumped the oaken club and beat the whole lot of them. Omelya came home and lay on the stove.

But complaints were taken to the King about Omelya. And a policeman was sent by the King. "Come along, Omelya. The King wants you. What have you been up to? What have you done to the good folk of the town?"

Says Omelya, "At my request, and at the pike's command, up with you, oak club, and break his arms and legs. Why do you come bothering me?" And the oak club smashed the policeman all to pieces.

Then comes a Counsellor. He was clever. He brought along candy, and all sorts of good things, yes, and dried raisins. "Come along, Omelya, and see the King, he'll give you even better."

And Omelya says, "At my request, and at the pike's command, stove, carry me along to the King." Then the posts of the hut cracked, the walls flew apart, and off went the stove with Omelya to the King.

The King was looking out of the window. "What sort of a miracle is this?"

And they tell him, "This is Omelya coming riding to you on a stove." He came.

"What is this, Omelya, that you have been up to! How many good folk in the town have you knocked about?"

"Your High Kingship, I don't want to say I'm sorry to you." He turned round and was riding off again. But there was the King's daughter looking from a window. Says Omelya, "At my request, and at the pike's command, Princess, come riding with me." And the Princess went riding with him on the stove.

And the King was bitter mad with him. And the King caught them, and shut them up tight in a barrel and fastened it with iron bands, and took the barrel out to the sea, and left them in the waves. The Princess cried, "Oh Omelya, what have you done, and what have they done with us?"

Says Omelya: "At my request, and at the pike's command, blow, strong winds, and throw the barrel on to dry land near the King's house." And the barrel went flying up on to dry land and broke to pieces. "At my request, and at the pike's command, build here a crystal palace." And there was the crystal palace. "And now build a bridge of pearls to the King's house, with silver hand-rails." And then there was the bridge with silver rails. He sent a messenger to bid the King visit him. And the King came and sat at the table. And Omelya asked him: "Do you know whose guest you are, and at whose table you are sitting?"

"I don't," says the King.

"You are sitting at the table with Omelya, your son-in-law,

who came riding by on a stove, and this is your daughter, and now is the wedding feast." And so it was and from that time on the King and Omelya were for ever feasting, now in the King's house and now in the crystal palace.

As for the red kaftan, red boots and the red hat, the brothers brought them from the fair just in time for Omelya to wear them at the wedding.

The Costly Ring

Once upon a time — I do not know where and when — a certain man lived and died. That is an ancient custom in this world — man lives for a time, and dies. Well, this man died, and for a legacy he left a ring; not any kind of a ring, but with a precious stone in it. Behold what kind of precious stone there was in that ring: a hundred towns and a hundred villages was the price of it, and if I had thrown my old wife into the bargain it would not have been too much. The dead man left the one ring, but he left three sons to share it — Kiko, Hecho and Vano. And the trouble was not that they had such names; the real difficulty was, how to divide the ring. If you and I had thought for a hundred years we should not have thought of a way, but the old woman, the mother of the lads, thought of it at once. She seized the ring and hid it.

"If you have it," says she, "somebody will steal it."

"Matoushka," the eldest son, Kiko, began to beg her, "give me my patrimony. Who will steal from me? Why, I stole the eggs of the raven out of her nest when she was sitting on them, and she did not stir."

"That is not much to boast of," said the middle brother, Hecho. "You forget that when you were climbing up the tree after the raven's eggs I took your trousers off your legs and you never noticed it."

"But I am as good as either of them," took up the youngest son, Vano. "Why, I cut the soles off their slippers while they were climbing up the tree. Give the ring to me, Matoushka."

"No," said the old woman, "I will not give it to you. Truly says the proverb: 'Do not give a legacy to a stupid son, for it will bring him no good.' And you are actual fools, stealing eggs from the raven, and trousers and slippers from each other. What sort of profit was there in that?"

Now, over and above her three sons, the old woman had a

daughter of such beauty that when you looked at her and for a long time afterwards you had to rub your eyes with your fingers as if you had been looking at the sun. And her mother loved and cared for her more than for her own soul; for she was an old woman of intelligence; well she knew that such a beauty might marry a prince and a rich one at that, and then she, as mother of the princess, would have great honour in the house of her son-in-law, especially if she gave as her daughter's dower the ring that was worth a hundred towns and villages.

The old woman cared for her daughter as for her own eyes, and was for ever telling her: "Do not go, O my darling daughter, into the forest on the Black Mountain. In that place, so they say, lives a terrible, hairy Ndemi giant. If he sees you he will carry you off. How could he help carrying off such a beauty? Think, all the young men, for a week's journey on the roads, pay court to you; like pebbles in the stream are your admirers — peasants, merchants, noblemen, princes — and I have not yet chosen out the richest and most gracious as a son-in-law for myself. How would it be for me in the years of my old age, if I were to have as a son-in-law a hairy Ndemi in the forest?"

But her spoilt daughter did not pay much attention to her. She would take herself off and go after flowers or nuts into the forest on the Black Mountain. And once she walked and walked, but did not come home at night; she had fallen into the paws of the hairy Ndemi.

The old woman sobbed; she wept, she scratched her face, she tore out her hair; she beat herself with her fists, both on the breasts and on the head. She called her sons to her and said to them: "Ah! my sons, my brave lads! Go and look for your sister, my daughter, the light of my eyes, get her away from the wicked Ndemi, and bring her back to me, O my little bright sunshine! To the one of you who does this, to him I will give his father's ring, which is worth a hundred towns and a hundred villages."

Instantly the youths made ready, Kiko, Hecho and Vano,

and went to look for their sister. But where were they to seek her in the great wide world? They walked far and wide over the mountains, through the forests, through muddy swamps, over the quicksands and they came in the depths of the wilderness to a little hut. And at the threshold of the hut there sat an old woman so filthy and so ugly that the very sight of her would turn you sick.

"A good journey to you, young men," says the old woman. "Whither are you going?"

They told her. Says the old woman to them: "Well, you will not find this Ndemi, though you wander for a hundred years, unless I tell you the way. But if you want me to help you, let one or other of you marry my lovely daughter. Already for twice forty years she has been waiting for a lover; and where is one to look for him in this wilderness?"

The brothers thought and thought. "There is nothing to be done — we must find our sister and earn the ring." They drew lots, and it fell to the eldest brother Kiko to marry the old woman's daughter.

When the old woman led the bride out of the hut poor Kiko nearly fell backwards. The mother was terrible, but the daughter was still more abominable. And the old woman praised her daughter, caressed her, and told her, moreover: "See, my darling, a husband has been found for you. He will give you food and drink, and will love you, and dress you in garments of gold. And I, the old woman, will come with you and eat his bread until I die. You hear that, young man? If I give you my daughter, you must give shelter to me."

There was nothing to be done. They had to find their sister and earn the ring. And so the young man Kiko married the old woman's daughter, and they went on further, now five together. Oh, far they went, and into dark places, and they met many terrible things. They saw the savage Ochokochy folk, who live in the impassable forests and do not talk like people but howl like wolves, and do not know fire, which is the gift of God. They saw the water-sprite, the Chinka, as small as a two-year-old child, but its hair is silvery to the heels. They heard the Hadjee crying from far away, the lovely woman of the woods with green hair. And they did not go far from that place where the Tzaritsa of all the witches, the terrible Rokapi, is chained with bonds of hair to an iron pillar, a hairy skeleton with eyes that gleam like fire. They all went on and on together, and came at last to a little hut in an unknown place. And before the hut there was sitting an old woman, still older and still more loathsome than Kiko's mother-in-law.

They greeted her. They told her whither and for what purpose they were travelling. But the new old woman said to the first: "That is right, little sister; you have brought suitors; already my little daughterkin has been waiting for them for twice fifty years. If a loving bridegroom from among these young men takes her in marriage, I will help my son-in-law to send to sleep the Ndemi who has taken their sister and guards her day and night. And if he does not put him to sleep he will never get his sister from him, for this Ndemi crushes a hundred men with his finger as if they were flies."

There was nothing to be done — they had taken it upon them and they had to rescue their sister and earn the ring — so they drew lots, and it fell to the middle brother, Hecho, to marry the old woman's daughter. He spat and spluttered when he saw his bride, old, huckle-backed, and armless too; but he had to marry her. Hecho married, and they all went on together, now seven in number. They went on and on, no small way — farther than from the mouth to the nose — and they saw many wonderful things, and came in the end to a third little hut; and on the threshold of the hut there was an old woman sitting. She was bent altogether into a bow, her nose rested in her bosom, and she was as bald as a knee.

Kiko and Hecho and their mothers-in-law exchanged greetings with her, and told her whither and for what purpose they were travelling. But she said: "Well, I thank you, dear aunts, for bringing me a lover; I have already been waiting for him twice sixty years. What a pity that dear mother is dead; she would have rejoiced on my account. Well, young man," she said to the youngest brother, Vano; "since you wish to rescue your sister and earn the ring, cherish me, a maid, as your wife. If not, you will not see your sister, even though my little younger aunt should show you where the Ndemi lives, even though my other aunt still has the herb her grandmother left her which has the power of putting that Ndemi to sleep. How will you bring the herb near him if I do not help you? Offer it to him? Why, he tears every stranger instantly asunder. But me he will not touch, because I am his gossip, and from old times have kept my friendship with him. I will put him to sleep with the herb, and bring you your sister. Only marry me, sweetheart, if you please!"

What was to be done? When the young man Vano only thought of such a wife he turned sick at once. But there was no escape from the marriage. They had to rescue their sister and earn the ring. And his elder brother said to him: "What! Are we to have married our old hags for nothing? Marry, you also. It will be all the easier for you. At least you will have no mother-in-law."

The young man Vano married the old woman who for twice sixty years had been waiting for a lover. She said to him and his brothers: "Now wait for me here; in three days' time I will come back and bring you your sister alive and in good health."

And she went off. As she said, so she did. In exactly three days she came back and brought the young men their sister, alive and in good health. The brothers were about to rejoice over their sister — kissing and embracing each other — but the old women put a sudden stop to all that.

"There is no time for that sort of thing," they said, "we must escape. We have a long way before us, and the Ndemi has only fallen asleep for seven days and for seven nights. He will wake up, he will overtake us, no one of us will escape from death, unless we teach a place where many people dwell."

And they all started off, now nine in number, on the return journey. The seven days passed, during which the Ndemi slept, but they had not nearly reached the places where men live. And suddenly thunder sounded in the mountains behind them, the tall trees shook from side to side and cracked, and rocks rolled from the tops of the hills.

"Oh misfortune!" cried the old women, "that Ndemi has waked and is pursuing us."

And the mother-in-law of the eldest brother, Kiko, flung a spindle behind her. There rose up tall, tall mountains, to the very sky, and the Ndemi had to pass over them. The travellers ran on. Suddenly the wind howled again behind them, the earth shook; the Ndemi had passed over the mountains, and was overtaking them. The mother-in-law of the middle brother, Hecho, flung behind her a comb. There grew up behind them, for a three-day journey, thick black forests; a snake could not crawl between the trees. But through that forest the terrible Ndemi forced his way, and broke a road for himself — it is still to be seen — and once more overtook the travellers. Then the wife of the youngest brother, Vano, flung a looking-glass behind her, and there spread behind them a wide sea. The forest-living Ndemi could not go into the water, and so he stopped on the shore. And then quickly they came in sight of the dwelling places of men, and after that the brothers, with their sister, with their wives, and with their mothers-in-law, made their way to their own village.

The old mother rejoiced unspeakably over her beloved daughter, and without dispute gave her sons their father's ring, that was worth a hundred towns and a hundred villages. And then there began among the brothers a quarrel as to which of them was the owner of the ring. The eldest brother, Kiko, said: "If had not married, how should we have learnt where to find our sister? Yes, and my mother-in-law was the first to think how to stop the Ndemi when he was overtaking us. Mine is the ring!"

"What of that!" said the middle brother Hecho. "If I had not married and my mother-in-law had not given the herb of sleep, how should we have taken our sister from the Ndemi? I will not give up the ring."

Nor would the youngest brother, Vano, give way. "I," says he, "am the youngest, but my wife is older than either of

246

yours, and on that account I should receive our father's ring. Besides, my wife brought our sister to us, and she put the Ndemi to sleep, and she, too, it was who finally put an end to his pursuit of us."

So the quarrel went on — oh misfortune! They went from words to deeds; they came to blows; wives took their husbands' parts, mothers their daughters'. Clamour, uproar yelping; the women, as is the custom, tugged at each other's hair. Well, they fought and fought, and saw at last that however much they struggled there would be no end to their dispute. So they took the ring and went into the village, in order that the old men should come together and decide between them.

The old men came together, drank wine, which the brothers provided for them, and began to judge the matter. From the redness of the sky in the morning to the redness of the sky at night, they all sat there, forming their opinions, disputing and being reconciled. In the end they adjudged that the ring should be divided equally among the three brothers. They looked for the ring. It was nowhere to be found. Someone had stolen it. Some said that a thief had come to the village and in the bustle had stolen the ring; others that they had seen how the raven from whose nest Kiko had stolen the eggs had flown away with the ring. But who knows the truth? The ring was lost that was worth a hundred towns and a hundred villages; it was lost and has not yet been found.

And the young brothers, Kiko, Hecho and Vano, were left without riches and with ancient wives. The two elder had mothers-in-law as well. I should like to tell you that their old wives turned into young and beautiful princesses, but what is the use of telling you if it did not happen. You may say "Honey, Honey" for all you are worth, and there will be no sweetness in your mouth.

And as for their sister, rich people no longer wanted to marry her. There is no more honour for a maiden if she has been taken from her father's house, even if by a Ndemi of the forest. Indeed I, a poor man, married her from pity and not at all gladly. My old woman has such a character. Ah me!

Anyone can see that she brought all the wickedness of the Ndemi away with her. And so I am ready to give her for nothing, with the tale into the bargain. Anybody want her, good people? Be so kind. But if you will not please an old man in this way, at least do not send him away without a present on account of the story.

A Chapter of Foxes

The Fox and the Jackal

Once upon a time the little hungry Jackal was trotting in the fields, when he met the Fox who was going along carrying a little bit of paper in his teeth.

"Good evening, my dear," says the Fox, "whither are you hurrying?"

"I do not myself know whither. Wherever there is food to be had."

"Now if you yourself do not know, we will go together. There close at hand a flock of lambs is grazing. We will carry one off for our dinner."

"There is nothing better than lamb," says he, "only there are very vicious dogs about."

"But what of this that I have in my teeth? Do you know what this paper is?"

"How can I tell? I am no scholar."

"Look you. It is an order that the dogs are not to bite anybody if he wishes to eat the lambs. Go ahead, my good friend, and pick the best."

The Jackal rushed into the middle of the flock. As soon as the dogs saw him they leapt upon him and began to tear him to pieces. They worried him so that the fur flew! And he yelled out:

"Ai! Ai! O Fox! Give quickly thy order, quickly I beg thee... Oh my pain ..."

"Ah," said the Fox, "do not complain. Who knows these dogs?" he shouted to the Jackal. "They do not wish, I see, to read or to listen. You must get out of it, my friend, by yourself, and as well as you can."

And he ran away.

The Fox and the Barkantz

A Barkantz is a little lean hairy devil, who walks with his feet turned backwards. There was in hell a Barkantz-Dev so cunning that every day he carried in baskets to Satan the people he had deceived. And this Barkantz grew proud: "There is nothing," he thought, "in the world, which I have not deceived." Among devils thought is speech: all one. And, behold, a little devil heard his thought, and said:

"I have heard that of all things in the world the Fox is the most cunning. Have you tried to compete with him?"

The crafty Barkantz immediately sprang out on earth, and sought the Fox, and said to him:

"Now, let us make a wager together: he wins who deceives and dupes the other."

But the Fox rebuked him:

"What, what, Barkantz-Dev. It is now Lent. We cannot busy ourselves with such things. Come next Sunday, in the morning during the time when flesh is permitted; then we will contend."

On the following Sunday the Barkantz hurried up to the Fox. He was standing by his hole, leaning his back against an enormous rock. He saw the Barkantz and cried out:

"Clear off and do not get in the way. Never shall I be able to contend with you in cunning. You see I am holding up this rock so that it shall not crush in my earth. I cannot abandon it even for your sake: and, moreover, I have no sack for my trick; I have left it at home."

"Allow me; I will hold up the rock," says the Barkantz-Dev, "while you run for the sack."

The Fox agreed. The Barkantz-Dev supported the rock with his shoulder, and thought: "At this point I will loose the rock and let it crush the Fox."

He loosed it. The rock stood, as it stood before.

"Well now, get along with you, stupid Barkantz," cried the Fox from his earth, "you are fooled already."

"Ah, Satan commend me not," said the Barkantz, "truly you have tricked me this time. Let us try once more, and not count the matter as settled."

"What next?" replied the Fox. "Would you like me to take you to the river and bring you back again and not allow you to drink?"

The Barkantz-Dev set off with the Fox on this wager. They went to the river. They came to it. Suddenly the Fox looked round and said:

"But where are the witnesses?"

"What witnesses?" asked the Barkantz-Dev.

'Why you will say that you drank the water: I shall say that you did not drink. And so there will be no issue to our wager. We will go and seek witnesses."

They went back again. They passed by the Fox's earth and the Fox said:

"O Barkantz, were you just now beside the river?"

"I was."

"And did you drink the water?"

"No."

"Well, what more do you want? Get away home, and in future do not have the impertinence to contend with me."

The Black Fox

In a certain village near that place where the river Tiberda flows into the Kuban, where, they say, there are stones from the old castle of Chuan and Sinta, there lived in the old days an elderly man, by name Sheraluko, and he had a son, Shamil.

Now this Shamil was the most courageous of men, a tireless walker, a faultless marksman, but he had no luck. And without luck, do what you may, you will not succeed, and however well you aim you will only waste your bullets on the crows.

So it was with Shamil: he grew to manhood but acquired nothing for himself save a tattered kaftan.

It happened that Shamil went out for a whole week and killed nothing: no wild beast, no bird came in his way, and he turned home with an empty bag, scarcely alive from starvation. He turned home, but the old man, Sheraluko, his father, was already dead from hunger.

The young man wept from grief and from bitterness at his fate.

"Oh God!" said he. "Where then is thy truth? The idle ones, women in men's caps, give life and rejoice and feed their parents, but as for me, do what I will, my hair has gone grey from age, and the only end has been that I have killed my old father from hunger."

And Shamil left those parts, going whither his eyes led him. He went over our mountain, over the mountain of the crows, over the mountain of the magpies. He travelled as much country as there is between the mouth and the nose. He looked round; above him on a rock an eagle was sitting.

"Very well," thought Shamil. "If an eagle, then an eagle." And he took aim. But the eagle spoke to him in the voice of a man:

"Stay, O hunter Shamil, and do not kill me! What sort of food is my flesh? Better that I should drive up a goat for you and be able to be of use to you again."

Shamil lowered his gun and the dark-blue eagle rose and flew away and drove up to him a wild goat. When the huntsman shot it and began to prepare its flesh, the Eagle flew down to him, perched on a stone beside him and said:

"Shamil, here is a feather for you from my wing. If you think that I can be of service to you, burn this feather, and I will immediately fly to you, though you should be at the ends of the world."

The hunter took and hid away the feather, and went on. He had not gone far when suddenly a wild he-goat leapt out directly in front of him, and stood as if rooted to the ground at seeing a man.

Shamil was just throwing up his gun, when the he-goat spoke to him in the voice of a man:

"Do not shoot me, O Shamil; you are satisfied and you have still food to spare. Take rather a tuft of hair from my beard; if I can be of service to you, singe it, and I will appear, even if you should be beyond the seven seas."

Shamil spared the life of the he-goat, took a tuft of hair from him, and went on further.

He went on and on. He went far, he went a long way, God alone knows how far, he exhausted himself with weariness and hunger, and came at last to the great river Edil, or Volga, which, beyond the wandering Calmucks, flows into the Caspian Sea. Shamil lay down on the bank and looked into the water. He looked, and close under the bank a great Pike was quietly resting. He thrust his hand into the water of the river, caught the Pike by the gills, jerked it out on the bank,

and was just going to drive a dagger into it, when the Pike spoke in the voice of a man:

"Do not stab me, O hunter Shamil! Poor sort of food is my pike's flesh. Better for me to drive up to you as many little fish as you can want, and be able to be of use to you again."

Shamil granted this, and spared it. The Pike dived into the river, splashed with its tail, and Shamil had not time to look round before little fish came to the bank in crowds. So closely they came that you could see nothing in the water but the backs of fish. And from the midst of them the Pike spoke to him:

"O Shamil, step upon the backs of the fish and do not be afraid. On them, as if on dry land, you shall go over to the other bank."

And Shamil crossed over the great river Edil on the fish as if on a bridge. The Pike gave him one of its little scales and said:

"Take this scale. If can be of service to you, burn it in the fire, and I will appear, though you should be on the summit of Oshchamach where as yet no human foot has trod."

The hunter went on further, over desert plains and deep sands. He had not eaten or drunk for a whole day when suddenly from a mound leapt out a black Fox. Shamil took aim with his gun, but it called out to him:

"Hold! Do not shoot me, O Shamil the hunter! My flesh is not good and I can be of service to you."

The marksman lowered his gun, and the Fox said:

"Keep always straight on along the track on which you are going. You will come to a great town where the Princess has already been the death of ninety and nine suitors. Fearlessly ask her in marriage. When, unavoidably, the last difficulty is upon you, then burn in the fire this hair from my tail — it is the only white one of all that I have — and I will appear to help you, even though you should be above the seventh cloud."

He spoke and disappeared, as if he had sunk into the earth. Shamil hid away the white hair from the black Fox and went on further without eating. For twelve whole days he

255

neither ate nor drank but always went on and on. And the further he went the braver and the gayer he grew. He came to a big town, white and red. He almost danced.

"May you live long yet, baboushka," said Shamil to an old woman whom he met. "May you yet be the delight of two husbands!"

"What are husbands to me, my son! I have already outlived five. Whither are your legs carrying you?"

Shamil told her, and the old woman said:

"In our town lives that very Princess who has already been the ruin of ninety-nine suitors. She orders each of her suitors to hide himself three times. If she finds him all three times he loses his head from his shoulders. If even once she fails to find him, that man will she take as her husband. Only how should she fail to find him when she has, so they say, a magic tube, through which she sees every grain of dust in all the world? The Princess is of unspeakable loveliness."

"Well, I shall go and ask her in marriage, for it is all the same to me," said Shamil.

"Ah, handsome one, do not go, unless you have a spare head in your pocket. But if you go, do not forget; you are the hundredth suitor; the Princess will allow the hundredth to hide a fourth time. Then remember me."

The old woman was and she was not. She vanished, only at a corner it was as if there flashed the tail of a black Fox.

Shamil went up to the Tzar's palace, and told the Tzar that he wished to be a suitor for his daughter. The Tzar was a kind man. For a long time already he had been tired of seeing them cut off the heads of young suitors on account of the Princess. Moreover Shamil was pleasing to him, and he began to dissuade him.

"No," said. Shamil. "My life is such that should your daughter cut off my head, it will be no loss to me."

And the Princess called from another room:

"Round my garden runs a hedge which is not yet quite finished. On ninety-nine stakes are the heads of my suitors, but the hundredth stands uncrowned. Your head will fit this stake precisely. Well, rest today from the road, and tomorrow hide for the first time."

All night long Shamil considered where best to hide, and could think of nowhere. In the morning he walked out in the country and remembered the eagle's feather. He kindled a fire, burned the feather: the eagle came flying.

"What do you need, O hunter Shamil?"

"Hide me, if you can, so that the Princess shall not find me."

"Get on my back."

And the Eagle took him to the far-away mountain Gurd-jeesh, where its nest was, hid him in its nest, and sat itself above him.

In the morning the Princess went out on the roof and began to look round with her magic tube. She looked to the right, she looked to the left, before and behind, above and below: she did not see Shamil. Midday came and she saw him: how the Eagle hid the hunter in its nest but had not noticed that a corner of his kaftan could just be seen. By this little corner the Princess found Shamil.

The next morning Shamil burnt the goat's hairs. The goat was instantly before him.

"Oh hide me," said Shamil, "so that the Princess shall not perceive me."

The Goat took him into the far-away hills, and hid him in a narrow cave, and itself blocked up the entrance. All day long the Princess sought for the hunter and could not see him. It was already near evening when the Goat shook a fly from its head: and the Princess found Shamil.

On the third day he summoned the Pike. The Pike swallowed him and went off with him into the river Edil, into a deep pool. The Princess looked and looked, from early morning till the evening. The sun was actually setting and Shamil was nowhere to be seen. She was just going to put away the tube, when she looked round. The Pike held out no longer, opened its jaws to swallow a fish, and there was Shamil sitting in the Pike.

"So that is where he got to," said the Princess. "Well, he is clever, but all the same tomorrow he will be without a head."

Shamil presented himself before the Princess and asked her to allow him to hide another time, the fourth. Perhaps because he was pleasing to her, or because he was the hundredth, or because the Tzar, her father, asked her, she agreed.

"Very well," she said, "hide yourself for the last time. It is all the same. If not tomorrow then on the day after tomorrow, you will be without a head."

And Shamil, the hunter, this time became thoughtful. It was not terrible to him to die, but it was terrible not to win the Princess. He went in the morning into the country, and set fire to his last hope, the fox's hair. Scarcely was the hair alight before the fox was beside him.

"Good day," said he. "And what do you wish?"

"Now, O Fox, save me," begged Shamil. "The unavoidable difficulty has come upon me. I must hide from the Princess or she will not take me for her husband."

258

The black Fox unfastened the sack of his wiles and turned into a red-bearded Jew, and made Shamil a flea. As soon as the Princess was awake the Jew went up close to the palace and cried out:

"Behold! Fine wares for the young Princess! See my fine wares!"

The Princess heard and ordered that the merchant should be summoned. He undid his bundle of goods, and Shamil the flea hopped out, and hid in the bosom of the Princess, under her bodice, and sat there, dissembling himself.

All day the Princess looked from the roof of the palace. The evening came, the sun set, black night began, and no Shamil anywhere to be found. The Princess clutched her magic tube, and in vexation dashed it on the stones. The Tzar, her father, came and asked her:

"Well, little daughter, have you found the young man?"

"No, batiushka, he has outwitted me. Most probably he is frightened and will not even now show his face."

Instantly the Flea leapt from under the Princess's bodice, fell on the ground — and Shamil stood before the Princess.

"No, Princess, here I am! All day long as a little flea I have hidden in your white bosom."

The Princess grew red. But the Tzar, her father, rejoiced, and laughed till his sides shook.

"You are outwitted," said he, "little daughter. You have had enough of sitting unwed. Marry the cunning one. He will make a good husband for you."

And the poor hunter Shamil married the Princess. And he became Tzar on the death of his father-in-law. Cleverly he ruled his state, and vanquished all his enemies.

Concerning the Poor Man Covetous

The poor man, Avner, and his wife, Iska, had seven children, and nothing with which to feed them. Things came in the end to such a point that their little youngest son grew weaker, and yet weaker, until he was at the point of death from hunger.

"We'll get out of the house," said Iska to her husband; "perhaps you do not know that, according to the custom, it is not permissible for a father to be present at the death of his child? Go along, solicit alms, or we shall all die of hunger."

Avner set out. He wandered this way and that; nobody gave him a morsel of bread, for his people were as poor as himself. He was just going to turn back to his hut, when suddenly there came to meet him a venerable old man, well dressed in the ancient manner, with stern eyes. This old man called the beggar, and questioned him: was he of the true faith, did he obey all the rules of the Sabbath, did he not eat forbidden food? All these things he inquired in detail. But when Avner confessed that from bitter need it happened to him to sin against the law, the old man took out of his bosom a little copper bowl, and from his pocket a gold three-rouble piece, gave them to the beggar, and said: "This ducat will suffice you to bury your son and to get food for your family until the Sabbath. And on the night of Friday you must place this bowl under your pillow. In the morning you will find a gold piece in it, and so it will be every week, in order that you shall not sin from poverty."

A ducat is a rich alms, and Avner rejoiced in it even more than in the bowl. Thinks he: "It must be that the old man is laughing at me. What miracles are there in our sinful days?" But on Friday evening, all the same, he put the bowl under his pillow. His wife urged him to it.

"Why not put it there? Put it. It is not as though there could be any harm in doing that."

In the morning they looked, and in very truth there was a new ducat in the bowl. The law, of course, did not allow them to take it on the Sabbath; but it was permissible to look at it. They set out, Avner and Iska, to examine the bowl, a very simple, polished, little copper bowl. Only, on the edge of it was engraved a certain strange mark, and at the bottom of the bowl was a ducat, new and shining. On the next Sabbath there was again a ducat in the cup, and a week later again another.

"This is good," said the husband. "It is sufficient for our necessities, and other things I can earn."

"Much you will earn!" replied his wife. "Think! If in place of a single ducat two were produced, why then it would be possible to put something by, and set up some sort of business. Do you know what I wonder? Whether all its power is not in the sign which is on the bowl. One sign, one ducat. Take the bowl to the engraver Nachshon and tell him to engrave another sign on it exactly like the first."

"But what if the bowl is altogether spoilt?"

"What! Because of such a tiny little sign! Tell Nachshon to grave carefully, and not too deep."

The husband also had a mind to see if he could not receive more money. He went to Nachshon, the engraver, and Nachshon the engraver graved a sign for him on the edge of the bowl in every particular like the first. Friday came, and they put the bowl under the pillow. All night long they did not sleep. They could hardly wait till the morning. And when they looked in the bowl they saw not one, but two gold pieces!

"Well! Didn't I tell you? Take the bowl back to the engraver, and let him place signs all over it, both inside and outside."

"But what if it is spoilt altogether?" said the husband. "We had better try once more. Let him again place but one third little sign."

The engraver placed a third sign, and on the next Sabbath there appeared three ducats. After that the husband was no longer afraid. He and his wife began to count together; how many signs there was room for on the bowl, how many ducats they would get every week. They counted a great number. Then they began to think what they would do with the money.

Avner said: "I am going to buy up carpets from the makers and gold and silver things, and cart them to the big town. Good merchants make much profit by that — double."

But Iska disagreed: "So that's your idea! You will ride to town, but I am to sit here and have no peace with the children! I, too, wish to live in the big town. I wish to wear fine clothes, gold, precious stones. I wish to live in a fine house of my own and have many servants. I wish to go to the bath every week and live like the rich merchants' wives."

They argued and argued. They quarrelled, and the husband gave his wife a thrashing. Now, this had never happened before.

Next morning as soon as it was light, Avner took the bowl and ran with it to the engraver. Nachshon, the engraver, looked it over, and considered, and said: "There is a deal of work to this. I shall not take less than three gold pieces."

There was nothing to be done, and Avner agreed to the price. He had the last three ducats still untouched, but there was nothing left of the two from the week before. "We will rub along," he thought, "somehow or other, even if we go on short commons. And it will be for the last time!"

On the Friday morning Avner got his bowl. The whole of it, outside and inside, was covered with signs, and every sign was exactly like the first. Not for nothing did the engraver take his three gold pieces. They began, Avner and Iska, to count the signs. They counted all day, and made out one thousand and fifty and two.

"Oh what a pity the bowl is so small," said Iska, and her husband was also sorry that the bowl was not larger.

The sun went down and the night came, and with it the joyful Sabbath descended on the earth. Iska laid the supper on the table — nothing but a pot of millet gruel, and for that she had borrowed the millet from a neighbour. It was a poor Sabbath meal. Well, no matter, it was the last of its kind, and the next day there would be the whole pile of gold.

Suddenly somebody knocked on the door. Now, a guest to the Sabbath meal is the ambassador of God. Avner threw open the door and there came in that same old man who had given him the bowl and the ducat.

"May the Holy Sabbath be bright for you, good people!"

"You are too kind, father," Avner replied.

"But why do you make so poor a meal? Why, you have not even lit a candle for the holiday. Does not my bowl help you? Where do you keep it?" The bowl was standing on a shelf close to the table. The old man took it, looked it over, and said: "Truly, insatiable is the heart of man; there is no limit to his greed for gold! Better it is to be the poor man's son, for his poverty is his justification, than to be the son of the rich. Eh! What is that over there in the corner?"

They all looked round at the dark corner, but there was nothing there. They turned again to the old man, and he was nowhere to be seen. He had disappeared, and the bowl had disappeared with him.

And so it came about that the poor man Avner had again to beg for charity. He asked for alms, and said to everyone who gave to him: "Spit in my face, good man, and smite me. I deserve it."

The Little Cattle

There was a lad named Ivan, who kept an inn, on the great road from Novgorod to Moscow. And in those days the vodka was good warming liquor, and the pedlars and drovers and pilgrims going north and other travellers would rest their legs at Ivan's inn, and wet their gullets before getting on along the road. And there was good straw and even soft rushes in the loft where men slept who stayed the night through. And Ivan was a good fellow and was not one of those who are afraid to take a drink themselves so that other men may drink the sweeter. But, for all that, the inn was unlucky. Few who slept there one night had any wish to sleep there again. And fair-minded guests would often go off in the morning without paying, offering blows instead of money, aye, even if fresh rushes had been laid for them, and they given a double share of straw for their bedding.

And the reason for that was the rats and the mice that ran upon that inn like flies in summer on a dried fish, and even built thickets through the straw at night, and filled the quiet of the dark hours with their weddings and feastings and running to and fro.

It was they that gave the inn a bad name. There was hardly a pedlar or a drover who took that road who would not raise his voice to curse his sleepless nights in Ivan's inn. And this though Ivan was a good fellow and his vodka had no water in it.

One night — it was about the time of the cattle fair in Novgorod — a night with a clear moon it was, and the back end of the year, Ivan was sitting in his inn, waiting for folk to call in and ask for vodka and hot tea, when the door opened, and an old drover fellow came over the threshold. He was just like any other drover, with a fur cap, and a tall stick. He was just like any other drover, all but his eyes.

And those eyes of his were quiet eyes. They did not look at Ivan as if to see what could be made out of him. They looked as if they were afraid of nothing, and wanted nothing.

And the old drover smiled at Ivan, and bid him a good evening. And Ivan smiled at the old drover and gave him the same greeting. He could do nothing else, with those eyes upon him.

And the drover calls for a glass of vodka. "For it's cold travelling this night," says he, "and there's frost under the moon."

And Ivan pours him a glass of vodka.

"You'll have a glass yourself," says the stranger, smiling with those quiet eyes.

And Ivan pours a glass of vodka for himself.

With that they fell to drinking their vodka, and talking of many things. And so the time went by.

And at last the old drover, he fixes Ivan with those quiet eyes of his, and he says, "It so happens that I have not a silver rouble on me, nor yet a copper piece. And so, brother, you'll have to thank me for the vodka. I'll pay you some time, never fear."

Now Ivan was a good fellow, but no fool, and he'd have thrashed the life out of you and me, if we'd had a drink of good vodka, and then let out that we had no money to pay for our warm gullets. But he looked in the eyes of that old drover, and he did not lift a finger.

"God be with you," says he, "pay me when you can. And let us have another glass of vodka together, and think no more of that."

So Ivan and the drover had another glass of vodka apiece, and fell to talking again. And the more they talked the friendlier they grew, until at the last they were like brothers back from the wars, smiling in each other's faces, and it was Ivan who was sorry when the old drover took his stick, and gave him the blessing of God, and said it was time he was getting on his way.

And says he to the drover, as one friend to another, "What are you driving tonight? Is it big cattle or little? Oxen or sheep?"

And the old drover smiled at Ivan, and he says, quietly: "Tonight I am driving very little cattle."

And with that he was out of the door.

The inn seemed cheerless without him, and Ivan got up, and went to the door of the inn, to look after him going down the road.

And there was the drover, striding away in the moonlight with his tall stick. And for a minute Ivan was looking for his cattle, and could not see them. And then, suddenly, he saw the road before the drover was grey and moving. And there on the road were thousands upon thousands of rats and mice, moving in the moonlight. And behind them walked the old drover, never looking back.

From that day on the sleeping at Ivan's inn was as good as any in Russia. There was not a mouse or a rat in the place. The old drover had driven them all before him along the road to Novgorod.

And some time after that, it happens that Ivan had business with a neighbour who was known for a cunning fellow. And to get the better of the neighbour, Ivan thought it would be just as well to burn a candle to Saint Nicholas and get the Saint's help in the affair. So off he goes to the church, and buys his candle, and lights it, and is praying for help in the business, when, just as he reaches up to set the candle before the holy picture of Saint Nicholas, he looks up and sees the eyes of the holy picture smiling down upon him. And the eyes were the quiet eyes of the old drover who drove the very little cattle on the road from Ivan's inn.

And there, beside the candle, just below the picture, was the price of the two glasses of vodka.

The Gypsy and Saint George

Once upon a time there was a Gypsy who lived honestly and so had nothing to eat. Things went so badly for him that he had nothing to drink, and that was worse. So this Gypsy, he ups and walks along the high road thinking how he shall get a pint of ale.

This Gypsy he comes to a stand in the road, a-twisting of a straw in his mouth, a-listening to the cuckoo, and a-thinking he could well do with a drop of something to make his own throat as easy as the bird's.

And just as the Gypsy was thinking that thought there comes Saint George himself, riding round the corner of the road, on a great white horse, with silver armour on him, and a gold bridle in the horse's mouth, and reins to put the sun out for jealousy, and golden stirrups, and the horse's hooves all covered with pure gold. And Saint George, he was leaning over his horse's neck, and the gold hooves were beating on the road, and the horse was all in a lather, and his nostrils blowing flecks of foam.

And this Gypsy, he stands in the middle of the road, and he shifts a straw from one side of his mouth and puts it in the other with a twist of his tongue, and he says, "Good day," says this Gypsy, "and what is the hurry?"

"I ride to Heaven," says Saint George.

"And what for?" says this Gypsy, stroking the horse's nose and looking at the golden bridle.

"For orders," says Saint George, "how each man is to live, and what he is to do for a living."

"Tell Please-God about me too," says this Gypsy, "and ask him how I am to make ends meet."

"I'll tell him," says Saint George, and with that he clattered off along the road, galloping, galloping, on his way to Heaven, so that there was no seeing the glitter of his armour for the cloud of dust raised by the golden hooves.

And this Gypsy he twisted his straw back to the other side of his mouth, and watched Saint George till he was out of sight, and then he lay down at the side of the road and waited till evening.

At evening by the light of the moon Saint George comes riding home, the great horse going step by step lifting his golden hooves like ton weights and putting them down as though he were tired of them, with the golden reins loose on his neck, and Saint George all of a hunch in the saddle, like a man asleep. And this Gypsy he ups and stops Saint George and rubs his horse's nose.

"You are not in a hurry," says he.

"I am not," says Saint George.

"And why is that?" says this Gypsy.

"I ride from Heaven," says Saint George.

"Did you tell Please-God about me and ask him what I am to do for a living?"

"I did not."

"And why not?" says this Gypsy.

"I forgot," says Saint George, and with that he rode on slowly down the road, with the moonlight on his silver armour. And this Gypsy, he stood in the road, looking after him, a-sucking on his straw.

Next morning this Gypsy was waiting in the road at the same place, a-sucking of his straw, a-listening to the cuckoo, and a-thinking of his thirst. And sure enough Saint George comes riding like the wind on his way to Heaven to take his orders from Please-God. And again this Gypsy asks him: "Tell Please-God about me and ask him what I am to do to keep body and soul together."

"I will," says Saint George, and rides on, and this Gypsy sleeps through the day till late evening when the moon was high and Saint George comes riding slowly back.

"And have you asked him?" says this Gypsy.

"I forgot," says Saint George, and goes riding on his way like a man asleep.

And there was this Gypsy real mad, for his thirst would not bear thinking of, and he had nothing to eat.

The third day Saint George would have ridden by and not spoken to this Gypsy, he was in such a hurry and tear to be on his way to Heaven. But this Gypsy he catches the great horse by his golden rein, and he ups and says to Saint George, "Now, this time, will you tell Please-God about me and ask him what I am to do for a living, or will you not?"

"Let go of my horse," says Saint George, but this Gypsy, he holds tight, and rubs the horse's nose, and asks again:

"Will you tell him?"

"I will," says Saint George, "but you let go of my horse."

"You will forget," says this Gypsy.

"I will not forget," says Saint George.

"Give me one of your golden stirrups," says this Gypsy. "I'll keep it till you come back. Then, perhaps, you will not be forgetting."

And Saint George, he was in such a tear and hurry to be on his way to Heaven, that he off with one of his golden stirrups, and gave it to this Gypsy. And this Gypsy loosed the horse's rein, and Saint George, he gave a shout, and the great horse plunged, and they were out of sight in a moment.

So Saint George left the Gypsy looking at the golden stirrup, and galloped and galloped, till he came to the Gate of Heaven, where Saint Peter nodded as he rode by, and Saint George, he nodded to Saint Peter. He rode through Heaven and came to Please-God, and took his orders, how this man was to be a baker, and that man a blacksmith, how this man was to be a shepherd and that man a learned doctor with more books than most folk would read in a lifetime and a half. And when he had his orders he was riding slowly through the Holy Gate out of Heaven on his way back to this world, when Saint Peter who was sitting in the gateway keeping count of them that came in, looks up at Saint George as he sat there hunched in the saddle on the great white horse, and says he, "Why, George, you have lost a stirrup."

"Stirrup," says Saint George, "why brother of mine, that's to remind me of that Gypsy fellow away there down the road. I'd all but forgotten him again." And with that he turns his horse and rides back into Heaven, and tells Please-God how a Gypsy stopped him in the road and asked what he was to do for a living.

"This shall be the trade of that Gypsy," says Please-God. "What he gets, that shall he keep, and the way of it shall be cheating and lying."

Saint George rode off, passed the time of day with Saint Peter at the Holy Gate, and at night found this Gypsy waiting in the moonlight at the roadside, a-sucking of his straw.

"Well, Gypsy," says he, "you were right. If you hadn't kept the stirrup, I'd have forgotten you again."

"I thought so," says this Gypsy. "But you'll never forget me now. Every time you look at your stirrup you'll remember me. But tell me, what did Please-God say?"

"He said that what you get that you shall keep and the way of it will be lying and cheating."

"Thank you," says this Gypsy. "He said that, did he?" and this Gypsy, he settled his straw in the corner of his mouth, and turned on his heel and walked off.

"Stop a minute," says Saint George, "where are you off to? What about that stirrup?"

"What stirrup?"

"Why, my stirrup, my golden stirrup, the one you took."

"I never took a stirrup from you. I never saw you in my life before," says this Gypsy. "Shame upon you! Here's a great gentleman, and a saint at that, saying a poor gypsy stole his golden stirrup. I've never taken a stirrup from anybody, and how would I take one, tell me that, from such a man as you. So help me God, I know nothing at all about it."

Well, they argued for a long time, and Saint George gave this Gypsy a thrashing, but that did not mend matters. And the end of it was that Saint George rode home without his stirrup, and rode to Heaven next day without it, and has ridden with one stirrup ever since.

But this Gypsy he shook himself, and twisted his straw to the other side of his mouth, and took the golden stirrup out of

273

the bushes where he had hidden it, and went off to look for a buyer. And he sold it, and stole it, and sold it again, and lives well to this day, eating well and drinking well, cheating and lying and never doing a stroke of work.

The Blacksmith in Heaven

There lived in the world a blacksmith who never took any money for his work. He would mend a wheel or shoe a horse for you, and when you would be asking him what was to pay, he would smile at you and say, "Nothing at all, friend," and wish you good luck on your journey.

People came to know that he never took any money for his work. They did not offer it to him. But when he had shoed a horse for them they said, "May God reward you!" and rode away with their money jingling in their pockets.

Time went on, and the blacksmith grew old, and died, and went to the other world. He went walking through the other world till he came to the Gate of Heaven, and through the gate he could see the shining grass of Paradise and the saints walking to and fro upon it picking flowers. And there was the Holy Peter standing at the gate jangling his golden keys.

And Peter looks at the blacksmith, and says he: "Why have you come here?"

"Well," says the blacksmith, "I have died, haven't I? Where should I go?"

And with that the Holy Peter opened the Gate of Heaven, and let the blacksmith through.

So the blacksmith walked through the Gate of Heaven into Paradise and walked there upon that shining grass, looking at the saints and other folk. And far before him, in Paradise, he saw a great and blazing light, and he went towards it and came to it, and saw, as he came nearer, that it was God Himself, sitting on his golden throne.

God saw the blacksmith, standing there with his cap in his hand, and God beckoned to him.

So the blacksmith went up to the very throne of God, and stood at the foot of the golden throne, and waited.

"Many folk have prayed that I should reward you for your

good work," said God. "Tell me now how you would wish that I should reward you."

And the blacksmith stood and scratched his head. At last says he: "O Lord God, I need nothing at all. But if You wish to reward me, perhaps, just for one day You would let me sit on Your golden throne, and see the angels walking below me on the shining grass of Paradise."

"Very well," says God to the blacksmith; "sit you here."

And with that God got up from His throne, and came down the steps, and went off to walk and to amuse himself in Paradise. And there was that blacksmith, scratching his head and looking at the empty throne.

For just a moment the blacksmith was afraid; but then thinks he to himself, "I may never have the chance again." And with that he runs up the golden steps, and sits him down on the very throne of God.

No sooner had he sat down there than the world lay open before him. There was no secret for him in the world. Nothing was hidden from him in the earth or on the earth, on the sea or in the sea, and he knew the very hearts of the birds flying in the blue air. It was no pleasure to him, but sorrow more terrible than he could bear. For he saw all that went on in the dealings of men with each other, cheating and lies and hate and little biting malices. He knew each secret thought of everyone in the world. The whole meanness and wickedness of man was clear to him. He tried to jump up from the throne, but could not. He tried to cry out and curse mankind for the evil of their hearts, but the words were choked in his throat. And suddenly he saw that God Himself was standing there below the throne watching him.

"No," says God to him, "sit you there, and watch and suffer. You, who cannot sit there for one minute, see only what I see. I sit on that throne for ever, age after age, and see all the evil that is done or dreamed, and am patient with it. Let you be patient too."

But the blacksmith fell senseless from the golden throne at the feet of God on the shining grass of Paradise. And God lifted him tenderly in His arms and said:

"Every just soul is patient at the sight of wickedness. But no man's soul is strong enough to bear the sight of all the evil with which the world is filled. The soul of man is saved alive only because it does not know the whole evil of the world. You did not know what it was you asked of Me. Better if I myself choose how to reward you. This shall be the reward of your good life, that you shall go back to earth and be a good man, as you have been so far."

And God kissed him, and went up the golden steps, and sat once more upon the throne, looking beyond Paradise, and seeing the wickedness of all the world.

The blacksmith, staggering like a drunken man, passed out through the Gate of Heaven. And the Holy Peter, standing at the gate, jangled his keys and wondered.

Somewhere or other the blacksmith lives on earth today, shoeing horses and taking no money but content if people ride on their way leaving nothing behind them but the words, "May God reward you!"

277

The Soldier and Death

A soldier served God and the Great Tzar for twenty-five years, earned three dry biscuits, and set off to walk his way home. He kissed his companions with whom he had served so long, and boasted of the feasting there would be in the village when he should come marching home with all his wars behind him. Singing at the top of his voice he was as he set off. But as soon as he was alone on the high road, walking through the forest, he began to think things over. And he thought to himself: "All these years I have served the Tzar and had good clothes to my back and my belly full of victuals. And now I am like to be both hungry and cold. Already I've nothing but three dry biscuits."

Just then he met an old beggar, who stood in the road and crossed himself and asked alms for the love of God.

The soldier had not a copper piece in the world, so he gave the beggar one of his three dry biscuits.

He had not gone very far along the road when he met a second beggar, who lent on a stick and recited holy words and begged alms for the love of God.

The soldier gave him the second of his three dry biscuits.

And then, at a bend in the road, he met a third old beggar, with long white hair and beard and loathsome rags, who stood shaking by the roadside and begged alms for the love of God.

"If I give him my last dry biscuit I shall have nothing left for myself," thought the soldier. He gave the old beggar half of the third dry biscuit. Then the thought came into his head that perhaps this old beggar would meet the other two, and would learn that they had been given whole biscuits while he had been given only a half. "He will be hurt and affronted," thought the soldier, "and his blessing will be of no avail." So he gave the old beggar the other half also of the third of his three dry biscuits. "I shall get along somehow," thought the soldier, and was for making forward on his way. But the old beggar put out his hand and stopped him.

"Brother," says the old beggar, "are you in want of anything?"

"God bless you," says the soldier, looking at the beggar's rags, "I want nothing from you. You're a poor man yourself."

"Never mind my poverty," says the old beggar. "Just tell me what you would like to have, and I am well able to reward you for your kind heart."

"I don't want anything," said the soldier; "but if you do happen to have such a thing as a pack of cards about you, I'd keep them in memory of you, and they'd be a pleasure to me on the long road."

The old beggar thrust his hand into his bosom among his rags, and pulled out a pack of cards.

"Take these," says he, "and when you play with them you'll always be winner whoever may be playing against you." And here's a sack for you as well. If you meet anything and want to catch it, just open the sack and tell beasts or birds or aught else to get into it and they'll do just that, and you can close the sack and do with them what you will."

279

"Thank you kindly," says the soldier, throws the sack over his shoulder, puts the pack of cards in his pocket, and trudges off along the high road singing an old song.

He went on and on till he came to a lake, where he drank a little water to ease his thirst, and smoked a pipe to put off his hunger, resting by the shore of the lake. And there on the lake he saw three wild geese swimming far away. "Now if I could catch them!" thought the soldier, and remembered the sack the old beggar had given him. He opened the sack and shouted at the top of his voice: "Hi! You there, you wild geese, come into my sack!"

And the three wild geese splashed up out of the water, and flew to the bank and crowded into the sack, one after the other.

The soldier tied up the mouth of the sack, flung it over his shoulder and went on his way.

He came to a town, and looked for a tavern, and chose the best he could see, and went in there and asked for the land-lord.

"See here," says he, "here are three wild geese. I want one of them roasted for my dinner. Another I'll give you in exchange for a bottle of vodka. The third you shall have to pay you for your trouble."

The landlord agreed, as well he might, and presently the soldier was seated at a good table near a window, with a whole bottle of the best vodka, and a fine roast goose fresh from the kitchen.

When he made an end of the goose, the soldier laid down his knife and fork, tipped the last drops of the vodka down his throat, and set the bottle upside down upon the table. Then he lit his little pipe, sat back on the bench and took a look out of the window to see what was going on in the town.

And there on the other side of the road was a fine palace, well carved and painted. A year's work had gone to the carving of every doorpost and window-frame. But in all the palace there was not one whole pane of glass.

"Landlord," says the soldier, "tell me what's the meaning of this? Why is a fine palace like that standing empty with broken windows?"

"It's a good enough palace," says the landlord. "The Tzar built the palace for himself, but there's no living in it because of the devils."

"Devils?" says the soldier.

"Devils," says the landlord. "Every night they crowd into the palace, and, what with their shouting and yelling and screaming and playing cards, and all the other devilries that come into their heads, there's no living in the palace for decent folk."

"And does nobody clear them out?" asks the soldier.

"Easier said than done," says the landlord.

Well, with that the soldier wishes good health to the landlord, and sets off to see the Tzar. He comes walking into the Tzar's house and gives him a salute.

"Your Majesty," says he, "will you give me leave to spend one night in your empty palace?"

"God bless you," says the Tzar, "but you don't know what you are asking. Foolhardy folk enough have tried to spend a night in that palace. They went in merry and boasting, but not one of them came walking out alive in the morning."

"What of that?" says the soldier. "Water won't drown a Russian soldier, and fire won't burn him. I have served God and the Tzar for twenty-five years and am not dead. A single night in that palace won't be the end of me."

"But I tell you: a man walks in there alive in the evening, and in the morning the servants have to search the floor for the little bits of his bones."

"None the less," says the soldier, "If your Majesty will give me leave..."

"Get along with you and God be with you," says the Tzar. "Spend the night there, if you've set your heart on it."

So the soldier came to the palace and stepped in, singing through the empty rooms. He made himself comfortable in the biggest room of all, laid his sack in a corner and hung his sword on a nail, sat down at the table, took out his bag of tobacco, filled his little pipe, and sat there smoking, ready for what might come.

Twelve o'clock sharp and there was a yelling, a shouting, a blowing of horns, a scraping of fiddles and every other kind of instrument, a noise of dancing, of running, of stamping, and the palace cram full of devils making themselves at home as if the place belonged to them.

"And you, soldier?" cried the devils. "What are you sitting there so glum for, smoking your pipe? There's smoke enough where we have been. Put your pipe in your pocket and play a round of cards with us."

"Right you are," says the soldier, "if you'll play with my cards."

"Deal them out," shouted the devils, and the soldier put his pipe in his pocket and dealt out the cards, while the devils crowded round the table fighting for room on the benches.

They played a game and the soldier won. They played another and he won again. The devils were cunning enough, God knows, but not all their cunning could win a single game for them. The soldier was raking in the money all the time. Soon enough the devils had not a penny piece between them, and the soldier was for putting up his cards and lighting his pipe. Content he was, and well he might be, with his pockets bulging with money.

"Stop a minute, soldier," said the devils, "we've still got sixty bushels of silver and forty of gold. We'll play for them if you'll give us time to send for them."

"Let's see the silver," says the soldier, and puts the cards in his pocket.

Well, they sent a little devil to fetch the silver. Sixty times he ran out of the room and sixty times he came staggering back with a bushel of silver on his shoulders.

The soldier pulled out his cards, and they played on, but it was all the same. The devils cheated in every kind of way, but could not win a game.

"Go and fetch the gold," says the oldest devil.

"Aye, aye, grandfather," says the little devil, and goes

scuttling out of the room. Forty times he ran out, and forty times he came staggering back with a bushel of gold between his shoulders.

They played on. The soldier won every game and all the gold, asked if they had any more money to lose, put his cards in his pocket and lit his pipe.

The devils looked at all the money they had lost. It seemed a pity to lose all the good silver and gold.

"Tear him to pieces, brothers," they cried, "tear him to pieces, eat him and have done!"

The soldier tapped his little pipe on the table.

"First make sure," says he, "who eats whom." And with that he whips out his sack, and, says he, to the devils, who were all gnashing their teeth and making ready to fall on him, "What do you call this?"

"It's a sack," said the devils.

"Is it?" says the soldier. "Then, by the word of God, get into it!"

And the next minute all those devils were tumbling over each other and getting into the sack, squeezing in one on the top of another until the last one had got inside. Then the soldier tied up the sack with a good double knot, hung it on a nail, and lay down to sleep.

In the morning the Tzar sent his servants.

"Go," says the Tzar, "and see what has happened to the soldier who spent the night in the empty palace. If the unclean spirits have made an end of him, then you must sweep up what is left of his bones."

The servants came, all ready to lament for the brave soldier done to death by the unclean, and there was the soldier walking cheerfully from one room to another, smoking his little pipe.

"Well done, soldier! We never thought to see you alive. And how did you spend the night? How did you manage against the devils?"

"Devils?" says the soldier. "I wish all men I have played cards against had paid their debts so honestly. Have a look at the silver and gold I won from them. Look at the heaps of money lying on the floor."

The servants looked at the silver and gold and touched it to see if it was real. But there was no doubt about that. I wish I had more in my pocket of the same sort.

"Now, brothers," said the soldier, "off with you as quick as you can, go and fetch two blacksmiths here on the run. And let them bring with them an iron anvil and the two heaviest hammers in the forge."

The servants asked no questions, but hurried to the smithy, and the two blacksmiths came running, with anvil and hammers. Giants they were, the strongest men in all the town.

"Now," says the soldier, "take that sack from the nail and lay it on the anvil and let me see how the blacksmiths of this town can set about their work."

The blacksmiths took the sack from the nail.

"Devil take it, what a weight," they said to each other.

And little voices screamed out of the sack: "We are good folk. We are your own people."

"Are you?" said the blacksmiths; and they laid the sack on the anvil and swung the great hammers, up and down, up and down, as if they were beating out a lump of iron.

The devils fared badly in there, and worse and worse. The hammers came down as if they were going through devils, anvil, earth, and all. It was more than even devils could bear.

"Have mercy!" they screamed. "Have mercy, soldier! Let us out again into the world, and we'll never forget you world without end. And as for this palace... no devil shall put the nail of the toe of his foot in it. We'll tell them all. Not one shall come within a hundred miles."

The soldier let the blacksmiths give a few more blows, just for luck. Then he stopped them, and untied the mouth of the sack. The moment he opened it, the devils shot out, and fled away to hell without looking right or left in their hurry.

But the soldier was no fool, and he grabbed one old devil by the leg. And the devil hung gibbering, trying to get away. The soldier cut the devil's hairy wrist to the bone, so that the blood flowed, took a pen, dipped it in the blood, and gave it to the devil. But he never let go of his leg.

"Write," says he, "that you will be my faithful servant."

The old devil screamed and wriggled, but the soldier gripped him tight. There was nothing to be done. He wrote and signed in his own blood a promise to serve the soldier faithfully wherever and whenever there should be need. Then the soldier let him go, and he went hopping and screaming after the others, and had disappeared in a moment.

And so the devils went rushing down to hell, aching in every bone of their hairy bodies. And they called all the other unclean spirits, old and young, big and little, and told what had happened to them. And they set sentinels all round hell, and guards at every gate, and ordered them to watch well, and, whatever they did, not on any account to let in the soldier with the sack.

The soldier went to the Tzar and told him how he had dealt with the devils, and how henceforth no devil would set foot within a hundred miles of the palace.

"If that's so," says the Tzar, "we'll move at once and go and live there, and you shall live with me and be honoured as my own brother." And with that there was a great to do shifting the bedding and tables and benches and all else from the old palace to the new, and the soldier set up house with the Tzar, living with him as his own brother, and wearing fine clothes with gold embroidery, and eating the same food as the Tzar, and as much of it as he liked. Money to spend he had, for he had won from the devils enough to last even a spending man a thousand years. And he had nothing to spend it on. Hens don't eat gold. No more do mice. And there the money lay in a corner till the soldier was tired of looking at it.

So the soldier thought he would marry. And he took a wife, and in a year's time God gave him a son, and he had nothing more to wish for except to see the son grow up and turn into a general.

But it so happened that the little boy fell ill, and what was the matter with him no one knew. He grew worse and worse from day to day, and the Tzar sent for every doctor in the country, but not one of them did him a half-pennyworth of good. The doctors grew richer and the boy grew no better but worse, as is often the way.

The soldier had almost given up hope of saving his son when he remembered the old devil who had signed a promise written in his own blood to serve the soldier faithfully wherever and whenever there should be need. He remembered this, and said to himself: "Where the devil has my old devil hidden himself all this time?"

And he had only just said this when suddenly there was the little old devil standing in front of him, dressed like a peasant in a little shirt and breeches, trembling with fright and asking: "How can I serve your Excellency?"

"See here," says the soldier. "My son is ill. Do you happen to know how to cure him?"

The little old devil took a glass from his pocket and filled it with cold water and set it on the sick child's forehead.

"Come here, your Excellency," says he, "and look into the glass of water."

The soldier came and looked in the glass.

"And what does your Excellency see?" asked the little old devil, who was so much afraid of the soldier that he trembled and could hardly speak.

"I see Death, like a little old woman, standing at my son's feet."

"Be easy," says the little old devil, "for if Death is standing at your son's feet he will be well again. But if Death were standing at his head then nothing could save him."

And with that the little old devil lifted the glass and splashed the cold water over the sick child, and the next minute there was the little boy crawling about and laughing and crowing as if he had never been sick in his life.

"Give me that glass," says the soldier, "and we'll call it quits."

The little old devil gave him the glass. And the soldier gave back the promise which the devil had signed in his own blood. As soon as the little old devil had that promise in his hand he gave one look at the soldier and fled away as if the blacksmiths had only that minute stopped beating him on the anvil.

And the soldier after that set up as a wise man and put all the doctors out of business, curing the boyars and generals. He would just look in his glass, and if Death stood at a sick man's feet, he threw the water over him and cured him. If Death stood at the sick man's head, he said: "It's all up with you," and the sick man died as sure as fate.

All went well until the Tzar himself fell ill and sent for the soldier to cure him.

The soldier went in, and the Tzar greeted him as his own brother, and prayed him to be quick, as he felt the sickness growing upon him as he lay. The soldier poured cold water in the glass, and set it on the Tzar's forehead, and looked and looked again, and saw Death standing at the Tzar's head.

"O Tzar," says the soldier, "it's all up with you. Death is waiting by your head, and you have but a few minutes left to live."

"What?" cries the Tzar. "You cure my boyars and generals and you will not cure me who am Tzar, and have treated you as my own born brother? If I've only a few minutes to live I've time enough to give orders for you to be beheaded."

The soldier thought, and thought, and he begged Death: "O Death," says he, "give my life to the Tzar and kill me instead. Better to die so than to end by being shamefully beheaded!"

He looked once more in the glass, and saw that the little old woman Death had shifted from the Tzar's head and was now standing at his feet. He picked up the glass and splashed the water over the Tzar, and there was the Tzar as well and healthy as ever he had been.

"You are my own true brother after all," says the Tzar. "Let us go and feast together."

But the soldier shook in all his limbs and could hardly stand, and he knew that his time was come. He prayed Death:

"O Death, give me just one hour to say goodbye to my wife and my little son."

"Hurry up!" says Death.

And the soldier hurried to his room in the palace, said goodbye to his wife, told his son to grow up and be a general, lay down on his bed and grew iller every minute.

He looked, and there was Death, a little old woman, standing by his bedside.

"Well, soldier," says Death, "you have only two minutes left to live!"

The soldier groaned and, turning in bed, pulled the sack from under his pillow and opened it.

"Do you know what this is?" says he to Death.

"A sack," says Death.

"Well, if it is a sack, get into it!" says the soldier.

Death was into the sack in a moment, and the soldier leapt from his bed well and strong, tied up the sack with two double knots, flung it over his shoulder and set out for the deep forest of Brian, which is the thickest in all the world. He came to the forest and made his way into the middle of it, hung the sack from the topmost branches of a high poplar tree, left it there and came home singing songs at the top of his voice and full of all kinds of merriment.

From that time on there was no dying in the world. There were births every day, and plenty of them, but nobody died. It was a poor time for doctors. And so it was for many years. Death had come to an end, and it was as if all men would live for ever. And all the time the little old woman, Death, tied up in a sack, unable to get about her business, was hanging from the top of a tall poplar tree away in Brian forest.

And then, one day, the soldier was walking out to take the air, and he met an ancient old crone, so old and so ancient that she was like to fall whichever way the wind blew. She tottered along, blown this way and that, like a blade of withered grass.

"What an old hag," said the soldier to himself. "It was time for her to die a many years ago."

"Yes," says the old crone, with her toothless gums mumbling and grumbling over her words. "Long ago it was time for me to die. When you shut up Death in the sack I had only an hour left to live. I had done with the world, and the world had done with me, and I would have been glad to be at peace. Long ago my place in Heaven was made ready, and it is empty to this day, for I cannot die. You, soldier, have sinned a sin that God will not forgive. I am not the only soul in the world who is tortured as I am. Mine is not the only place that is growing dusty in Heaven. Hundreds and thousands of us who should have died drag on in misery about the world. And but for you we should now be resting in peace."

The soldier began to think. And he thought of all the other old men and women he had kept from the rest that God had made ready for them: "There is no doubt about it," thinks he; "I had better let Death loose again. No matter if I am the first of whom she makes an end. I have sinned many sins, not counting this one. Better go to the other world now and bear my punishment while I am strong, for when I am very old it will come worse to me to be tormented."

So he set off to the forest of Brian, which is the thickest in all the world. He found the poplar tree, and saw the sack hanging from the topmost branches, swinging this way and that as the wind blew.

"Well, Death, are you alive up there?" the soldier shouted against the wind.

And a little voice, hardly to be heard, answered from the sack: "Alive, little father!"

So the soldier climbed up the tree, took down the sack, and carried it home over his shoulder. He said goodbye to his wife and his son, who was now a fine young lad. Then he went into his own room, opened the bag, lay down upon the bed, and begged Death to make an end of him.

And Death, in the form of a little old woman, crept trembling out of the sack, looking this way and that, for she was very much afraid. As soon as she saw the soldier she bolted through the door, and ran away as fast as her little old legs could carry her. "The devils can make an end of you if they like," she shrieked, "but you don't catch me taking a hand in it."

The soldier sat up on the bed and knew that he was alive and well. Troubled he was as to what to do next. Thinks he: "I'd better get straight along to Hell, and let the devils throw me into the boiling pitch, and stew me until all my sins are stewed out of me."

So he said goodbye to everybody, took his sack in his hands and set off to Hell by the best road he could find.

Well, he walked on and on, over hill and valley and through the deep forest, until he came at last to the kingdom of the unclean. There were the walls of Hell and the gates of Hell, and as he looked he saw that sentinels were standing at every gate.

As soon as he came near a gate the devil doing sentry go calls out:

"Who goes there?"

"A sinful soul come to you to be stewed in the boiling pitch."

"And what is that you've got in your hand?"

"A sack."

And the devil yelled out at the top of his voice and gave the alarm. From all sides the unclean rushed up and began closing every gate and window in Hell with strong bolts and bars.

And the soldier walked round Hell outside the walls, unable to get in.

He cried out to the Prince of Hell:

"Let me into Hell, I beg you. I have come to you to be tormented, because I have sinned before God and before man."

"No," shouted the Prince of Hell, "I won't let you in. Go away. Go away, I tell you. Go away, anywhere you like. There's no place for you here."

The soldier was more troubled than ever.

"Well," says he, "if you won't let me in, you won't. I'll go away if you will give me two hundred sinful souls. I will take them to God, and perhaps, when he sees them, he will forgive me and let me into Heaven."

"I'll throw in another fifty," says the Prince of Hell, "if only you'll get away from here."

And he told the lesser devils to count out two hundred and fifty sinful souls and to let them out quickly at one of the back doors of Hell, while he held the soldier in talk, so that the soldier should not slip in while the sinful souls were going out.

It was done, and the soldier set off for Heaven with two hundred and fifty sinful souls behind him, marching in column of route, as the soldier made them for the sake of order and decency.

Well, they marched on and on, and in the end they came to Heaven, and stopped before the very gates of Paradise.

And the holy apostles, standing in the gateway of Paradise, said: "Who are you?"

"I am the soldier who hung Death in a sack, and I have brought two hundred and fifty sinful souls from Hell in hope that God will pardon my sins and let me into Paradise."

And the apostles went to the Lord, and told him that the soldier had come, and brought with him two hundred and fifty sinful souls.

And God said: "Let in the sinful souls, but do not let in the soldier."

The apostles went back to the gateway, and opened the gates and told the souls they might come in. But when the soldier tried to march in at the head of his company they stopped him, and said: "No, soldier! There's no place for you here."

So the soldier took one of the sinful souls aside and gave that soul his sack, and told him: "As soon as you are through the gates of Paradise, open the sack and shout out, 'Into the sack, soldier!' You will do this because I brought you here from Hell."

And the sinful soul promised to do this for the soldier.

But when that sinful soul went through the gates into Paradise, for very joy it forgot about the soldier, and threw away the sack somewhere in Paradise, where it may be lying to this day.

And the soldier, after waiting a long time, went slowly back to earth. Death would not take him. There was no place for him in Paradise and no place for him in Hell. For all I know he may be living yet.

The Two Brothers

There were once two brothers, Ostap and Ivan. Ostap was the elder by one year, but they loved each other like twins. And when their father died, and left them the little farm and what there was with it, they did not leave each other. They did not draw lots for the property. No: what was Ostap's was Ivan's, and whatever Ivan had Ostap was welcome to make what use he could of it. And so they lived, with never a bitter word between them.

Eh, but it was ill living for peasants in those days. Up before dawn to work for the gentry and slave away till evening, every day alike. A man had no time for the tilling of his own earth, unless he was to kill himself with labour. Only a strong man could live. And so it was that Ostap died, and left Ivan alone.

And Ivan, the younger brother, lamented bitterly. And wept for his, brother. For as I told you they loved each other like twins.

He tried living alone, but, when his day's work was done for the gentry, he had no heart for the tilling of his own earth, now that he could not look up from the plough and see his brother at the far end of the furrow.

He sat at the table with his head in his hands and asked himself what he could do with his life, to make it worth living, so that he could face God with a glad heart and not curse his fate from morning to night.

And, thinks he, "I will marry. I shall not be alone all the time. And even if things are wicked, it is easier for two than for one." And with that he put his cap on his head, and went and asked the Elder of the Village to find him a good wife of an honourable decent family.

A bride was found for him, and all was fixed up for the wedding. His wife-to-be went round the village with her friends, inviting relatives and acquaintances to the wedding feast.

And Ivan thinks to himself and, says he, "I will go to the graveyard, to my brother, and ask him to the wedding, and in memory of my wedding, lay acorns on his grave."

So Ivan came to the graveyard, to his brother's grave, and took off his hat, and crossed himself, and laid the acorns at the foot of the grave. And he thought of how he loved his brother better than all else in the world, and how he had no other friends. And he threw himself on his face on the grave and said, "Oh, brother of mine, I beg you come to my wedding, for I have wearied of sorrowing alone, and today I shall be married."

He had hardly said these words when the earth opened before him. And there in the earth was a deep vault, and in the vault there was Ostap his brother, sitting and smiling as he used to smile on earth.

And, says Ostap, "Come you to me, Ivan, and let us talk things over."

And Ivan went down into the vault, and the earth closed behind him.

Ostap lit a wax candle, and the two of them sat there, in the vault in the graveyard, talking, as if they had met after a journey, with the wax candle throwing shadows of them on the wet walls.

And Ivan told his brother how hard was life up there in the world.

Ostap listened, slowly nodding his head.

But when Ivan had done, Ostap said to him:

"Truly life is hard in the world. But folk in the world are unhappy because they do not live in the right way. Listen now, how we live here, and you will learn how folk should live in the world above ground."

And Ostap took a heavy, stout old book from a shelf and set it in the light of the wax candle and began to read, down there in the vault, to his younger brother Ivan who had come to visit him.

And in this book everything was written as it should be. Folk loved one another. There were no rich and no poor, no strong and no weak. All men were equal. And each man called all men his brothers. In that book there was no working for rich gentry till your back was nigh breaking before evening came and you were free for the tilling of your own scrap of land. Many, many were the good things that Ostap read out of that book. And Ivan listened, and did not think of stirring.

And the wax candle burnt out.

Ostap lit a second candle, and read on. And Ivan listened with his head in his hands and the tears running through his fingers as he heard of the life in this book and thought of the life he knew on earth.

And the second candle burnt out.

Ostap looked up from his reading, and says he, "What about that wedding of yours? Don't you want to be going home? You have been here a long time."

"No, brother, no," says Ivan. "Let me hear a little more of your book. Eh," says he, "but it's fine to think of living like that, among some good kind folk, with justice to be had everywhere and not be carried up by the folk's money bags. Just a little longer, let me think that the world is like that."

So Ostap lit a third candle, and read on, while Ivan listened.

And he heard how there were no wars, and no quarrelling; how if one man had too much, he gave to his neighbour; how there was no weeping; and how men lived like children, trusting each other and God.

And the third candle burnt out.

And Ivan stood up, remembering the wedding that was to be. And he said, "Oh brother, I could listen to your book for hundreds of years and never have enough. But now it will be time for me to go home, or they will be waiting for me."

"Go," says Ostap. And the earth opened before Ivan, and he stepped out of the vault, and the earth closed behind him, and he stood there rubbing his eyes.

He was in the graveyard by his brother's grave. But at the foot of the grave was a huge oak.

"It's a queer thing," says Ivan to himself, "but it seems to me there was no tree there when I came, and yet look at this great tree."

And says he wondering, "I did not think there were so many graves."

He crossed himself again before his brother's grave, and went home, wondering, rubbing his eyes, and staring at all he saw.

He knew the road well enough: but it seemed changed. There were some cottages that he remembered. And the cottages seemed different. There were children in the road and they did not know him. There were old people, and he did not know them.

He came to his own farm. The place was the same, but the building was different. And there were barns and outhouses that he could not call to mind. And people came out of the house, strangers: and he wondered what they had been doing in his house.

And these strangers whom he did not know came out of his own house and asked him what he wanted.

"What do you mean?" says Ivan. "This is my house, and was my father's before me. And my grandparents lived here. I am Ivan. Don't you know who I am? I have been to my brother's grave to bid him come to my wedding today."

And the strangers, coming out of his own house, laughed in his face.

"Eh, good man," say they, "why do you try to make fools of us? Why do you talk empty folly? We don't know you." Others of the village came round, and stared at him and listened. One said: "He has got hold of the old tale, how three hundred years ago a man lived here who was going to marry and who went to his brother's grave and was never seen again."

And the others said, "Aye. We have heard that tale, but we know nothing about you. Off with you and don't come bothering busy folk with your nonsense."

And Ivan turned away from his own house and went through the village.

He knew now what had happened, and that while one candle burned itself out down there in the vault, a hundred years went by, up in the world. And he remembered what he heard when Ostap read to him out of the great book. And his soul grew bitter and sad at the sight of the world and its sorrow and evil, and he wished to tell people all that Ostap had read to him, so that here on earth also folk might live rightly and joyfully.

He went up to the folk he met on the road, and began telling them the happy truth of how folk live in the other world. And he said how on earth also people might live justly and with happiness.

But very few were ready to listen to him. They turned from him angrily, or told him to go off on his business, or took no notice of him at all, as if he had not been standing there and opening his mouth to tell them the good news. And of those who did listen to him, some did not believe him, others did not understand, and some even laughed at him.

He went with his good news from village to village through the world. And wandering, he came at last back to his own village. It was a rare cold night in autumn, and in his own village, he had no welcome, and stood in the road there by his own house, without a bed, with no food, not knowing where to go next.

And Ivan went to his brother's grave, where the great oak grew that he had planted three hundred years before. He fell on his face on the ground, and said: "Let me come in to you, brother, for there is no place for me on earth. I can be of no use to anyone at all."

And the earth opened. And Ivan went down into the vault and greeted Ostap his brother. And the earth closed above them. And, while the earth goes on as badly as before, Ostap and Ivan sit in the vault, and read out of the great book by the light of wax candles. As one candle goes out, they light another, and read on, and with each candle the world is older by a hundred years — and no wiser.

Arthur Ransome
Trust

www.arthur-ransome-trust.org.uk

**"I seem to have lived not one life,
but snatches from a dozen different lives."**

Arthur Ransome...

Arthur Ransome is best known today as the author of the
Swallows and Amazons series of children's books. Rightly celebrated
for their understanding of childhood imagination and play, they
offer a refreshing approach to responsibility, risk and adventure.
All have been continuously in print since they were first published
between 1930 and 1947. They are currently available in hard and
softback print editions, as well as e-book and audiobook formats.

But there was much more to Arthur Ransome's life than
Swallows and Amazons alone. In total he published over 40 books,
contributed to many more, and wrote over 1,500 newspaper and
magazine articles. His subjects reflected his interests and life.
As a young man he was a romantic and a Bohemian, fascinated by
the craft of storytelling. The First World War and Russian
Revolutions turned him into a war reporter and political journalist,
who played chess with Lenin, married Trotsky's secretary,
debated enthusiastically with Karl Radek, helped Estonia gain
independence and was recruited by MI6.

Arthur Ransome
Trust

A keen fisherman and sailor, with a life-long love for the Lake District, Ransome was above all an accomplished and professional writer who, in addition to children's literature, made significant contributions to sailing and angling writing, literary criticism and political journalism.

...the Arthur Ransome Trust...

The Arthur Ransome Trust (ART) is a charity (no: 1136565) dedicated to helping people discover, re-discover, appreciate and enjoy Arthur Ransome's fascinating life and works.

ART's main aim is to establish a public Arthur Ransome Centre in the Lake District, Arthur Ransome's spiritual home.

Whilst working towards a centre, ART arranges exhibitions, displays and lectures. The Trust also has projects to develop teaching materials, for use in schools and virtual resources for use by visitors to the Lake District.

If you want to know more about Arthur Ransome, about the Arthur Ransome Trust's aims and projects, or think you might like to help to fulfil them, then please do visit us at:

www.arthur-ransome-trust.org.uk

Arthur Ransome
Trust

...and Buried Treasure

Buried Treasure is the Arthur Ransome Trust's publishing project.
Its aim is to uncover out-of-print Ransome works, making them
available again in new editions with informative
explanatory introductions.

This volume of Arthur Ransome's Russian Tales combines
Ransome's classic *Old Peter's Russian Tales*, first published
in 1916, with *The War of the Birds and the Beasts*,
which has been out-of-print for a number of years.

For more information about current and forthcoming
Buried Treasure publications, visit:

www.arthur-ransome-trust.org.uk

**"I spent the morning in working out
a synopsis in twenty chapters, took a sledge,
drove into Moscow and bought a lot of typing paper.
I had made up my mind to write..."**